Secrets Worth Killing For

A Founding Fathers Mystery

Jamison Borek

Secrets Worth Killing For

ISBN-10: 0-9915366-6-5
ISBN-13: 978-0-9915366-6-5

Published by:

Shrewsbury
Press

www.shrewsburypress.com

∞ I ∞

If you are seized with a chilliness or shaking, followed by a fever, bad headache, pain in the back and loins, sick stomach or vomiting, uneasiness about the breast, soreness of the eyes or pain in them, immediately get bled; and take one of the powders of jalap and calomel, so successfully used in 1793. They may be had at the apothecaries with proper directions for using them. Drink very freely of molasses and water, or tamarinds and water. If this method does not carry off the disease, send for a physician.

Philadelphia, September 6th, 1797

It was a bright, sunny October day when Bridget LeClair breathed her last, lying there in her bed in the hospital. No one thought very much of it when she died – no one, that is, except for Doctor Dobel, the doctor who was treating her, and her fellow servant Annie Dawson.

Her death was but one of many, after all. The deadly yellow fever had returned to Philadelphia just months before, in July of

1797. It wasn't as bad as the epidemic of 1793, when thousands of people had died. The lesson had been learned. Everyone who could manage it fled from the city to the safety of the countryside, leaving the poor and the unlucky to die.

Bridget was one of the unlucky ones. She was a kitchen maid working for Mr. and Mrs. Waln, one of the city's wealthiest merchant traders with ships travelling all over the world. They were preparing to leave Philadelphia, like so many others, but he was waiting for a ship to return from China.

When she showed signs of the fever, Bridget was sent to the Wigwam Hospital. A former tavern situated at the foot of Race Street by the Schuylkill River, now it was set aside for the yellow fever victims, being well away from the settled parts of town.

She didn't want to go, but she had no one else to turn to. Her father had died when she was small, run down in the street by a carriage. Her mother and her husband had died of the yellow fever in 1793, and her brother had died of it also just a few weeks before. They all lay in the churchyard at Saint Mary's now and soon she would lie there too.

Bridget lingered for a week in her hospital bed, growing daily sicker and weaker. On the seventh day, early in the evening, she breathed her last.

Doctor Dobell happened to come by just moments before it happened. Watching helplessly as her life slipped away, he felt surprise along with his pity. He'd been so certain that she'd be one of the few who would recover. Earlier that day her pulse had been strong, not weak and broken like the others. She'd had no difficulty breathing and she wasn't yellow with jaundice. These were signs, in his experience, that she would survive, that she'd be able to walk away from the hospital rather than being carried out lifeless to her grave.

As he closed her eyelids and drew the thin bed sheet over her body, he was struck by how much the girl had been sweating. Her nightclothes and the sheet were practically dripping with moisture, a veritable flood it seemed.

He turned to the nurse who stood beside him.

"How long was she sweating like this?"

The nurse shook her head, gesturing at the room around them. It was crowded with beds, so far beyond capacity that there was scarcely room to walk between them.

"There's so many coming in these days, how can I keep track of them? They come, they stay a while, they die."

"Yes of course." It was true enough. He couldn't blame her. He himself was tired beyond measure. "Do you remember anything about her symptoms?"

"She had a spell this afternoon, according to the nurse on duty. First it was cramps, tossing in her bed and moaning. Then a bit later on, when I came on, she was like to puke her guts out. A proper mess it was, I can tell you." The nurse made a face at the recollection.

Doctor Dobell shook his head, perplexed. Bridget's case was very curious. According to Doctor Benjamin Rush's observations, sweating – especially great sweating like this – was always a sign that the patient would survive the fever. Dr. Rush had seen literally thousands of cases, he said, and not a single one where the patient had died after sweating heavily. Yet here was this girl who had sweated and died, and with no jaundice, no weak and broken pulse, but cramps and nausea. It was strange, very strange indeed. Had she really died of the yellow fever?

As Doctor Dobell rose from Bridget's bedside, a wave of dizziness came over him. He felt so light headed and weak that he feared he would fall, and he reached for the bed frame to steady himself. His face felt flushed and hot. A sense of dread overcame him. Was he merely overtired? Could it be that he'd caught the yellow fever himself?

Surely he was just overtired, he told himself. Desperately tired, to be honest. There were so many who'd fallen ill, far too many to attend to. He'd hardly seen his dear sweet wife, whom he'd married just a few months ago. For weeks, he had hardly slept at all.

Home again, very late that evening, he had a late supper and a glass of port and felt somewhat recovered. He made notes in his journal about the curious symptoms of the sweating girl and penned a short letter about it to Dr. Rush, to pique his curiosity.

As Dobell sealed the letter, he stared at the blob of bright red sealing wax with fascination. How much it was the color of blood – such bright, arterial blood, and how exactly! Blood, so much like blood . . . With a start, he realized that he wasn't thinking clearly. He forced himself to rise and go to bed, leaving the note to Doctor Rush in the hall.

The next morning, he could barely lift his head. He was jaundiced and his body was burning. It wasn't just a matter of overwork; that was now undeniable. After months of treating yellow fever patients, he'd succumbed to the disease himself.

Doctor Rush came by the day afterwards. He'd gotten the strange, cryptic note about Bridget's case and come to discuss it, but Doctor Dobell was so weak that he could barely manage a word of greeting. Doctor Rush spent his time purging and bleeding his colleague and friend.

To no avail. Doctor Dobell would not be the one to contradict Doctor Rush's theories. He was desert dry; not a drop of sweat escaped his pores. His pulse was broken and his breathing was labored and difficult. On the sixth day after Bridget's death, Doctor Dobel also breathed his last.

ᘯ 2 ᘰ

Jacob Martin stepped onto the dock from the little three-masted ship with an overwhelming sense of relief and gratitude. He'd sailed up and down the coast many times, first to attend the Continental Congress and now as a United States Senator. He'd even sailed back and forth to London once, across the entire Atlantic Ocean in a small and leaky wooden ship. These last twelve days sailing up from Charleston to Philadelphia, however, had been the worst of his entire life.

The weather had been stormy and raw; rain, snow, and hail had beat down on them incessantly. The ocean had tossed the tiny ship up and down, a fragile wooden toy in the maelstrom, as wave after giant wave rose up high over them, taller than even the mainmast, and then came crashing down.

More than once, Jacob had been sure that he'd never see land again, that the angry sea would be his grave. Now here he was, miraculously landed. Somehow they had all survived.

In his heavy black wool greatcoat, sturdy boots, and cocked beaver hat, Jacob blended in to the crowd of passengers disembarking. A slim man of average height, he wore his thick dark hair long and ribbon-tied in a queue behind him, and he dressed in a deliberately conservative style. A lawyer by trade, a plantation farmer by inheritance, he looked as he was, an honest and honorable man. Only a shrewd observer might see more, behind the carefully controlled exterior – the sharp intelligence that glinted in his dark brown eyes and the fiery nature that smoldered within.

There had been other, wilder times in his younger days, when he studied law at the Inns of Court in London. Times cut short by the Revolution, when he came swiftly home to fight for a new and independent land. He was a Patriot, to the extreme disgust of his stubborn, self-righteous, Loyalist father.

His father's assets were all confiscated once the Revolution was won, as a punishment for being a Loyalist, and an unrepentant one too. So it fell to Jacob, as the eldest son, to take on the role of head of the family. He started paying off his father's debts and supporting them all. His father, a scornful, disapproving, broken man, never forgave him.

Jacob's father and mother had passed away some years before and his brother was now a successful doctor, but Jacob still supported his sister and her charming but ne'er-do-well husband. They lived in Georgia and took care of Jacob's two children, Jacob and Louisa, ever since his own wife died in childbirth.

Sometimes he wondered if he'd paid too high a price, accepting so dutifully the role fate seemed to have handed out to him. But what else could he have done? Could he have left his mother, brother, and sister to live in poverty?

He paused a moment on the dock to savor the view of Philadelphia as it was best seen, from the water. The city was built long and low, a thin crescent of buildings that hugged the Delaware River shore, for the sea-going trade was the lifeblood of the city. The merchant's wharves and warehouses clustered along the river's edge, with the waterfront taverns and merchant's mansions behind them. Rows and rows of densely-packed red-brick townhouses lined the broad, straight streets beyond. Rising above it all were the tall spires of the city's public buildings and churches, the majestic steeple of Christ Church chief among them. Just visible, some five blocks away, was the weather vane-topped white cupola of Jacob's destination, Congress Hall.

The inhabitants of Philadelphia, numbering well over forty thousand, had long been proud of their city, with its outstanding institutions of science, medicine, and education. The economy was booming too, as fortunes were recovering from the long years of war. The great merchant families of Philadelphia were perhaps the richest in America. For the past seven years, they'd also had the honor (if honor it was) of being the nation's capital, until the government moved permanently to the newly-created District of Columbia.

Jacob had only been gone a few months, since the last session of Congress had ended just after Independence Day. It had been an extraordinary session, called by President Adams to deal with the crisis in French relations. As the two nations teetered precariously on the brink of outright war, the depredations of French privateers were devastating the economy. They were seizing ships not only on the open seas, but even in American coastal waters and harbors. More than three hundred ships had been lost in the past twelve months alone, to say nothing of all their precious and expensive cargo. American cargoes were "legally" awarded to the privateers by compliant French authorities in the Caribbean.

American captains had been tortured and crews imprisoned or left impoverished on foreign shores.

It was a crisis indeed, one that threatened the very survival of the fledgling nation. The United States was virtually defenseless, with no army, no navy, and the revolutionary militias now disbanded. The country was in worse shape militarily than it had been in 1776. Thanks to the bitterly partisan nature of politics these days, however, the extraordinary session had accomplished nearly nothing. The Federalists and the Republicans spent their time fighting each other instead.

President Adams had proposed a series of measures to protect the country and its trade, but the Republicans opposed any measures to improve things. They still considered the French to be friends and allies, for all their insults and attacks, and blamed President Washington for causing the conflict. He was too cozy with the British, they said. He'd violated the French alliance and any measures to strengthen defenses could only aggravate things. The best and only way to improve relations with the French, they said, was to elect a Republican as President. The only significant thing the whole session had managed to agree on was to send (yet another) mission to Paris, in the hope that things could be improved by diplomacy.

Now the next regular session would be starting soon. Jacob wondered if it would be any better.

He slowly became aware that his fingers and toes were numb, thanks to the piercing cold wind blowing off the river. He was hungry too. He felt as if he hadn't eaten a decent meal since he set sail from Charleston, as indeed he hadn't. He badly wanted warmth, drink, and food, preferably in that order. His rented rooms in the city would be cheerless and cold, however, so he arranged for his baggage to be taken there and he made his way to the City Tavern.

"Good day, Senator Martin!"

The doorman greeted Jacob heartily, as befitted a long-time, prominent patron of the establishment. Jacob had been going there for over twenty years, ever since he'd come to Philadelphia as a delegate to the Continental Congress. He remembered how he and the others had marched in parade from the City Tavern to Carpenters' Hall, where they would write the Declaration of Independence. These days, most of the tavern rooms were reserved for the Merchant's Coffee House and Place of Exchange, a club where merchants, captains of vessels, and other business gentlemen could sip coffee, brandy, or what they pleased, as they did their deals and traded the latest intelligence.

Soon Jacob was comfortably settled in a high-back red leather chair, close to a cheerfully blazing fire in the marble-fronted fireplace. He had only moments of peace and comfort, however, before he was rudely interrupted.

"Senator Martin!"

It was no greeting of welcome this time, but rather a sharp and peremptory command, such as one might use to summon a lazy servant. Jacob knew the speaker all too well – Theodore Sedgwick, Senator from New Hampshire. Sedgwick was all New Hampshire granite without any leavening of charm, forceful, blunt, and passionate in his prejudices.

Sedgwick pulled up a chair and sat himself down next to Jacob.

"I left you messages at the Senate and your rooms, but you haven't answered," he began without preliminary. The way he said it, it sounded like he was accusing Jacob of deliberately avoiding him. He peered at Jacob suspiciously.

"I wasn't here," Jacob answered evenly. It was curious that Sedgwick of all people wanted to see him so urgently. The man was what they called a "High Federalist," fiercely conservative in his views. He disapproved, to say the least, of Jacob's more moderate and independent positions. "As a matter of fact, I've only just gotten off the ship from Charleston."

"Ah, yes?" Sedgwick's attitude mellowed ever so slightly. "Then you could do with some hot punch, I suppose. It must have been a rough voyage, if the weather was anything like it was reported to be."

At Jacob's surprised and grateful nod, Sedgwick signaled to the bartender through the doorway. Catching his eye, he pantomimed drinking from a punch bowl. Soon a steaming bowl of punch arrived, fragrant with orange, nutmeg, and rum. There was silence for a moment, as they passed it back and forth until it was finished. It was almost – almost – companionable.

"All right then," Sedgwick resumed, "as I said before, I've been wanting to talk to you."

"About what?" Jacob looked at Sedgwick with a wary eye. There was business enough to be sure, once the session started. National defense, for one thing. Day by day, hostilities with the French were worsening.

"Have the French declared war? Has it come to that?" Jacob asked worriedly.

"Not yet, thank God." On this one issue at least, Sedgwick and Jacob were in agreement. "What a disaster that would be, with them well on the way to conquering the world and us so pitifully defenseless. They've already subdued the Italian states, as I'm sure you know, even the Papal territory and Austria. I hear they're planning to invade Britain too. It seems there's no stopping that young Corsican fellow, General Bonaparte."

"Senator Blount, then?" Jacob tried again. "Has the House of Representatives finished its investigation?" According to reliable reports, Senator Blount had been the mastermind of a treasonous conspiracy. He'd been plotting with the British to fight against Spain, a country the United States was at peace with. Blount would raise his own army of Americans and Indians to invade and conquer the Spanish Louisiana territories, and the British would provide money and equipment. The Senate would be holding the very first impeachment trial, just as soon as the House of Representatives adopted the Articles of Impeachment.

"Not yet. I can't imagine what's taking so long, when the situation is so perfectly clear to begin with. The whole Blount conspiracy is a plot by the French, quite obviously. I expect the Republicans are trying to delay the investigation and report, to keep the truth from becoming public."

Jacob's eyes widened in astonishment.

"A French plot? You can't be serious. He was working on behalf of the British. His whole plot was aimed against the French, to keep their ally Spain from giving them Louisiana and control over the Mississippi trade."

"That's what they'd like people to believe, but can you really be so credulous?" Sedgwick looked at Jacob narrowly, as if trying to decide if he was being devious or just dumb. "Blount's a Republican, after all, and he's not such a fool as he pretends to be. The French plan was to entrap the British, to ensnare them in a treasonous plot against the United States and then to expose their perfidy. Why else would Blount write a letter telling of his plot and then send it to someone who was bound to make it public?

To harm the British, that was the plan all along – and it worked, didn't it?"

Jacob was impressed despite himself. Sedgwick made this crazy theory sound almost plausible.

"Which leads to my question, in a way," Sedgwick went on. "Did you know that Senator Bingham's been going around saying we should make you the President *pro tem* for this session? That's if our most honorable Vice-President doesn't show up on time and preside himself," he added contemptuously. "Since Jefferson can never bring himself to show up on time, I think that's a safe assumption."

"Senator Bingham's been saying I should preside?" Jacob's surprise was genuine. "I didn't know, in fact. He hasn't said or written anything to me about it."

Sedgwick shrugged.

"Well, that's Bingham's plan, no doubt about it. Maybe you left Charleston before the letter arrived, or maybe the damned postal carrier just left it at some tavern. Bingham's already lining up support, so he must assume you'd accept if offered. It's hard to imagine my voting for it, I have to say. To be fair, however, I told him I'd talk to you."

"Talk to me?" Jacob had a pretty good idea what Sedgwick meant, but he wanted him to come right out and say it.

Sedgwick didn't hesitate.

"It's about your political sympathies, of course. You say you're a Federalist, but given your past voting record, I'd have to say that your Federalist credentials are pretty questionable. Between your behavior in the Senate and your efforts to save Jefferson's precious life, I'd say your sympathies were decidedly Republican."

"You know very well –" Jacob began, his temper rising. Talk about "saving Jefferson" again – would there be no end to it? At the farewell dinner for George Washington in March, a waiter was poisoned, but it seemed that the poison was really intended for Thomas Jefferson. Soon charges were flying that President Adams, or someone in his Federalist Party at least, was trying to murder their chief Republican opponent, Thomas Jefferson. It was President Adams himself who insisted that Jacob solve the crime, but the task was difficult and thankless. When Jacob couldn't find the murderer quickly, the crisis escalated. The bonds that held the fragile young nation together were coming apart, as people came to believe that the Federalists had abandoned the Constitution and meant to stay in power through political assassination. Jacob himself had been ruthlessly (and inconsistently) attacked by his colleagues and in the press as incompetent, complicit in a cover up, and even engaged in a dastardly secret plot with Jefferson to fake the murder attempts.

"Oh I know what you're going to say," Sedgwick cut off Jacob's protest. "You say you only got involved because President Adams asked you, but do you really think he meant for you to take it so seriously? He had to do something to deflect the charges that he was the one behind it all. He only asked you for the sake of appearances. And then there's your voting record as well – hardly what one would expect from a committed Federalist." Sedgwick paused and looked at Jacob haughtily. "If you want my vote, then in return I want some assurances. Can you swear to me that as President *pro tem* you'd be more reliable?"

"Do you mean, will I always vote the way you think I should, no matter my own opinion?" Jacob asked sharply. "Is that what you mean? If that's your question, Senator, the answer is no. No, most assuredly."

"That's not what I meant." Sedgwick looked annoyed, as if Jacob was being unreasonable. "You take offense so easily, you southerners. Which, by the way, is another ground for concern, your being a southerner. Almost all the other southerners are Republicans, as you know, and you southerners tend to stick together."

It was only with a visible effort of will that Jacob held his tongue. He'd be damned if he'd lower himself to Sedgwick's level. Between the rigors of the journey, the insults, and the punch, however, it took nearly all of his self-control. The look he gave Sedgwick was purely lethal.

Sedgwick didn't seem to notice, or perhaps he was even amused. By now, the two of them had an audience. Behind a pretense of reading their papers or sipping their drinks, the other gentlemen in the room were listening with keen attention. Some were even betting in whispers amongst themselves, whether and when Jacob would lose his temper.

"The worst thing you've done, I have to say," Sedgwick went on, "is to work so hard to keep Jefferson from being murdered. He's a dangerous man, just like those blood-sucking French Jacobin terrorists he supports. Given a chance, he'd be happy to see us have a French-style bloody revolution. You know he's behind the efforts to foment insurrection here in the United States, trying to overthrow even President Washington by mob violence. I can't think why you'd want to make sure he survived, unless you were secretly one of them."

Jacob rose and bowed to Sedgwick with bare politeness. Aware of the others keenly listening, he raised his voice just enough for his words to be heard throughout the room.

"I thank you for the punch, Senator Sedgwick, but now I will take my departure. I don't give a damn what you think or how you vote, and I'll see you in hell before I care a whit for your opinion. As for the rest, I think you've insulted me quite enough, even for a man with your obvious lack of breeding. You should just be thankful that I swore that I'd never duel again, or my second would be visiting you this very evening."

With that, Jacob bowed to the Senator once again, turned his back, and left the room, leaving behind a hubbub of gossip, commentary, and settling of wagers.

By the time he reached his lodgings, the fires had been lit and his rooms, if not yet comfortable, were at least a few degrees warmer than the street outside. For a man hoping to recover from a long and trying trip, however, the prospect before him was hardly welcoming. The entry room, which served as his office and study, resembled nothing so much as a storehouse. Boxes, trunks and cases full of books and other belongings were still in heaps and piles, covering nearly half the floor space. The things he'd left behind were covered in dust, having sat there since last July. The things he'd taken home to Charleston and back again were cold and wet from the voyage.

He decided to put off the tedious job of setting things to rights again. All he needed for the moment was the small travelling case of toiletries and other necessities that had served him on his journey and a clean shirt and a fresh pair of stockings for the morning.

He opened the case and pulled out the book he had been reading, on and off, and looked at it dubiously. *A Vindication of the Rights of Women*, by Mary Wollstonecraft. It was not, truth be told, a book he ordinarily would have chosen. He meant to make a point with Elizabeth Powel, however. She'd been so sure he'd never read it. "Men just can't take women seriously when they speak of women's rights," she'd said, with a rare display of annoyance and even anger.

He sighed. Elizabeth Powel, how much he had missed her. He had been drawn to her from the very first meeting. It had been Bishop White who'd brought them together, just a few months ago. As the chaplain of the Senate, he knew Jacob well. He also knew Elizabeth as his parishioner.

"You two can talk about politics," the Bishop had told him, knowing politics was Elizabeth's weakness. She liked to say women should leave the political sphere alone, but she herself could never stay away from it.

Bishop White had been right that she and Jacob would get along. The initial meeting had quickly evolved into a regular weekly invitation. She would provide him with "tea and relishes" (that staple of Philadelphia social life) and he would provide her with the political news and gossip. Jacob had also valued her opinions and advice, for she was an acute and intelligent observer. Even George Washington had listened to her views. It was she, people said, who'd convinced him that he must accept a second term as President.

Always, however, Jacob felt an undercurrent of uneasiness and reserve in her attitude that left him wondering if his feelings were reciprocated. People said that the death of her husband and her sons had left her reclusive and withdrawn. Was that why she seemed so detached and cool, seemingly unwilling to open up again to any sort of deeper friendship? He would not dream of rushing to see her, for all that he longed to do so. He was always afraid a too-eager approach would frighten her. Instead, the next morning early, he spent several hours composing a two-sentence letter to inform her of his return. Then he anxiously awaited her answer.

⚯ 3 ⚯

James Mathers, a rugged and solid Irishman, had a spring in his step and a smile on his face as he sauntered down Chestnut Street toward the Senate. No matter that he was nearer sixty than fifty now (though not by much, he told himself). No matter that his black hair seemed a good deal grayer than it ought to be, whenever he chanced to look in a mirror. No matter that he couldn't climb up and down stairs quite as easily as he used to do and the wound in his leg (a souvenir from his fighting against the British at Yorktown) ached more and more often than he admitted. No matter, life had been good to him.

He had a grand job as the Doorkeeper for the Senate, plenty to eat and drink, and a room of his own to shelter him. Most of all, he had his hopes that the pretty young widow Rachel McAllister might someday come to fancy him, even half as much as he fancied her.

At first, he hadn't dared to try to gain her favor. She was so much younger than he was, so smart, attractive, and accomplished. Her husband had died, like so many, in the yellow fever epidemic of 1793. He'd been a printer and she'd been his assistant. Some even said she'd been the better printer and businessman. As skilled as she was, when he'd died she'd had no trouble finding employment. She worked for Thomas Dobson now, tending his bookselling and stationery shop and setting set type for his printing operation also.

Rachel hadn't lacked for suitors since her husband died, but she hadn't taken up with any of them. It seemed she quite liked her present state in life, with the rights and freedoms that women only enjoyed when they were widows.

Mathers hadn't summoned the courage to make his feelings known, but he couldn't stay away from her either. Dobson's was where the Senate bought its supplies, so he stopped by the shop whenever he could, on the pretext of picking up quills and ink and parchment. For this he had incurred the wrath of the Secretary of the Senate, Samuel Otis. It was the Secretary's prerogative to purchase stationery supplies, as Otis constantly reminded him. "A mere doorkeeper," Otis called him, with a haughty look down his patrician nose, bought lesser things like coal and wood for the fireplaces and hay for the horses. But Mathers was stubborn, large, and strong and Otis was small and timid.

"Does he really imagine he has any chance with her?" Otis sniffed to his clerks one day, knowing that Mathers could overhear him. "An old fool like him with such a young and attractive lass? Like they say," Otis added with a smirk, "there's no fool like an old fool."

It was worth any amount of Otis' scorn and derision, however, when Mathers's attentions at last awakened (or so it seemed) some spark of reciprocal interest. It was just a few months ago, after the dinner that Dobson had hosted to celebrate completing the seventeenth volume of his *Encyclopaedia*, the first ever published in America. After the plentiful feast and even more plentiful liquors, Mathers had summoned up the courage to ask if he could escort Rachel to her lodgings. To his joyful amazement, she'd said yes. She even let him take her arm, as they walked through the streets in the moonlight.

Since then, his hopes had grown but his courage hadn't returned, nor had Rachel given him the least encouragement. He would have given up long ago, but Rachel's colleagues urged him to keep trying. Notwithstanding how it might appear, he was special. It wasn't his fault that she seemed so uninterested. It was just she liked things just the way they were. She didn't want to go back to having a husband.

Mathers whistled softly to himself as he mounted the steps to the second floor of Congress Hall, where the Senate had its meeting Chamber, its committee rooms, and its offices. A two-story red-brick building with tall mullioned windows and a fine white cupola, it lay at the corner of Sixth Street and Chestnut, part of a larger complex of government buildings. Next to it were the city's newest and grandest attractions – the New Theater, Rickett's Circus, and Oeller's Hotel. Beyond, stretching further westward toward the Schuylkill River, development fell off rapidly, and the red brick buildings gave way to trees, fields, and pastures.

A few steps down the Senate hall, Mathers turned into the first room on the left where the staff had their offices. Most of the room was devoted to the desks, supplies and other equipment that belonged to Secretary Otis and his clerks. Mathers's own domain, the "Doorkeeper's Lodge," was only a small space against the farthest wall, with a desk, a chair, and a tall cabinet with pigeonholes for the Senators' mail, newspapers, and messages.

He settled himself in his chair and began to sort the mail. All around him was peace and quiet. Secretary Otis had wandered off on some errand, it seemed, and his clerks were gone also. He savored the silence and, even more, the absence of demands and interruptions. With the Senate not in session, there was a blissful absence of Senators.

Still he looked forward to when the session resumed again. He loved the hustle and bustle of his job and it suited him perfectly. A spot of peace and quiet was all very well for a change, but there was such a thing, in his opinion, as too much of it. Indeed, he was just drifting off to sleep, when a shout from the hallway awakened him.

"Hallo, Mathers, are you about?"

It took him but an instant to recognize the voice and his initial annoyance quickly vanished.

"Good day, Senator Martin," he called back as Jacob appeared at the doorway.

Mathers quickly rose and helped Jacob out of his coat.

"It's good to see you again, Senator, and that's the truth. What are you doing back so early? The Senate isn't set to start for nearly two weeks yet. You'd not be bringing me another murder investigation, would you now? That would make my day for certain."

He was joking, but only in part. Unlike Jacob, he'd quite enjoyed tracking down Jefferson's would-be murderer. Not only was finding the murderer satisfying in itself, but it had also greatly enhanced his standing with the Senators. He wasn't just "the doorman" any more. He was "that clever fellow Mathers who'd helped find the murderer."

"Why does everyone have to keep talking about it?" Jacob responded irritably. "Can't they leave it in the past? You must excuse me," he added quickly, realizing he sounded rather petulant. "For me though, as you know, the whole experience was highly unfortunate. Anyway, it's good to see you again. I've come to see if I've gotten any mail or messages."

"Sure and there is something, as I recall." Mathers reached out to one of the cubbyholes and retrieved a small packet of folded paper sealed with bright red wax. "It came on the mail stage just a couple days ago."

Jacob glanced quickly at the name of the sender and felt a stab of apprehension. It was from his business agent in New York, the one who handled the sale and shipping of the rice he grew on his plantation. Was it good news or bad? Much depended on the answer. It might report that payment had been made, a welcome infusion of cash that was sorely needed. Then again, it might say that the ship had been taken by French privateers, in which case he'd lost everything. He should have insured his shipment of course, but these days no one could afford it. Thanks to the privateers, insurance premiums had gone sky-high and they were climbing ever higher.

He decided to save the letter to read later on and tucked it away in his pocket.

Before their conversation could resume again, there was once again a shout from the hallway.

"Good day, good day. Is anyone around yet?"

Senator Bingham arrived at the office door and smiled at them cheerily. And why shouldn't he be cheerful, after all? He had a beautiful wife, the largest and finest mansion in town, and he was the richest man in Philadelphia – perhaps the richest in the entire nation. He cut quite a figure himself as well, with his well-tailored black velvet suit, his ruffles of lace, and his shoe buckles of sparkling diamonds. He wore his hair in the older style and his wig was elaborately curled and powdered.

"What luck to find you here," he cheerily observed, clearly addressing himself to Jacob. "I need a private word, if you will." He turned and headed for the Committee Room across the hall, leaving Jacob little choice but to follow him.

"I hope you've had a pleasant summer?" Bingham politely began, once he'd closed the door and they'd seated themselves at the green baize-covered table.

"Yes, though it was over too soon. I always hate to leave Charleston."

"There are consolations in Philadelphia though, I believe." Bingham smiled and winked conspiratorially. "My aunt has been asking about you, for example. My wife's aunt that is," he added, just to be certain that Jacob understood.

"Oh yes?" Jacob couldn't help but brighten. Bingham's wife's aunt was none other than Elizabeth Powel. "Has she really been asking about me? You must give her my best regards, now that I'm back in Philadelphia."

"There's a bit of gossip about you two, you know. I don't credit it though. Too bad for you, I'm afraid, if you've any hopes in that direction. My wife is quite sure that her aunt is committed to her widowhood now, forever mourning the death of her sons and her husband."

He paused and fixed Jacob with a quizzical stare, as if giving him a chance to comment. Jacob, however, said not a word. Gossip? About him and Elizabeth? Part of him was horrified. If only it were true, whispered another part, and the gossip be damned. He sighed. His life had been far too full of "if only"s.

"But down to business," Bingham went on smoothly, perceiving that he'd get no further response. "I didn't chase you down to talk about my relatives. The question I wanted to ask you is this – how would you like to preside over the Senate? Until Jefferson gets here, that is, but he's already written to say he'll be late. I've been talking with some of our colleagues and I think we can get you elected. The other Federalists agree that we may have been hard on you the last session, and that you ought to have a second chance. Well, most of them do. I'm afraid that, well –" he paused uncertainly, but Jacob rescued him.

"The day I arrived, I ran into Senator Sedgwick at the City Tavern," Jacob informed him with a wry smile. "He was as tactful and diplomatic as usual."

"Then I don't have to tell you." Bingham was obviously relieved not to have to explain, even more than Jacob realized. As blunt as Sedgwick had been with Jacob, it was mild compared to what he'd said to Bingham. "The man's nothing but a lackey for the Jacobin scum," he'd snapped, "a fool at best and at worst a traitor. You might better propose a Republican to preside. At least a Republican would wear his true colors honestly."

"All the same," Senator Bingham went on, still wincing inwardly at the memory, "I don't think we need Sedgwick's vote to win. So what do you say? Will you do it?"

"I'd be honored to have the chance," Jacob answered sincerely, "and I thank you."

"You may not thank me, when you've actually got the job," Bingham said lightly. "It won't be any more amusing from the President's chair. I doubt we'll be able to accomplish much, with the Republicans fighting tooth and nail against us."

Jacob frowned. Of course this session would be as contentious and unproductive as the last one. Any hopes that it would be otherwise were naive. President Washington hadn't even been gone a year now and already you had to wonder what things were coming too. The fragile bonds that held the fractious, self-proud states together were fraying and growing thin, powerful enemies surrounded the United States on all sides, and Congress was paralyzed by political hatreds. Sometimes it seemed like his father was right, that the United States would never survive as an independent country.

"Good then, we're agreed." Bingham reached over and shook Jacob's hand. "We'll go ahead and get you elected. I warn you though, many of your colleagues still suspect you're really Jefferson's man, even if they're giving you the benefit of the doubt for the moment. If I were you, I'd watch my step pretty carefully. 'Go along to get along,' as they say. Whatever your true feelings, you'd do well to pay more attention to appearances."

∞ 4 ∞

Elizabeth Powel sat at her desk, quill in hand, wearing a flowing gown of embroidered white muslin with a light shawl loosely wrapped about her shoulders. She'd bought the desk from George Washington just months before. It had been his desk when he was President. The desk was an elaborate French-style bureau of mahogany and maple inlay, taller than she was and nearly twice as heavy, amply supplied with drawers and pigeonholes. In one of the drawers, she'd found love letters to him from Martha. She hadn't read them, of course, just enough to realize what they were, and then returned them, teasing him about having a secret love affair.

She missed him so much, and the entire United States would surely miss him also. He had always stood above the fray, seeking only the good of the country. The others – Mr. Jefferson especially – seemed in comparison such calculating, scheming men, tainted by their lust for power.

Every morning, without fail, she sat at her desk and tended to her extensive correspondence. She wrote letters about her business affairs, to her acquaintances and friends, and to her family. She even wrote to her niece Mrs. Bingham, who lived right down the street. One letter, however, she had set aside, strangely unwilling to answer it. It was the note from Jacob announcing his return to Philadelphia. Time and again over the past months she had missed his companionship, and yet she was hesitant to see him again. The prospect awakened troubling feelings that she'd thought to leave far behind her. Attachments only led to pain, she knew too well. She'd learned that the hard way.

The room was cold, the fires having been lit not long before, but, enrapt in her thoughts, she was oblivious to the temperature. As she wrote, the carefully crafted sentences took shape slowly, graceful lines of black ink traced across the creamy white paper.

Her maid Lydia stood anxiously at the doorway, twisting and untwisting her apron in her hands, torn by indecision. Her employer did so hate to be interrupted, she knew, but she was in a terrible state of agitation. Her employer could go on writing letters for hours and hours!

At length the sheer intensity of Lydia's turmoil penetrated Elizabeth's concentration and she looked up.

"Yes? What is it, Lydia?" she asked, a tinge of reproof in her tone, when she saw the maid standing there at the doorway.

Lydia's relief was evident.

"I know as I shouldn't interrupt, but it's troubling me so that I just couldn't help it. Oh, Mrs. Powel, I'm sorry, I really am."

"What is 'it,' my dear?" Elizabeth's tone was gentler now as she perceived the depth of Lydia's unhappiness. "What is it that is troubling you so?"

"It's about Bridget, Mrs. Powel, my cousin Bridget. You remember Bridget? The one who died of the yellow fever?"

Elizabeth nodded.

"Only it wasn't – it wasn't the yellow fever after all!" Lydia's words came out in a rush, her voice breaking with emotion. "It wasn't the yellow fever that killed her. At least, that's what Annie says. What Annie says is, it was, it was – oh Mrs. Powel, it's just so awful." At this, a fit of sobbing overtook her.

"Slow down now, Lydia," Elizabeth said firmly. Really, Lydia was like a child sometimes. The least little thing could upset her so. "Take a deep breath before you go on and begin at the beginning. Who is this Annie and what exactly did she say?"

Lydia took a deep breath, and then another.

"Annie said –" Catching herself, she began again. "Annie Dawson, I mean. She was Bridget's friend. They worked together at Mr. and Mrs. Walns. You know, the merchant?"

"Yes, go on." Elizabeth nodded and smiled encouragingly.

"I ran into her this morning, Annie that is, at the market. That's when she told me. Bridget didn't die of the yellow fever, she said. It was much more terrible. She said Bridget was, she was – she was murdered."

"Murdered? What a thing to say. Don't tell me you believed her?"

"I know it sounds crazy," Lydia said defensively, "but it made sense, the way she told it. She says it was on account of the people Bridget knew and the things she knew. Terrible secrets, she said, worth killing for."

"Now really, Lydia –"

"Bridget knew important people," Lydia went on stubbornly, "like that Senator, the one who's in trouble. He had an eye for the pretty girls, Annie says, and he gave Bridget expensive presents.

Annie was worried there'd be trouble right along, she says, even before the yellow fever."

"Senator Blount? Senator Blount from Tennessee? Is that the Senator she's talking about?" Elizabeth's attitude underwent a subtle change. She was still skeptical, but she also felt a flicker of curiosity. She'd withdrawn herself from the social whirl, but she still closely followed the world of politics. If Lydia's cousin Bridget had really been involved with Senator Blount, that just might be something interesting.

"Senator Blount? That sounds like what she said, I guess." Lydia hadn't the least idea of political things and she said it somewhat doubtfully. "It might have been Blount, or something like it."

"What exactly did Annie say?"

"Oh Mrs. Powel, I couldn't follow it all." Lydia wrung her hands in helpless frustration. "Bridget was murdered, she said, on account of this Senator Blount, or whoever it was. On account of what Bridget knew, what he must have told her. It all made sense, what she said, when she said it, but it was all so very complicated."

Elizabeth sighed. Lydia was a good girl but so naive, so very young and inexperienced. If she ever met this Annie, she'd certainly give her a talking-to for filling Lydia's head with such nonsense.

"There, there, Lydia. Why don't you go lie down for a bit? I'm sure that you'll be the better for it. I wouldn't pay too much attention to what Annie says. She couldn't possibly know what she's talking about. I expect that she's just very upset herself, losing her friend like that so suddenly."

Obediently, Lydia left the room, but this was not the response that she'd been hoping for. Something wasn't right about Bridget's death, she was sure. She'd felt it, she told herself, from the beginning.

almost certainly she didn't. But if not that, then what was it that killed her?

One by one, Rush considered the other possibilities. Tainted food? However careful the hospital might be, that was always possible. It might have been a small thing, not affecting other patients, something brought by a visitor, perhaps, or perhaps she was especially sensitive.

What about death from inflammation of the stomach or bowels? This was also a possibility, if the inflammation was severe and longstanding. But if so, was it likely there'd have been such a misdiagnosis, as to think it a case of yellow fever? Could she have been taken with some ordinary fever, perhaps, and then dosed (or overdosed) with something that killed her? Again, that was a possibility. The doctors at Wigwam Hospital were entirely competent. The nurses, however – well, that was a different story. They were often little more than maids. Common girls, most of them, hired because they were willing to risk their lives by working at the hospital.

And yet there was Doctor Dobell's cryptic note, that he felt it was a "quite suspicious" death. And Dobell had a flair for accurate diagnosis.

∞ 6 ∞

Annie's suspicions festered and grew in Lydia's mind, despite Elizabeth's attempts to reassure her. She couldn't stop thinking about it and, as she did, she grew ever more certain that her cousin's death wasn't due to yellow fever at all. The cause was darker and more terrible.

Nearly every time Lydia spoke to Mrs. Powel she found some way to refer to her conviction and concern, directly or indirectly. Lydia's pestering was (for the most part) respectful, but stubborn and unrelenting. Frankly, Elizabeth told herself, it was getting to be quite annoying.

Sheer repetition finally wore Elizabeth down. She decided to talk to Doctor Rush to see if he could help put the whole matter to rest. He was her personal physician, and that of her late husband as well, and Lydia had always been in awe of him. Perhaps if she could persuade him to talk to Lydia, he could convince her there was nothing to worry about.

So Elizabeth invited Doctor Rush to tea. She was somewhat surprised that he accepted immediately. His note of acceptance came back to her right away, so he must have told the messenger to wait there while he wrote it.

"I would be glad of a chance to talk to you," he said, "without the need for any elaborate tea or other preparations. If you chanced to be free this afternoon, I would be happy to be at your disposal."

He duly arrived that afternoon. Elizabeth greeted him in the upstairs withdrawing room.

"It's just a simple tea," she apologized right away, though the array of food on the table before her was more than ample. "I do have coffee, tea, or chocolate, as you wish. You must try one of these orange biscuits too, they're really quite excellent. And a bit of butter cake as well," she added, as she began to heap his plate high, "and some sugared almonds and candied apricots."

"You are a sublime hostess my dear, but a terrible temptress," he protested, only partially joking. "You have sweets enough for three of me, at least. As you know, I firmly believe that moderation is the best preventative of illness." He accepted two biscuits and a piece of cake all the same, and a cup of tea to wash them down with.

"But you didn't invite me here just to feed me," he said, after a bite of cake and a few sips of tea. "It's actually a fortunate coincidence, for I have been thinking I ought to talk to you. Ladies first, however. What did you want to tell me?"

Elizabeth briefly recounted Lydia's conversation with Annie.

"So you see," she concluded, "Lydia is quite convinced that something is amiss, and I hope that you could help me to reassure her. I would love to set her mind at rest as she is pestering me quite unmercifully."

Doctor Rush thoughtfully studied his plate.

"Oh no, no more cake or biscuits," he said quickly, as Elizabeth reached for the cake to give him another portion. "It's only that I'm not sure what to say. I'm troubled by this new information, I have to say. I'm afraid that I am unable to provide you with any reassurance. To the contrary."

Elizabeth's eyes widened in surprise.

"To the contrary? You can't mean that there's any truth to this wild tale?"

"To say that it's true would be going a bit too far," Rush replied carefully, "but the circumstances are certainly suggestive. Doctor Dobell himself had very serious doubts about the case, I'm afraid. In fact, his view was perhaps the same as this Annie's."

"He thinks she was murdered?"

"Not quite that, perhaps, but it's a complicated thing. He'd sent me a note, you see. A note about Bridget's case and how odd it was. The note was unfortunately rather cryptic. I went to see him, to find out more, but discovered that he was gravely ill himself with the yellow fever. He died, I'm afraid, and I never did get a chance to talk to him. Recently, however, I assisted Mrs. Dobell in organizing her husband's effects and papers and found his journal."

Doctor Rush took another sip of tea, looking grave and thoughtful.

"The fact of the matter is, he didn't think the yellow fever killed her at all. Partly it had to do with her symptoms and partly on my theories on pulse and sweating."

"Pulse and sweating?"

"I have observed that in cases of yellow fever," he explained, "the presence or absence of certain symptoms indicate strongly whether a patient will live or die. In my experience, for example, when the patient has a certain type of soft, broken pulse, the patient inevitably succumbs to it."

Rush looked at Elizabeth to see if she was following his explanation. Satisfied that she was, he continued.

"When a patient sweats greatly after the first or second day, on the other hand, it is a sign that he will surely recover. It seems, according to Doctor Dobell, at least, that Bridget's symptoms were not of the fatal sort. I'm quite sorry he didn't live to tell me more about it." He paused, realizing how that sounded. "I'm so sorry, that sounds quite heartless of me, doesn't it?"

"Not at all." Elizabeth smiled gently. "I understand you entirely. As a doctor and a scientist, you must be passionate in seeking the truth in such things, must you not? Even when it contradicts your own thoughts and theories. Is it significant, though, in terms of Lydia I mean? As you yourself told me, not so long ago, there are other forms of fever that are fatal as well. Does it matter so much, whether it was the yellow fever or some other disease that killed her?"

Doctor Rush took another sip of tea, considering. How much should he say? He didn't want to upset things unnecessarily. Mrs. Powel, however, was strong-minded and intelligent. And with this story about Bridget and Senator Blount – well, perhaps it was best to tell her everything.

"I'm afraid that Doctor Dobell didn't think it was any kind of disease at all. He seems to have found the whole thing, as he put it, 'quite suspicious.' In the morning, he'd been quite confident she'd survive, yet she died that very evening. Her symptoms, moreover, weren't at all what you'd expect for a fever of any sort. It seemed to him more like an acute inflammation of the stomach or bowels, such as one might have from tainted food or even poison."

"Poison?" Elizabeth's eyes widened with shock. Could this Annie Dawson's suspicions possibly be right – could Lydia's cousin really have been murdered?

"He didn't express a definite opinion, mind you," Doctor Rush quickly cautioned her. "But he did say it was 'suspicious,' and that her death should perhaps be further investigated. Moreover, in light of what you say about Bridget and Senator Blount, it does seem to take on a greater significance. Is it certain that she was involved with him?"

Elizabeth was silent for a few moments, still absorbing this startling news. Then she realized that Dr. Rush was awaiting a response to his question.

"Bridget and Senator Blount?" She shook her head. "It's all a bit uncertain, I'm afraid. Wholly uncertain, to be strictly accurate. Lydia wasn't even entirely sure that Annie was talking about Senator Blount. She was upset and she is wholly ignorant of politics. She only remembered it was 'that Senator who is in trouble.' But it would have to be him, don't you think? No other Senator is 'in trouble' – at the moment, anyway. At least not that I know about."

"That does sound like Senator Blount," Doctor Rush agreed, "but I think we should know more before coming to conclusions. Maybe someone should talk to Annie, to try to get a more coherent and detailed story?"

"Yes, someone should talk to her," Elizabeth said thoughtfully. "And I know just the 'someone' who should do it."

∞ 7 ∞

Jacob would not be eager, Elizabeth knew, to involve himself in Lydia's problem. The task of finding Jefferson's would-be murderer earlier in the year had been such an ordeal that Jacob had sworn he'd never again get involved in anything like it. She had hopes, nonetheless, of persuading him. She was counting on his sense of justice and regard for the truth, and also she knew (though she didn't want to dwell on the reasons why) that it would be hard for him to resist her if she begged him for a favor.

An agreeable disposition would be best achieved, she thought, after a meal with ample food and wine. So she invited him to supper instead of merely to tea. She presented it as simply resuming their social get-togethers once again, giving no hint of her ulterior motive. She wasn't really deceiving him, she told herself. She'd told him the truth, just not all of it.

Not that she intended for Jacob himself to talk to Annie Dawson. He'd cross-examine her as if he was in a courtroom. She would be frightened and overawed, and he'd get nothing useful out of her. The Senate Doorkeeper, on the other hand, was a solid, sensible, and reassuring sort of fellow. Annie would surely open up to him and he could give a reliable report. And Jacob was obviously the one to ask him.

Once Jacob had been invited to dine (and of course he'd promptly accepted), she suffered after-thoughts of anxiety and regret. Had she done the right thing, asking him to come so soon after his return? Would he misunderstand her motives for inviting him? This last July, she'd allowed things to go too far and in the wrong direction. She blamed it on the stress of having been herself a murder suspect at the time, when the Philadelphia authorities, knowing how much she hated Thomas Jefferson, had decided she was the one who was trying to murder him. In her relief at Jacob's finding the true murderer and proving her innocence of the crime, she'd (quite understandably) been carried away by her sense of gratitude.

Even if she was inclined to allow herself a romantic interest once again (which she was not, most assuredly), Jacob Martin was a very poor choice for it. He was a visitor, just passing through. Their relationship had no future prospects.

Thank heavens the Congress had ended and he'd gone back for months to Charleston. Thinking about it these past few months, she'd decided that for their relationship to go on, they must begin again on a different footing. They should be friends, not terribly close friends even. More like very friendly acquaintances.

Such were the thoughts that occupied her mind. Why then did she await his arrival with such impatience?

Jacob, for his part, had no such concerns. As he walked the familiar route to her house, in the soft purple glow of a lingering twilight, he found himself humming a silly popular tune and smiling.

Third Street between Spruce and Walnut, where she lived, was in the city's most prestigious neighborhood. Stately townhouses lined the streets for blocks around, their stolidity and expensive architectural details proclaiming that here lived wealthy and prominent citizens. Elizabeth Powel's house was no mansion, to be sure, nothing like the Bingham's house that lay beyond it. Nonetheless, it was tasteful and attractive. The brickwork was carefully laid in Flemish bond, with bands of granite marking the division between the floors and a carved white dental molding edging the roofline. Each of the mullioned windows had white wooden shutters, also nicely carved, and decorative brick lintels with granite keystones in the middle.

Most impressive of all, though, was the entry-way. The doorway was flanked by two tall Doric columns supporting a massive carved pediment, all painted white to match the dental molding and the shutters. Within this imposing frame was a substantial paneled door with a delicate fan window above it.

At Jacob's knock the door was opened by Lydia herself. Knowing why her mistress had asked him to come, she'd shooed the footman away and lingered in the hallway awaiting him. Lydia gave him a welcoming smile, took his coat, and escorted him up the broad mahogany stairs to the withdrawing room.

The withdrawing room was a comfortable room intended for informal entertaining, in contrast to the grand formal ballroom that adjoined it. It was furnished with a folding game-table, a large curtained bookcase, a tea table, and a number of upholstered mahogany chairs. At one end was the fireplace, with a nicely crackling fire, at the other end two tall windows hung with heavy silk draperies overlooked the formal back garden. A fashionable paper with a Grecian border adorned the walls, along with a large circular mirror and a judicious selection of original engravings and oils, the fruits of Elizabeth's husband's European travels. As Jacob entered the room, the thick Brussels carpet in jewel-like tones cushioned his feet and softened his footsteps.

Elizabeth sat at the tea table by the fire, wearing a fashionable high-waisted dress of fine muslin sprigged all over with tiny silver-spangled flowers. She looked as lovely as Jacob remembered. A Kashmiri shawl with a pink and green design on a cream wool background rested gently about her shoulders and a sheer white linen cap with a delicate lace edging set off her chestnut-colored hair. Jacob didn't wonder that men still wrote her poetry. He'd even written a verse or two himself, if only he dared to show her.

"Please do sit down." Elizabeth gestured at an empty chair across the table. "It's good to see you. It's been so long." She was disturbed to hear the wistful longing in her tone. You're just friends, just friends, she scolded herself.

"Yes, it has been nearly half a year since we've seen each other." Jacob took his place at the table, contriving to move his chair even closer to her. He could smell her perfume – jasmine and sandalwood, undoubtedly Parisian. She must have bought it long ago, before the French Revolution put an end to such luxuries. Feeling her presence so near, all his good resolutions to maintain a dignified reserve started to melt away. It was all he could do not to reach out and touch her.

"I've missed our times together," he said warmly, "if I may say so."

Elizabeth felt herself flush.

"Would you like a glass of claret?" she asked awkwardly. "There's coffee, chocolate, and tea also, but the claret is very good."

Hastily, on the pretext of getting the decanter of claret, she moved her chair a more comfortable distance away. Really, she thought, this is just too absurd. Shall we be moving our chairs round and round the table?

Chagrined, Jacob drew away in turn.

"Yes, I'll take the claret, thank you."

Once he had glass in hand, he took a healthy swig and surveyed the table.

There were so many blue and white porcelain serving dishes arrayed before him that he could barely see white damask cloth beneath them all. There were slices of roast beef and ham, cold pork pies, fried fish filets, and chicken fricassee with onions, and on the side, stewed apples, sweet potato pudding, and eggs with gravy, along with bread, biscuits, butter, and cheese. And after all this, there would be the desserts as well. Knowing the cook's specialties, there might be almond custard in addition to sweetmeats and cake, or perhaps a whole apple, perfectly spiced and baked in a crisp and buttery puff of pastry. As Elizabeth was well aware in planning the menu, Jacob had a not-so-secret weakness for sweets.

They sat in companionable silence while Elizabeth filled his plate with the first of several helpings.

"How have you been, since I saw you last?" Jacob asked with careful politeness, determined not to upset her a second time. "I heard that there was another epidemic of yellow fever. I was worried, I must confess. I hope that it has not touched your friends or family?"

"No one close," she said guardedly, "but there's a curious story there. I'll tell you later on, if you're interested. But first, tell me about yourself. How was your time in Charleston?"

He took another sip of claret before he answered. The truth was, the months in Charleston had been full of unwelcome surprises, as he discovered just how much damage the public attacks on his integrity and competence during the protracted murder investigation last session had done to him.

"Well enough," he answered simply. "My sister brought the children to Charleston for a visit. It was wonderful to see them again."

Noting Jacob's reluctance to say more, Elizabeth turned the conversation to the safer subject of politics.

"How do things stand with Senator Blount? Have there been any further developments?"

"I know little more than you do, I expect," Jacob responded. "The Senate hasn't been involved since we expelled him last July. The House of Representatives Impeachment Committee is apparently still investigating."

"Do you think the British had actually agreed to give him money and weapons? Do you think things had really gone that far? I read British Minister Liston's denials, but of course that's what he would say. He'd hardly admit it, would he?"

Jacob shrugged.

"It's anyone's guess, how far the British had committed themselves. I think it was Blount's own idea, however, at least originally. He'd speculated deeply in Tennessee land from what I hear. If Spain gave the Mississippi delta to the French, given how we're practically at war, the French would probably cut off our shipping. Then Blount's land would be valueless and he would be ruined."

"It's a wild scheme, but he's a wild man," Elizabeth said judiciously. She'd met Senator Blount a time or two and she found the unfolding story perversely satisfying. He seemed a charming fellow on the surface but she'd always thought that, underneath, he was thoroughly and ruthlessly selfish.

This naturally led to a discussion of the session soon to begin and to the disastrous state of French relations. As their conversation flowed on, Jacob cleaned his heaping plate of food and, as he had hoped, some of his favorite desserts had been brought to the table. The baked apple had been especially delicious and was most quickly consumed. Elizabeth, smiling, helped him to another. It was time, she decided, to broach the subject of Bridget's murder.

"To change the subject just a bit," she said casually, "I wonder if I might beg a favor? It concerns Mr. Mathers, actually, your Senate Doorman, but I thought you might speak to him for me."

Jacob's warning instincts were dulled by sugary contentment, and he graciously nodded.

"Your wish is my command."

"I mentioned before that there was a curious story to tell, about the yellow fever?

"Yes?"

She took a deep breath and hoped for the best.

"Well, now I shall tell you. Lydia has a cousin, Bridget LeClair, who died during the yellow fever epidemic, a little over a month ago."

"Bridget LeClair? A French name, but I thought that Lydia was Irish."

"Yes, Irish as they come. It's Bridget's husband who was French."

"So sorry, I interrupted," Jacob said contritely. "Please do go on."

"It seemed a straightforward matter at first, her cousin's death, what with the epidemic and so forth. Then Lydia spoke to one of her cousin's friends, someone who works – worked – with Bridget. They were both employed by Mr. and Mrs. Waln, I gather. The friend, Annie Dawson, filled Lydia with fanciful ideas about how her cousin's death was suspicious."

"Was there any good reason for her suspicions?"

"I don't really think so, but there's one little thing." Elizabeth frowned. This was the part that even she had trouble entirely dismissing. "According to this girl's story, Lydia's cousin was intimate with Senator Blount, at about the time he was planning his conspiracy."

"Senator Blount?" Jacob's eyes narrowed ever so slightly.

"Yes, the very same. It seems that he was a seducer as well as a schemer. Or anyway, that's what Lydia thinks that Annie said."

Elizabeth took a deep breath and then plunged on into the crux of it.

"Lydia didn't really understand it all, I'm afraid, and her account is rather incoherent. She's been on and on about it though, to the point that my nerves are quite frayed. So I'm wondering if Mr. Mathers could speak to Annie himself, to find out what she really told her? Of course, it's absurd to think it could really be murder."

"Murder, you say?" Jacob set his teacup down with a clatter. "On the word of some flighty servant girl?"

"That's just the point, isn't it?" Elizabeth asked reasonably. "It's probably all some foolish fantasy, but Lydia's story is so muddled, I hardly know what to make of it. It would be just a little talk, to get the story straight and see what he makes of it. To set Lydia's mind at ease, for her sake and also so she would stop pestering me. It would be nothing for you to ask him, and I'm sure he wouldn't mind it."

"I imagine he would," Jacob said dryly, "but as for myself . . ."

"I wouldn't ask you, I really wouldn't, but I'm at my wit's end, really." Elizabeth sighed helplessly. Portraying a woman in distress was turning out to be easier than she thought. "Someone has to talk to Annie, and I don't know who else to ask to do it." She looked deep into Jacob's eyes and smiled very sweetly. "You did say, just a moment ago, that you'd be happy to do me a favor?"

Jacob sighed. She was right; he'd already said he would. There was no option but surrender.

"All right. But just this one thing, that's all. Mathers will go and talk to this Miss Dawson and that's the end of it. Are we agreed on it?"

"Let us see what Mr. Mathers says," she responded cautiously. "As you say, it's likely just the foolish idea of a flighty servant girl. I certainly hope that's all there is to it."

∽ 8 ∾

To no one's great surprise, Congress didn't actually begin on November thirteenth, the day it was officially supposed to. The gathering that morning was nine short of a quorum, as only eight of the thirty-two Senators had managed to arrive in Philadelphia.

To be sure, there were many perfectly valid excuses for delays in travel. Ships were prey to storms and carriages were prone to drunken coachmen, or to losing a wheel in the deep rutted paths that passed for roadways and overturning into some nearby ravine. For many, however, the late arrival had simply become a convenient habit. Jacob, who had always made a point of being punctual, was annoyed.

He and a handful of others lingered for a while in the Senate Chamber, gossiping amongst themselves and hoping for (but not expecting) a tardy appearance by more of their colleagues. It was a handsome room, more grandly conceived and expensively furnished than the House of Representatives Chamber on the floor below it. Each of the Senators had his own free-standing mahogany desk with a locking drawer and a matching chair up-holstered in red Moroccan leather. The floor was covered by a specially-made rug of immense proportions hand-knotted in bright colors. In the center was a great American eagle holding an olive branch, a scroll reading "E PLURIBUS UNUM," and thir-teen arrows, surrounded by a circle of shields bearing differing symbols, representing each of the thirteen states.

The House Chamber below, on the other hand, was a plain white room where the hundred and six members sat packed close-ly together on plain, straight-backed chairs at three long, curved rows of continuous tables. It only made sense, any Senator would tell you, for the Senators were (in their own estimation at least) manifestly of a higher standing. In the beginning, there was even talk of Senators having titles. The Representatives ridiculed them mercilessly, however, greeting them with comic bows and sarcas-tic greetings – "Your Highness of the Senate" and so forth, until the Senators (with bad grace, it must be said) gave up on it.

Jacob eyed the raised dais facing the rows of Senators' desks, where the Vice-President would be when he was presiding. It was styled as a sort of throne, with a tall upholstered chair under a canopy of crimson silk damask, matching the elaborately swagged and tasseled damask curtains that adorned the windows. Jefferson hadn't arrived yet, to no one's great surprise, so if Bingham was right about the vote count, Jacob would be sitting there himself once there was a quorum.

Once there was a quorum. After that first day, the scenario was repeated day after day. Every morning Jacob arrived at the Senate promptly, only to leave again. And every morning, when he saw James Mathers, he winced inwardly. He hadn't yet spoken to him about talking to Annie Dawson. His conscience nagged him but he ignored it until at last he could ignore it no longer. He'd be seeing Elizabeth again soon and he'd better have talked to Mathers before then.

Mathers was there every day, of course. He arrived well before eleven o'clock when the sessions typically began. After checking the messages and mail, he went about setting things in order – laying and lighting the fires, filling the inkwells, setting out sharp quills and candlesticks, and generally tidying up. After that, he had little to do but stand around, waiting and watching. His main task during the day's session was be to keep the visiting public in line, confined to the public gallery and not too rowdy. Until the session actually began, however, there wouldn't be any visiting public to speak of.

Today, after the Senators were once again dismissed for lack of a quorum, Jacob signaled to Mathers with a meaningful look and a tilt of his head in the direction of the Committee Rooms that lay behind the public gallery. Mathers met up with him there once the other Senators had departed.

"I have a favor to ask of you," Jacob began simply. "You needn't do it, if you'd rather not."

"I'd be glad to be doing you a favor, that I would," Mathers said honestly. "What is it?"

"You remember Lydia, Mrs. Powel's maid? I believe you have met her?"

Mathers nodded. He had met her a few months ago, when Rachel had been so ill that she almost died. Lydia had been taking care of her at Mrs. Powel's behest, bringing her food and fixing her supper, when he'd armed himself with a load of firewood and summoned the courage to visit her also.

"Lydia has a cousin. One of her many cousins, that is. This cousin died of the yellow fever, in early October I think it was. It seems pretty straightforward, but Lydia's very upset about it. She heard some odd story from one of her cousin's friends."

Mathers cocked a quizzical eyebrow.

"This friend – her name is Annie Dawson," Jacob continued, with a noticeable lack of enthusiasm, "worked with Lydia's cousin at the Walns. Mr. and Mrs. Robert Waln. I expect you've heard of him?"

"Of course." Everyone had heard of Robert Waln. He was only thirty-two, but he was second only to Stephen Girard among the city's most prominent merchants. He was active in politics as well. The year before, he had narrowly lost a bid for the House of Representatives. Everyone expected him to try again in the next election and then be elected.

"The problem is, this Miss Dawson seems to think there's something odd about Bridget's death, or so Lydia says she told her. Miss Dawson said that Bridget was involved with 'the Senator who's in trouble,' apparently, and that's why Bridget died. Lydia doesn't know anything about politics and her account to me was rather garbled. There's probably nothing to it," he concluded hopefully, "but Mrs. Powel wondered if you might talk to Miss Dawson, and see what it's really all about."

Mathers's face brightened with enthusiasm.

"A suspicious death, you're saying? You can be sure I'll talk to her, and with pleasure."

"I didn't say 'suspicious.' Just odd," Jacob corrected him sharply.

"No more murders, is that it?" Mathers winked at him, not the least bit bothered by Jacob's tone. "Never you mind about that, if that's what you're thinking. Looking into another murder would be lovely, to be sure, but it's some new tidbit about Senator Blount, is what I'm hoping for. Many's the drink I've bought for old Tom, to hear his tales about Senator Blount from the House Committee. It's about time he'd be buying the beer for a change."

At the mention of Tom Claxton, the Doorkeeper of the House, Jacob's frown grew even deeper.

"Now don't go spreading wild tales around. We've plenty enough going on this session, without adding in rumors and scandal. Just talk to this Miss Dawson and get a straight account, so Lydia can calm down and rest easy. I gather she's been pestering Mrs. Powel about it quite a lot."

What with one thing and another, it was few days before Mathers had a chance to go to the Walns. He found Annie outside the kitchen in the yard, hanging up freshly laundered shirts and shifts. She was a pert young thing, blond and shapely, wearing a long-sleeved gown of blue and white striped linen, with a short wool cape around her shoulders. It was chilly in the Waln's back yard, just barely warm enough for the clothes to dry instead of freezing, and she was hanging things up this way and that, in a hurry to be finished.

She looked askance at Mathers at first, seeing this tall and burly stranger. But he smiled in his most winning way and called her by name.

"I'm looking for Miss Dawson – that's you, isn't it? For I've been told to look in the yard for a comely lass, and here you are and no one could be prettier." Mathers eyed her appraisingly. With her delicate features and a figure to match, he wasn't very greatly exaggerating.

"And who are you to speak so bold, I ask you?" Annie's initial wariness had clearly mellowed. She wasn't any man's fool, but if this fellow wanted to flatter her, she didn't exactly mind it. "James Mathers at your service, Mistress. The Doorkeeper of the Senate."

She cocked her head and fixed him with a level gaze. "And what might the Doorkeeper of the Senate be doing here with me?"

"It's not Senate business, if that's what you mean. Though I did come here on account of a Senator. It's about a conversation you had recently with the maid Lydia, if you recall? She reported your conversation to Mrs. Powel, her mistress, and she told Senator Martin, and he told me."

"Lydia? Would that be Bridget's cousin Lydia that you're referring to?"

"The very same."

"And what's it to you – or her – or him?"

Mathers considered how best to respond. She seemed a shrewd girl and, according to Lydia's report, she did seem to care about her friend Bridget. She'd tell him the most, he decided, if he laid it right out for her.

"Well, Lydia was powerfully struck by what you said, but as upset as she was, and unfamiliar with things political, she only had a general impression, so to speak. When it comes to the details, she didn't really get them clear. So Mrs. Powel asked Senator Martin, to ask me if I could come around and see you, and ask you to tell it all again."

"About Senator Blount?" she asked shrewdly. "Is that what you want to know?"

"Yes, that and your suspicions. I gather you had suspicions about why she died?"

Annie sat herself down on the garden bench and wrapped her cloak tighter around her. She looked thoughtful.

"My 'suspicions,' you're calling it? Yes, I suppose that's what they are. Well, I'm happy to tell you. It's not a short story, though, so you'd better sit down. And sit close," she added sweetly, patting the bench just beside her, "close for warmth. It's powerful cold out here."

So Mathers sat down and she began to talk, taking her time and obviously enjoying it. Bridget was a popular girl it seemed, friendly and good-tempered. Also something of a beauty, according to Annie, but none too bright, to put it kindly.

"There was any number of men that she knew quite well, if you know what I mean," Annie said with a coy sideways glance. "Not that she was a wanton. She couldn't help it, could she, that she was such a pretty girl? She attracted the men and she wanted to make them happy. She didn't know any better. That's how she was."

"A nice girl, but maybe too innocent, even simple-minded?"

"Simple, that's a good way of putting it. To tell the truth, she didn't have as much sense as would fill a teaspoon."

"And what about Senator Blount? What was the connection there? How did she even know him?"

"Before she came here, she worked as a laundress, going house to house. She often got washing from the lodgers at the boarding house where he lived. She was friends with Mrs. Finch, the lady what ran it. Bridget had a regular business there – always very popular with the lodgers, she was, being so good at washing their clothes and pretty too."

"So that's how she met Senator Blount?"

"That's how it was. He took quite a liking to her. Even when she left off going to the boardinghouse and didn't do any more washing, he kept right on seeing her, giving her money and little presents."

"So you think there was something between them?"

Annie nodded emphatically.

"I surely do. She was seeing him. I'm sure of it. I even saw them together, and her so flushed and excited, it was clear what was going on. He'd come by here some times, asking for her, even when his wife was in town."

"It's not a pretty story," Mathers observed, "but why does it make her death suspicious? A rich gentleman, a pretty servant girl, that's nothing unusual. Things like that are happening all the time."

"Well, it may not seem like so much when I'm telling you, but Senator Blount isn't your ordinary gentleman, is he? Treason, that's what they say, and there's others who was in it with him. Other men they don't even know about, maybe. What if Bridget knew who they were? Maybe someone would kill her to keep it secret, wouldn't they? After all, she's only a servant girl, as you say."

It was speculation, nearly all of it, but if I was Annie, thought Mathers, I'd be suspicious too.

"Did you visit her, in the hospital?"

"I meant to, but I put it off too long. Maybe I was afraid to go there, afraid that I'd get sick too. And that's another thing. If she really had yellow fever, why didn't any of the rest of us get it too? Not even me, and I was sleeping right beside her."

Annie gave him a look that said "answer that, if you can," with a pert little smile and one eyebrow raised coquettishly.

"I'd better get back to the laundry now, but there's the tale, if that's what you came for. And one thing more. Toward the end, before Bridget died, I could tell she was worried. Something had scared her, scared her a lot. So much that she even wouldn't tell me."

After interviewing Annie Dawson, Mathers felt rather satisfied with himself. So he thought he might chance a visit to Dobson's book and stationery store – the Old Stone House, as people called it. It was only a few blocks out of his way. With any luck, Rachel McAllister would be there.

When he entered the shop, there was sadly no sign of Rachel. Her colleague Derrick Wilkins, a cynical old soul with a cheerful attitude, was tending the store alone.

"I know who you've come to see," Derrick greeted him with a broad wink. "Or am I mistaken? Surely the Senate doesn't need more ink and parchment, when they're not even yet in town? And as many times as you've been here, you must have stored up enough extra for several whole sessions, even if they used half the paper to light the fires."

"You're a witty one, aren't you? Is this how you treat your best customers? Perhaps the Senate ought to take its business elsewhere, where we get some respect." Mathers spoke as if gravely offended, but the effect was offset by the hint of a smile on his rugged features.

"So now you decide where to shop, do you?" Derrick rejoined lightheartedly. "I thought your Secretary Mr. Otis was the one in charge of purchasing stationery supplies, and you were running his errands on sufferance?"

Mathers scowled, this time in earnest.

"That's a sensitive subject, as you know very well – or ought to. You needn't rub it in. You know what I'm on about, so you can do me a favor and tell me. Where is fair Rachel McAllister?"

"Sorry, old fellow. She's not tending the store today. They've left me here all by my lonesome. Mr. Dobson's like a man on fire, trying to finish up the next volume of his *Encyclopaedia*, so he's dragged her off to help him with the typesetting. She learned it from helping her husband you know. Too bad she couldn't continue his printing business. There were too many debts, I suppose. I hear he wasn't the best of businessmen."

"Did you know him?" Mathers asked eagerly.

"Well yes, I did know him a bit." Derrick motioned Mathers closer. "And the publishing trade's rather close-knit, you know, so there's always plenty of gossip. I heard a thing or two, and there's many a story I can tell you."

"Tell me, then." Mathers was instantly attentive.

"Well, for one thing, did you know that her husband was her father's apprentice? They say she married him to please her father." Derrick stopped and looked at Mathers teasingly.

"Go on, tell me more," Mathers said impatiently. "What was he like, this fellow?"

Just then, the shop door opened. They both looked up at once and saw Rachel herself standing there at the door, looking at them and frowning.

Rachel wasn't beautiful, not exactly, but she had lively blue eyes and thick black hair, and her figure was petite and nicely rounded. In Mathers's own view, her presence lit up a room, especially when she smiled at him. She was dressed, as usual, in a plain and practical outfit – a long-sleeved gown of brown figured calico, with a substantial checked linen apron over it.

She looked at them searchingly, suspicious.

"What have you been talking about? You look like you're plotting something, you two. You're a proper pair of scoundrels."

"A deep, dark murder, is what it is," Derrick improvised.

A knowing look came over Rachel's face.

"Are you talking about Lydia's cousin?"

How in heaven does she know about that, Mathers wondered, when I've only myself just learned of it? But then he remembered that Rachel and Lydia had become friends a few months ago, when Rachel had been deathly ill and Lydia (at Mrs. Powel's insistence) had helped take care of her.

"I wouldn't say as it's murder, not yet," he said cautiously. "So far, it's only suspicions."

Derrick looked at them both with astonishment.

"Say, what's this all about? When I said we were talking about murder, I was only joking."

Rachel looked at him curiously. What had they been talking about then, if it wasn't about Lydia's cousin? Then she shrugged and turned her attention back to Mathers.

"Have you talked to Miss Dawson then?"

"I have just now, as a matter of fact. Do you know her?"

"Oh no, I've never spoken to her. I've never even met her. Lydia told me about her, that's all. About how she thought her cousin Bridget's death was suspicious."

"And why was that?" Derrick broke in again, full of curiosity.

"Annie – Miss Dawson, that is – says that Bridget was a bit too friendly with men, in a manner of speaking," Mathers said delicately, with an anxious glance to see if Rachel was shocked or offended. "Some of her 'friends,' like Senator Blount, maybe had secrets they didn't want known. Or they knew other people's secrets, perhaps. She thinks that Bridget learned something dangerous."

"That's a lot of maybes," Rachel said skeptically.

"But how thrilling if she's right." Derrick was enthusiastic. "High politics leads to murder – what a story! Just think of the scandal. So you're investigating again," he asked Mathers pointedly, "you and Senator Martin?"

Mathers shook his head.

"It's only suspicions, like I said, and only this one girl Annie Dawson. So don't get ahead of things. And Senator Martin's not so eager to investigate anything again, that's for sure, not after such a rough patch as he had last time."

"But what about you? Won't you find out what's going on?" Rachel looked at him with trust and confidence.

What else could he say?

"Of course I will. You can count on it."

∞ 9 ∞

President John Adams and Abigail were relaxing in the more casual dining room that the family used. The serving dishes and dinner plates had been cleared away, leaving just the drinking glasses and a dish of nuts on the table. Smiling contentedly at the memory of the roast goose he'd just devoured, Adams poured himself a nice glass of Madeira and picked up a newspaper. It happened to be *Porcupine's Gazette*, published by William Cobbett. For a man feeling wholly at ease and hoping to remain so, it was an unfortunate choice.

Cobbett's *Porcupine's Gazette* was a highly partisan and intemperate scandal-rag, like Bache's *Aurora and General Advertiser* but quite the opposite in terms of its politics. Whereas Bache was a rabid Republican, Cobbett was a monarchist, a British subject and totally loyal to King George.

Not long after the Revolution, when feelings still ran high against those who'd supported the enemy Great Britain, Cobbett had decorated the window of his offices with a large portrait of the King himself, with innumerable portraits and engravings of sundry other kings, queens, princes, bishops, and nobles surrounding it. It was a deliberately provocative display of his contempt for Independence. He was brave and also lucky that his window survived.

Everyone read the paper nonetheless, even those who vehemently disagreed with him, for Cobbett was a bold and extraordinarily witty man. His paper was a reliable source of amusement, provided that you were not the target of his pen. He never shrank from printing outrageous gossip or viciously clever opinions, and people couldn't help but want to know what he would say next.

Adams had hardly begun to read it when Abigail began to hear a tirade of furious mutterings, delivered in an ever-increasing volume.

"That blasted Cobbett, that madman!" Adams's face was suffused with an angry flush of crimson. "Even for him, this is beyond outrageous. I know he hates Jefferson but there's such a thing as libel." He thrust the paper fiercely in Abigail's general direction. "Just look at this."

Abigail rose from her armchair and picked up her spectacles. Really, she ought to insist he stop reading the Philadelphia newspapers. Every time he read them lately, he had a fit.

When she reached his side, Adams handed her the paper, jabbing a stubby finger at a paragraph set prominently in the middle of the front page.

"There. You see?"

Even without her glasses, Abigail had no trouble reading the heading. It was printed in large black capital letters: "WHAT SECRETS DID SHE LEARN IN SENATOR BLOUNT'S EMBRACES THAT LED TO HER DEATH?"

Oh dear, she thought, maybe this really is something to get upset about. Anxiously she read on.

"We recently learned of the curious case of a certain housemaid who died of the yellow fever, or so it was thought. Did she die from Doctor Rush's deadly ministrations, bled to death by way of a "cure"? In the opinion of other doctors, it wouldn't be the first time, but that was not the trouble here. We have it on good authority that the poor girl was poisoned. Now those in the know are asking, who gave her the poison, and why? She was only a housemaid, but she was beautiful and well-connected. Among her intimates, we are reliably informed, was Senator Blount. What secrets were revealed to her in the bedchamber, what deadly secrets worth killing for? Did she learn that a certain very highly-placed Republican official from Virginia, one might even say the highest, is, as has been rumored, part of Blount's treasonous cabal? Would he kill to keep his dangerous secret from being exposed? Knowing this man's limitless ambition to be President, can one have any doubts as to the answer?"

"'A certain highly placed Republican official from Virginia?'" Adams repeated furiously. "'One might even say the highest?' If this isn't libel, I don't know what is. He's plainly accusing Jefferson – my Vice President – of murder."

Instead of sharing his outrage, Abigail looked thoughtful.

"Do you think it could be true? As Cobbett says, there have been rumors, more than rumors really, that Mr. Jefferson was involved with Senator Blount. It's not as if Mr. Jefferson was above that sort of devious machination. Remember when he was Secretary of State, how he plotted with the French Minister Genet to overthrow President Washington. And I'm sure he was behind the Whiskey Rebellion. I've heard it on very good authority."

"Even if that's all true," her husband countered, "and I don't say it isn't, mind you – that's all just politics, not murder. Jefferson is weak, confused, uninformed, and ignorant, I'll grant you that, and he's eaten to a honeycomb with ambition. But murder? That's a different thing entirely. Frankly, I don't think he's up to it."

"He's not above murder for political reasons," Abigail persisted. "Remember how he defended all the killings by those revolutionaries in France. What if there was proof that Jefferson really was involved? Jefferson, a traitor to his country. Wouldn't that be a fatal blow to his beating you in the next election? I'm sure he'd rather see a housemaid die than give up his dreams of being President."

"You have a point," Adams conceded grudgingly, "but how could he do it? He left Philadelphia as soon as he could in July. He was still at home at Monticello when the girl died."

"For a man like that, it's no trouble. As you know very well, he's used to doing his dirty work indirectly through friends and agents. In Philadelphia these days, I'm afraid you could easily find someone to do a murder for money."

"My own Vice President accused of murder." Adams finished the last of his Madeira morosely. "It's so unseemly. And a mere housemaid, too. As if I didn't already have enough problems, between the Republicans, the French, and the hotheads in my own Federalist Party. Pity me, my dear. Washington was never plagued as much as I am. Everyone loved him. He could do no wrong. But he's the one who created the mess we're in now, and I'm the one who must deal with it."

"Don't worry about Mr. Cobbett's accusations, my dear." Abigail smiled at her husband fondly. "What's bad for Jefferson is good for you. Would you like another glass of Madeira?"

❧ IO ❧

Thomas Jefferson, still comfortably settled at his Monticello home, rose early as was his habit. He ate a light breakfast and then went to his study to tend to his correspondence. Some days he enjoyed it; some days it was a chore. Today, he found it positively hellish.

Last evening a fast-riding messenger had brought him a letter from Philadelphia. He had opened it eagerly (though, it must be said, with a tinge of apprehension) and thus had learned of Cobbett's accusations. Just so he didn't miss the point, his correspondent noted that the other papers would soon be following suit, not only in Philadelphia, but also in Boston, New York, and etcetera. So he could be assured, the friend helpfully informed him, that, soon enough, all the world would read that he was accused of murdering a servant girl.

Jefferson felt a rising sense of apprehension as he pondered the implications. He was every bit as calculating as Abigail and John esteemed him, and the next Presidential elections were scarcely three years away. It had been close the last time. Adams had only narrowly defeated him. He was determined that, next time, it would come out the other way.

Against all reason, however, people believed what they read in the papers, even if it was only based on rumor and innuendo, or even outright animosity. Left to his own devices, Cobbett would surely keep the scandal going as long as possible. It was obvious that if he didn't stop things soon, his chances of being President would be gravely harmed.

He had to intervene, to divert attention from himself and onto other possible suspects, but what could he do from so far away? Now he regretted delaying his departure for Philadelphia. He would have to manage the scandal long-distance. He needed help.

James Monroe came to his mind immediately. Monroe had helped him enormously so many times. Perhaps Monroe could write to the doorman James Mathers and encourage him to look into things? Given how the fellow had enjoyed it the time before, probably he wouldn't need much encouragement.

That wasn't enough, though, in a matter of such consequence. A lowly doorman wouldn't get much attention from the public and press. He needed someone who would make the headlines, someone who people would gossip about. Someone like Senator Martin. He was already notorious. And who knew? He might even find out who did it. After all, he managed to do it the time before, though he took a damnably long time about it.

Martin wouldn't be so easy to enlist as Mathers, though. "Never again, by God!" he'd loudly sworn, when Jefferson had jokingly suggested that he had a talent for finding murderers. He wouldn't be easy to persuade. He didn't seem to be very interested in the usual trading of favors or seeking of preferments that served as political currency.

Jefferson had a shrewd idea, however, that Mrs. Powel might be able to convince him to get involved. They seemed to be fairly close friends – even more than that, if one believed the current gossip. The problem was, he himself had no influence whatsoever with her. He'd lost the last tiny shred of her esteem her when he split with Washington. Ever since then, she had made it clear that she detested him.

She was close to her niece Nancy Bingham, though, and Mrs. Bingham still considered him a friend, despite her being the reigning queen of Philadelphia's Federalist society. She might be able to engage her aunt, and even think it was her own idea, if he handled it carefully.

His strategy decided, Jefferson carefully composed a letter to each, then made copies with his copy-press and carefully filed the copies. He was proud of his filing system, a series of tied-up bundles arranged alphabetically and chronologically. He could locate any letter in a minimum amount of time, or even instruct a servant how to find one.

His major task for the morning done, he looked up from his desk and out the window, surveying the view of his grounds with satisfaction. Being at home was a far better thing than suffering the tedium and hardships of Philadelphia.

Time for a cup of tea, he thought, and just then Sally Hemmings appeared, tea in hand, as if he'd conjured her. After she laid it down, she spent a few moments slowly massaging his neck and shoulders.

He closed his eyes and enjoyed the touch of her fingers. How much she reminded him of his beloved dead wife Martha. The resemblance was no surprise, since Sally and Martha were half-sisters. Sally's mother was a slave, so Sally was a slave, but Sally and Martha had the same white father.

When she had left the room, Jefferson sipped his tea, his troubled thoughts chased away by his current contentment. Sally was such a pretty girl, so warm and sweet. And so obliging.

∞ II ∞

J acob woke up to the sound of rain. Again. It had been raining for days and days and days now.

The dreary weather so precisely matched his mood that he almost welcomed it. A vague malaise had settled into his soul, so unaccustomed that he wondered at the cause. Was it was missing his children, so far away? Or maybe it was his precarious financial situation that was worrying him? Well, perhaps, and no surprise. It was enough to worry anybody. A large loan was coming due – like farmers everywhere, he lived on credit. If his rice wasn't sold and paid for soon, he hadn't the least idea how he'd pay it. Or was his sense of dread due to the sudden flood of rumors and accusations? It was the same chilling, dangerous mixture that had nearly ruined him just months before, politics combined with murder.

Trying to shake off his gloomy mood, he quickly dressed, made his way through the drizzle to the City Tavern, and found himself an empty chair in the Subscription Room, so-called because that was where they kept all the latest newspapers. A waiter hurried over with a cup of coffee, strong and black, and the other members greeted him pleasantly. Soon he was happily at ease, sipping his coffee and reading a copy of Noah Webster's New York newspaper, the *Minerva*. Perhaps things were not really so out of kilter, after all. The world – his immediate world, at least – seemed in order.

When he reached the Senate, however, things went downhill. To begin with, he encountered Senator Sedgwick at the stairway. Sedgwick greeted Jacob with a sullen grunt and together they climbed the stairs. Sedgwick turned to face him as soon as they reached the landing.

"Have you read about Jefferson's murdering that housemaid?" Sedgwick brandished the newspaper smugly. "It's partly your responsibility, you know. If you'd let things alone last spring, he wouldn't still be around to murder people."

Sedgwick was deliberately provoking him, of course. He seemed to consider it a form of entertainment. Yet somehow Jacob always felt compelled to respond. He just couldn't abide the way Sedgwick tortured the facts and twisted them.

"There isn't a scrap of evidence in the story, you know. As far as I know it's just malicious speculation."

"I knew it." Sedgwick was darkly gleeful. "I knew you'd leap to defend him. You can't stand to see him accused of anything. Next thing I know, you'll be off investigating again, to prove that he didn't do it."

"Every time I talk to you, you accuse me of something," Jacob snapped, his dark eyes bright with anger. "I'm quite done with investigating murders, thank you. But unlike some, I'm careful in my opinions. I don't believe every damn fool thing I read in the newspapers."

With a grimace of disgust Jacob walked off down the hall, annoyed with himself even more than with Sedgwick. Every time they met, it was always the same. Why did he let the man rankle him so easily? It wasn't a smart thing at all to lose his temper. The Senate had serious business ahead. He couldn't waste his credit and credibility on petty things, if he hoped to have influence on the outcomes. He needed all the good-will he could muster.

He didn't get far down the hall before he was intercepted once again.

"Ah, Senator Martin." James Mathers stepped out of his office and into the hall, effectively blocking Jacob's progress. "I've been waiting for you. I've talked to Annie Dawson as you asked me. She's a lively one, I have to say," he added, tracing with his hands the outlines of a voluptuous figure. "Can you spare me a moment to hear about it?"

Jacob looked at Mathers warily. He'd hoped that Mathers's talking to Annie would put the whole thing to rest, but the man looked far too cheerful and excited.

"If you must," he said grudgingly, with a backward glance to see if anyone else was coming. "But just a moment. I've things to do. And let's not discuss it here in the hallway."

They stepped into one of the Committee Rooms and Jacob carefully closed the door.

"So, what did Miss Dawson have to tell you? Make it short," he said impatiently.

"All right, all right," Mathers grumbled, having looked forward to a lengthy telling of the tale. "If you must have it quick, here's the long and short of it. Annie says sure enough, this girl Bridget was bedmates with Senator Blount, and I believe her. The whole thing's suspicious as can be, if you're asking me. You're right to think it should be looked into."

"I don't think anything of the sort, as you know very well." Jacob's dismay was edged with anger. "You've seen the papers, so you know what trouble this all will cause, all this crazy talk and accusations. So Annie's got you going too, has she now? Was her credibility enhanced by her pretty figure?"

"'Got me going,' is it now?" Mathers said huffily. "I did you a favor, you and Mrs. Powel, so there's no call to be insulting my judgment. I'm not saying as how it's murder, am I? I'm not saying that Mr. Jefferson's to blame. I'm just saying Senator Blount knew Bridget, sure enough, so it's something that wants looking into."

"Based only on Annie's story?" Jacob said skeptically. "The testimony of a housemaid? Housemaids are a flighty lot to begin with and this one's practically still a child. You can't mean you take her wild ideas seriously?"

"Annie's a down-to-earth, sensible sort of person." The more Jacob challenged him, the more stubborn Mathers became. "I'm a pretty good judge of character, you know, and I believe her. Apart from which, given that it's Senator Blount, it's a pretty good story to begin with. He's one to go for a pretty wench, he is, and everyone knows it."

Jacob frowned. Damn and blast it! If it were any other Senator involved with some housemaid, it would hardly warrant a second thought. It would only be a choice bit of gossip. With Senator Blount already under investigation, however, and for a treasonous conspiracy at that, there really might be some greater significance.

"Well, we should refer it to the House Committee then. They're the ones investigating him."

Anne paused as if overcome and dabbed at the corners of her eyes with a dainty linen handkerchief. "Sorry. Sometimes it hits me like that, that she's really gone. Anyway, once she took sick and was sent away, that was the end of it. I never saw her again."

"So why do you think it had something to do with Senator Blount, if there was others besides him?"

"Who else had secrets worth killing for?" Annie asked reasonably. "I know all about him and his treason. Mr. Waln's a great one for politics. So he talks a lot about political things, him and his gentlemen visitors. They go on and on, talking louder and louder. I can't help but overhear. I've heard what they're saying about Mr. Jefferson. What if he was involved with Senator Blount and Bridget knew it? That would be grounds for murder, don't you think so?"

"It would be a great blow to Mr. Jefferson, certainly," Mathers said cautiously. "Even if he escaped the legal consequences, it could kill his hopes of being President. Still and all, you don't really know that he was involved or that Bridget knew anything about it."

"What else could it be, but something to do with Senator Blount?" Annie said stubbornly. "What other reason would anyone have for killing her?"

Mathers sipped the last of his beer slowly and thoughtfully.

"What else could it be? That's just the question, isn't it? Maybe the other men she knew had secrets too. If they do, I aim to find them."

As they walked away from the Kouli Khan, Annie lost her footing on one of the cobblestones and stumbled. She would have fallen, perhaps, had Mathers not instinctively taken her arm to steady her. Before he could move away, she had wrapped her arm tightly around his, holding it firmly.

"I thank you, Sir, for a very fine time," she said sweetly, snuggling close beside him. "Now that I know what you're after, I'm sure I can find a way to help you more. I know others who know Bridget, and I'll think on it really hard. I'm sure I can come up with something useful. You can ask me out again and I'll tell you."

Walking along with a pretty girl on his arm, Mathers couldn't help but feel a bit proud. He stood straighter and felt taller. At the same time, though, he felt uncomfortable, even guilty. Rachel McAllister, that was his girl. At least, so he always hoped. Didn't he?

∞ 13 ∞

The warehouses, mansions, and counting houses of Philadelphia's richest merchants can be found close to their docks, in the blocks around Front and Water Streets. Each had his own particular dock, jutting out into the river from the shore, to unload the cargoes of their heavily-laden ships that returned from across the globe, over every ocean. They brought cottons from India, silks and porcelains from China, and English rugs and furniture, as well as rum, sugar, and tropical fruits from the Caribbean, wines and spirits from France, Spain, and Portugal, and exotic spices from far off Pacific islands.

By now, the Delaware was full of chunks of ice and soon it would be frozen over. Meanwhile, business continued at a frenzied pace while the river was still passable. The streets were filled with a motley crush of people, goods, and vehicles, all of them in constant motion. Dozens and dozens of great ships were coming, going, or waiting at anchor, finishing or setting off on their last winter voyages.

The men who make their living off the seagoing trade are men of every color, nationality, and social station. There are ships' captains, mariners and seamen, and all the others whose labors support them – the carpenters, joiners, chandlers, iron mongerers, and sail-makers; the scriveners, factors, men from the insurance companies, and clerks from the counting houses; the odd-jobs boys and messengers, and the carters and wagoners patiently waiting with their carts and oxen.

Rough men strain at the ropes to lift the heavy cargoes into or out of the hold of the waiting ships, while others roll the two-hundred pound barrels down the docks to the warehouses. Scattered here and there amongst the crowd are the well-dressed merchants whose money makes it all possible, watching the loading and unloading of their ships, going to and from their counting houses, or keeping an eye on their cargoes and laborers.

Here too, side-by-side, you can find the poorest of the poor, the vagrants and vagabonds, the drunken layabouts, the beggars condemned to a lifetime of squalor. Along with throngs of the unemployed, hanging about in the hopes of even an hour's paid labor. By day, they loiter around the docks, by the night, they can be found in their own habitual establishments – a dark and seedy bar, a small rented space in a crowded tenement or on an attic floor, or a pitiful shed or mean low box of wood in a narrow, reeking alley. In the morning, one might stumble over a drunk sleeping rough on the street itself, or on the floor of the Market House, lying nearly comatose in his own putrid vomit.

There are only a few women, here and there. Sturdy fisherwomen gather by the Dock Creek inlet to cry out their husbands' catch for sale, dressed in patched and stained gowns or jackets and petticoats. Gaudy prostitutes in second-hand silks run their daytime errands or look for an afternoon's extra bit of business. A tall woman with skin like ebony stood by her cauldron of pepper pot soup on a corner, while others with baskets of pies and pasties hawk their tasty wares to the crowd. The scent of the spicy soup mingled with the smell of the river, dead fish, and wet canvas, the ripe, pungent odor of many unwashed bodies, and a hint of salt from the distant ocean.

Mathers made his way carefully through it all, alert to avoid the refuse underfoot, the wayward cart, the escaping barrel. Then he turned the corner onto Dock Street and suddenly the crowds thinned. He took a deep breath and looked around him.

Dock Street, where Dock Creek runs the last few blocks to the river, was once a prosperous residential area. In the beginning, when Dock Creek was a sweet, pure stream, it was a choice locale for the merchants to build their mansions. In time, however, the creek became little more than a reeking open sewer and (after many pleas from the local inhabitants) it was finally covered over. Now there was Dock Street instead, curving gently from Second Street down to the Delaware. It was the only crooked street in town, and Dock Creek itself now flowed hidden underneath it.

Mathers stopped in front of a narrow house in a cluster of mean, two-storey structures, huddling together side by side, as if shrinking away from the grander homes around them. The brick was dark with grime and the mortar was crumbling here and there. The wooden door before him had once been painted, but what color remained was worn and peeling. The stoop was freshly swept, however, and the windows had been polished. Shabby though the house might be, the occupant still had pretensions to gentility. A sign by the door read "Jean LeClair, Teacher and

Translator of the French Language, with Attention to Secrecy and Dispatch."

Mathers knocked at the door. Not long afterwards it was opened by a man who, Mathers judged, must surely be Mr. LeClair, Bridget's father-in-law.

Mr. LeClair looked like many of the French refugees who had given up everything to flee from certain death in the Revolution – a proud man, once of middling or better station, now fighting a losing battle against poverty. His once-fashionable suit of clothes was fine silk to begin with, but now was patched and worn. His face was lined not only with age but also with strain and worry.

He was, as Annie had rightly said, very much "old fashioned." He welcomed Mathers in, seated him in a comfortable, though threadbare, upholstered chair, and offered him a very tiny crystal glass filled with a quite decent sherry. They toasted the King and Queen of France, wishing death and retribution to those who had beheaded them. Not Mathers's sympathies, at least not so very strongly felt, but he felt that he had no choice but to go along with it.

As they toasted, Mathers looked around the room. Like Mr. LeClair's suit, the furnishings had once been elegant and expensive but now were badly worn and faded. In the corner, a small desk was covered with untidy piles of books and papers. The room smelled of dust and disappointment.

"I'm sorry to trouble you," Mathers began sincerely. "As I mentioned at the door, I'm investigating the death of your son's wife, Bridget." He hoped Mr. LeClair wouldn't ask what business it was of his to be investigating. Mr. LeClair, however, merely shook his head with a sigh. He had long ago given up questioning official authority.

"I know little of my daughter-in-law since my son passed away." His English was slightly accented, but fluent and elegantly constructed. "I have suffered from so many tragedies. First my son dies before me, and now his wife is gone. And without children, that is the worst of all. I shall die alone and the LeClair name shall be ended. Alas, it is the will of heaven, which we cannot change." LeClair spread his hands and shrugged his shoulders in resignation. "Ask what you will and I'll do my best to answer."

"As you know from the newspapers I'm sure, it's possible that your daughter-in-law didn't really die from the yellow fever after all. I'm sorry to say it, I really am, but some are saying that it was murder." Mathers looked anxiously at LeClair, wondering if he was being too blunt and callous, but LeClair just sat there impassively. "So I'm wondering if you know anything that might clear things up. Do you know of anyone who might have wanted to murder her?"

"Alas, Monsieur, I know nothing that can help you," LeClair said regretfully. "After my son passed away, Bridgette would not come to live with me as she ought to. She did come to visit me from time to time, but we had little conversation. Perhaps she thought that I would disapprove of her ways. She was right, I assure you. From what I have heard, her life was a scandal. She was *une femme publique*, free to anyone, if you understand me."

Mathers quickly decided that Jean LeClair was right. The man knew nothing that would help him. It was no wonder that Bridget had not talked to him freely. He clearly thought her no better than a whore. He must have been a difficult father-in-law, for all his courtly manners.

As Mathers was considering how best to take his leave politely, there was a knock at the door and LeClair rose stiffly to answer it. A painfully thin, kindly-looking woman stood at the stoop, carrying a willow basket. Mathers felt an instant pity for her. She was young and had once been fair. Even now, had she not been so pinched and worn, she might have been quite attractive.

"Ah, Madame Callender, come in," LeClair greeted her graciously. "This gentleman, he asks about Bridgette. Perhaps you can tell him something of interest."

Mrs. Callender peered in at Mathers for an instant, looked back at LeClair, and then rapidly backed away from the open doorway.

"Oh no, Mr. LeClair, I've nothing to say. You mustn't ask me. I'm in a hurry now, going off to the market. I only came by to ask if you wanted me to buy something for you." Not even waiting for the answer, she gave a brief, anxious smile and disappeared, almost tripping down the step in her haste to leave them.

LeClair gently closed the door behind her.

"Madame Callender is one of my neighbors," he explained. "She has a difficult husband and many children. Bridgette would go there from time to time to help her. She may know something of use to you, in spite of her denying it. She is the type one may easily talk to – *très sympathique*, as we say."

"Mrs. Callender, you say?" Mathers made a note of it, though he was sure he would remember. "And her husband? He wouldn't be James Callender the journalist, by any chance?" James Callender was a more notorious a journalist than William Cobbett, with an even more venomous pen, if that was possible. He was a mean-spirited, angry man and he drank too much in the bargain. A Scotsman by birth, he hated authority, was contemptuous of humanity, and indulged his talent for invective with a total lack of restraint. Since coming to America he'd embraced the Republican cause and now wrote for Benjamin Bache's *Aurora and General Advertiser.*

LeClair took a pinch of snuff from a small silver box and sniffed it up with great ceremony. A copious sneeze followed. He offered the open snuffbox to Mathers, who declined.

"He is, I am quite sorry to say. The poor woman, I wonder how she manages. Her husband makes very little, I think, and it's little wonder. Who would pay for it, when he writes such terrible things, such lies and insults?"

Mathers felt a surge of excitement. So Bridget was connected to James Callender! Callender loved nothing more than ferreting out the dark secrets of powerful and prominent men and then going after them. If Bridget was intimate with his wife, spending time in their household, she might have learned any number of secrets. First Senator Blount and now James Callender too. The girl was a positive magnet for scandal.

Mathers left Mr. LeClair and made his way down Water Street and into the market area. Perhaps he could find Mrs. Callender, corner her, and get her to talk. From the way she ran away, he was guessing she might know something that she didn't want to tell him.

As he walked along, he paid little mind to where he was going. In part, he was scouting about for Mrs. Callender. In part he was admiring the fresh good looks of the young country girls who had come to town to sell their chickens and cabbages.

He knew that he wasn't so young as he used to be. His muscular frame was softening around the edges, and there was a good bit of gray in his once jet-black hair. His romantic interests moreover, as he now reminded himself, were firmly attached to Rachel. Still, he wasn't dead. He could still admire the sight of a pretty ankle.

In proof of which, when a particularly good-looking young lady passed him by, a rose red ribbon around her creamy white neck and her hips gently swaying, he turned his head and appreciatively watched her walk away down the street behind him. As a consequence of which, when a young lad pushing a heavily-laden cart came out of the alley just ahead, they very nearly collided.

"You blockhead. Can't you see where you are going?" Mathers shouted angrily. In the Senate public gallery, his angry words and fierce look served to control the most rowdy visitor. This young lad, however, wasn't in the least afraid. He smiled at Mathers smartly as if he had not just nearly run into him.

"That I can't, Sir, begging your pardon. The packages, they was piled too high."

Mathers glowered all the more, but his anger had lost some of its conviction. The boy was impertinent, to be sure, but at the same time, he was so innocent, bright, and cheerful. Besides, the boy looked familiar somehow. Maybe this was some son of a friend of his? If so, it wouldn't do to be overly harsh. He softened his tone.

"What's your name, lad?"

"James, Sir, but they call me Jimmy. I work for Mr. Girard."

The lad pointed proudly at Girard's counting house a short distance away. What he said was strictly speaking true, but also misleading. He worked for any number of merchants, doing odd jobs like carrying, carting, or running messages, by the hour and by the job.

"Hmmph. Mr. Girard, is it? Jimmy what? What is your full name, you heedless young fellow?"

"Tucker, Sir. Jimmy Tucker, Sir."

"Well, young Tucker, didn't your father teach you better than this – that you ought to watch out where you're going?"

At that, the boy's bright spirits dimmed perceptibly.

"I'm afraid I don't have the benefit of a father, Sir. Well, I did have," he added gamely, "but I never knew him."

Out of nowhere, for no reason he could see, James Mathers began to feel a sense of foreboding.

"What about your mother, then? What about her?"

"She's dead now, her and the baby with her. It would have been my sister, named Catherine after my mother. So I'm an orphan I guess." The boy looked down, and was silent. Then he stood up, straight and tall. "I'm come from Bristol to make my way in the world, and I've come to Philadelphia."

"Indeed." Mathers felt strangely hesitant to question him more. He had known a Catherine from Bristol once upon a time, his sweet, dear Catherine. It was seventeen eighty-one, five years into the Revolution. He would have married her, but he had to go off to fight. He had looked for her when he returned but he couldn't find her. It was sixteen years ago that he'd known her. To his eye, the boy looked to be about sixteen. Don't be foolish, he told himself. It couldn't be.

"I'm sorry about your mother, lad. And what was her name, her full name?"

"She was a Tucker, Catherine Tucker."

Mathers had been holding his breath, hardly realizing it. Now he exhaled, relieved. It was only a coincidence, that's all. His Catherine wasn't named Tucker.

"Well you'd better go on about your business then," Mathers ended the conversation abruptly. "You'd best be more careful from now on. You're just lucky you didn't do me any serious injury."

His quest for Mrs. Callender entirely forgotten, Mathers made his way back to Congress Hall, still feeling unaccountably uneasy.

❦ 14 ❦

Thanks to the hatreds all around – merchant versus farmer, northerner versus southerner, partisan of Britain versus France, and (most of all) Federalist versus Republican – this session of Congress was looking to be as unproductive as the last one. The Republican Senators were just biding their time, waiting for reports from the diplomatic mission to Paris and trying to keep the Federalists from doing anything in the meantime. Even so, there was a great deal of meeting and debating.

From James Mathers's point of view, the Senate was far too busy. He chafed at how long the sessions seemed to be and how the Senate business delayed his efforts at investigation.

He was itching to track down Mrs. Callender again, to see if he could get something out of her. He also wanted to talk to Mrs. Finch, who ran the boarding house where Bridget had first met Senator Blount according to Annie. Sunday was his only free day, however, and that didn't seem the best day to talk to them. He wanted to catch them at home alone, when Mr. Callender was gone and Mrs. Finch's boarders also.

At last one day the Senate ended earlier than usual. Seizing his chance, Mathers set out immediately for the Callenders. Mrs. Callender was out, however, or so the ragged urchin who answered the door informed him. He doubted that it was really true, but the firmly closed door left him little option. Mrs. Callender had managed to avoid him once again but she couldn't keep it up forever.

So he set off to see Mrs. Finch instead, hoping she'd be a fine old busy-body, full of gossip and happy to share it.

Her boarding house was on Eighth Street past Arch, an up-and-coming area at the northern edge of the city's development. It was a middling neighborhood overall, home to butchers, blacksmiths, and the like, with a sprinkling of common laborers. It was nonetheless an excellent location for Congressmen and Senators to lodge, being quite convenient to the Congress. Mrs. Finch's establishment catered almost exclusively to this particular clientele, Republicans in particular.

Mathers knocked on the door, waited a while and then, when there was no response, he knocked again more loudly. This time, after a further wait, he heard heavy footsteps coming down the hallway. The door was opened by a large woman, ample in all directions. She smelled of wood smoke, he guessed most probably from the kitchen fire, as she was wearing a vast, grimy linen apron over her petticoat. Her face was smudged with bits of soot and her straw-colored hair was escaping here and there, sticking out from under her cap in wayward tendrils

"Yes, what is it?" She was abrupt, as if she'd been interrupted from important business.

He bowed low, as would a gentleman to a fine lady.

"Good day to you, Madam." He spoke in his most formal and gracious tones, hoping it would help to thaw her. "I'm James Mathers, the Doorman of the Senate of the United States, at your service. Is it Mrs. Finch, that I have the honor of addressing?"

"I'm Mrs. Finch," she said, her tone more friendly.

"I wonder if you could spare a moment," he began, but got no further.

"Come in, come in," she stepped back to let him enter, then turned around and set off down the central hallway. "I expect you want to ask me about Senator Blount. Come follow me out to the kitchen. I'll tell you everything I know, if you tell me what's going on with those folks in the Congress. The cook's gone off on some fool errand," she called out over her shoulder as she padded quickly toward the kitchen, "so I've got to keep an eye on the roast and the chickens."

He followed her down the hall and out the back door, to the kitchen building behind in the courtyard. Inside, the only light was from the fire and two smallish windows, but it was warm and cozy. A low fire was burning in the large, well-accoutered fireplace. Four plump chickens hung down from an iron spit hung over the fire, tied on with sturdy twine that kept them rotating by twisting and untwisting. A giant roast of beef slowly turned on a mechanical spit, dripping fat and browning nicely. The room smelled of roasting meat and wood smoke.

"From the Senate, you say?" she asked quizzically over her shoulder as she bent to twist up again the twine on the chickens. "I should have thought you'd be from the House of Representatives. They're the ones who are investigating him, aren't they?"

"You seem to be well informed."

She turned back to face him, wiping her hands on her apron.

↞ 15 ↠

Stephen Girard, Jimmy's occasional and favorite employer, had one of the city's most considerable fortunes. Unlike many of Philadelphia's richest men, he wasn't one for lavish spending. He'd learned early on that money was merely a convenient thing. It couldn't buy happiness.

At the age of fourteen he'd been sent off to sea, to get him out of the way when he and his new stepmother couldn't get along, and he'd ended up in Philadelphia at the age of twenty-six, by purest accident. It was during the Revolutionary War and he was trading with the rebellious colonies. The prospect of capture by a British warship forced him to flee up the Delaware River to Philadelphia. It was a lucky chance, for he quickly established himself there as one of the city's most successful merchant traders.

His success was well-earned, for he loved his work and he was good at it. He loved it all – the feel of the quill in his hand as he wrote out a bill of exchange, the billowing sails of his ship setting forth to distant lands, the bustle of the docks and the smell of the river. He loved even the risks and dangers, loved calculating them against the potential rewards. Most of all, he loved the sense of satisfaction when things worked out the way he'd planned them.

This morning, like every other morning, Stephen Girard woke up early. Donning his dressing gown, cap, and slippers, he sipped a cup of tea and awaited the arrival of Monsieur Dorphin, his French barber. After the shave and trim, he powdered Girard's hair, a custom rapidly fading from fashion.

The barber draped a cape around Girard to shield his clothes and handed him a mask with a handle to hold it up, so Girard could shield his face from the powder also.

"I have learned a thing most curious the other day, shall I tell you?" The barber didn't wait for a reply. Girard was always interested in any tidbit of news. It was a rhetorical question only. "It concerns *la petite jeune fille*, that girl who died, the one they say was murdered. Her husband was French, did you know of it?"

"But of course." Girard made it his business to know everything of possible consequence.

"Not only was her husband French," the barber went on, "but her doctor was a Frenchman also. It was Doctor La Roche, as a matter of fact." The powdering done, he removed the cape and handed Girard a mirror.

"*Normalement*, I do not repeat what I am told, you understand. To you, however, I tell everything." The barber paused dramatically. "*La petite*, this little Bridgette, she was with child when she died. Monsieur La Roche, he is sure of it."

Girard's eyebrows soared upward.

"Aha," said the barber smugly. "I have told you something you did not know. Considering what the papers say, this is interesting, is it not? One must wonder, who was the father?"

Once the barber was gone, Girard went to work in his counting house. For him, the counting house was an extension of his home, connected by an interior door off a hallway near the kitchen. Quickly lost in his business affairs, he spared only a few moments' thought for the barber's parting question – if Bridget LeClair was pregnant, who was the father? Then he filed the information away in his mind for future reference.

In the afternoon, Girard dined and then relaxed, reading for a while in his extensive library. In the evening he returned again to his counting house.

Earlier that day, he'd summoned the lad Jimmy to come by that evening, so Jimmy was waiting in the kitchen. Girard's cook had offered him supper and he was eating it hungrily. Suppers were becoming rare for him these days. With the river now frozen over, the ships could no longer come and go. The sea-going trade had virtually disappeared and with it Jimmy's income.

The cook was generous and the leftovers were plentiful. In very little time, Jimmy had made his way through a considerable quantity of oysters, apple fritters, and leftover ham with gravy. He was just mopping up the last bit of gravy with a piece of bread, when he heard one of the clerks call out to him.

"Look sharp now, you're wanted. Mr. Girard is ready to see you."

Jimmy popped the bread in his mouth, mumbled his thanks to the cook, and took himself off to the counting house.

Girard was sitting behind his desk. His broad, heavy frame was bent forward over a fat, leather-bound journal lying open in front of him. His head was turned to the side to favor his good left eye, and he was studying the columns of numbers and words with concentration.

Jimmy stood in front of the desk, silent and respectful, until Girard looked up and spoke to him.

"Ah, there you are." Straight to the point, Girard spoke in brisk yet friendly fashion. "I have an errand for you, a message to deliver." He picked up a sealed packet from beside the journal and held it out. "Are you familiar with Mr. Robert Waln's house?"

"Yes, Sir, right there on Second Street." Jimmy was familiar with all the places that the merchants might be found. "That's where that girl was working, isn't it? Bridget LeClair, I mean?" He was hoping that Girard would share a bit of information. He and his friends, they prided themselves on knowing what was going on. There was status in being able to share some new and interesting gossip. "Do you think it's true what they're saying, that Jefferson poisoned her?"

"Vice President Jefferson," Girard corrected the boy sternly. He was, unlike most of Philadelphia's wealthier citizens, a staunch Republican. "And I'm certain that he didn't. He's as fine a man as you're ever likely to see. I'd advise you, young man, to be careful what you say. There's no merit in passing on malicious gossip."

"Begging your pardon." Jimmy was instantly contrite. "I didn't mean any disrespect to Mister – Vice President – Jefferson."

"Very well then." Girard paused and took a moment to study the boy. He had once been a similar lad himself, making his way on his own, albeit with greater advantages. This lad Jimmy could be impetuous at times, but he was good at heart, eager and resourceful. At the moment he was looking a bit thin, however, thinner than Girard remembered.

"How are you getting along, these days?" he asked with genuine concern. "With the river frozen over now, I suppose there isn't as much work for you?"

"Not as much as there was." Jimmy answered bravely. In fact there was almost no work at all. It was his first winter in Philadelphia and he hadn't realized what a difference the winter made. Pretty soon, if he hoped to survive, he was going to have to find another source of income.

"I expect you'll have to find some other occupation," Girard went on as if reading his mind, "to keep you going through the winter. I can give you some odds and ends of errands myself, but it won't be enough. Can you read and write and do sums?"

Jimmy looked down at the floor.

"Some. A little. I can read, that is, after a fashion."

"You're an honest young man, at least. And I have watched you work – you're energetic and reliable. When you learn your sums and writing, let me know. I might have some work for you in my counting house."

"Yes, Sir." It sounded like heaven, to be a clerk for Mr. Girard. It was only a dream though, for all that he tried to look earnest and hopeful. How could he ever learn his writing and sums? He had neither money nor time for an education.

"Well, be on your way then," Girard said kindly, turning back to his ledgers. "You needn't wait for an answer. Just deliver it, that's all. You can give the note to whoever answers the door, only make sure they know to give it to Mr. Waln directly."

After leaving the note and reporting back again, Jimmy made his way to the Man Full of Troubles, Mrs. Smallwood's tavern. These days, it was his home. In return for helping her out with this and that, she let him sleep on a straw pallet under the sloping roof in the corner of her attic. The attic was a storage area overall, and piles of chests and barrels, a few pieces of old furniture, and similar odds and ends were Jimmy's night-time companions.

Just before he lay down to sleep, he opened his leather trunk, took out a small wooden box, and opened it. For the most part, his "valuables" were really only mementoes and souvenirs, valuable only in terms of sentiment. His store of "savings" was very little, just a meager handful of varied coinage. In the small wooden box was the one truly valuable thing he owned – a dainty gold ring, wrapped in a scrap of calico.

He carefully took out the ring and held it in the palm of his hand. It was an unusual design, a rose-cut garnet in a finely worked gold setting. It was real gold, a large, richly-colored stone, and the craftsmanship was very fine, but he would never pawn or sell it. It belonged to his mother and he'd sooner starve. She said it was a gift from the father he never knew. She had worn it always.

He had never worn the ring himself. It was far too small for his fingers. Today, however, he'd thought of wearing it around his neck as a sort of talisman. He took a thin leather cord, strung it through the ring, and slipped it over his head after carefully knotting it. It might bring him luck. Heaven knows, he sorely needed it.

Clutching the ring to his chest, he drifted off to sleep. In his dreams, his mother was still alive, it was summer, and he wasn't hungry.

"Oh yes, I'm sure it was." Unfazed, Callender smiled lecherously. "The weather is always better inside the bedroom. But never mind. By the way, that fellow Mathers from the Senate has been nosing around, did you know? He was trying to question my wife about the murder."

"Your wife?"

"Yes, my wife. She did know the girl Bridget, actually. Her father-in-law lived next door and she came to our house from time to time. I can assure you though, my wife won't give him the time of day. Not a word about you," he added with a nasty smirk, "nor your household arrangements."

"The Devil he did." Jefferson frowned, his concern about Mathers even greater than his growing anger at Callender. Had he made a mistake getting Mathers involved? Or had someone else set him in motion?

Callender looked at him shrewdly.

"Don't worry. As I said, she knows when to keep her mouth shut. I haven't talked to him yet myself, but he'll get even less from me. It's a man's own business, isn't it, what he does on his own property – or with his own property, should I say? Not that I blame you. For a widower in his prime, the nights must get very long."

Jefferson gave Callender such a look that even he was shaken, as heedless and thick-skinned as he was. Then, just as quickly, the look vanished.

"Yes, your *History* is excellent," Jefferson coolly remarked, as if there'd never been any other topic of conversation. "If you can spare it, I'll take another copy or two to give to others."

Callender picked out two books from the pile and wrapped them in sturdy paper, tying the package snugly with twine.

Jefferson meanwhile opened his wallet and carefully counted out twenty-two dollars and thirty-three cents in notes and change.

"This should be enough for the *History* and something extra for you."

After a moment's reflection, he reached back in the wallet and pulled out two more dollars.

"Do give your wife my best regards as well. Perhaps you could buy her some little present? Please tell her it's from me, as a token of my regard." With a meaningful look, he handed Callender the money, picked up his books, and left him.

Jefferson arrived the next day at Congress Hall, a month after he was supposed to. Tall and lean, dressed in his usual blue frock coat with a bright red waistcoat and britches, he strode into the Senate Chamber without a trace of apology.

He was an elder statesman now, nearing sixty. His reddish gold hair was now faded and streaked with gray. As all eyes watched his entrance, he crossed the room and went directly over to Jacob, ignoring even his Republican colleagues along the way.

"Well, I'm here at last," he greeted Jacob with a broad and welcoming smile, "and I must say that I'm very glad to see you. You've been a splendid President in my absence, just as I would have expected. To say nothing of your other assistance."

With that, Jefferson breezed up to the front of the room and took his place on the dais. He settled himself in the President's chair and picked up the ivory gavel, ready to call the meeting to order.

Jacob took his seat, grimly furious. Just this moment, if he and Jefferson were standing paces apart with pistols drawn, he quite happily would have shot him. Everyone had watched the encounter with keen attention, and no one had failed to grasp the implications. All around the room, Federalists were staring at him with open hostility. Senator Sedgwick leaned over to a colleague and muttered "just as I thought," rather loudly.

"Damn the man," Jacob swore to himself. "What on earth is he playing at?" This little performance of Jefferson's (for it was clearly calculated) was going to cost him dearly.

He hadn't much chance of getting the twenty dollar fee for naturalization certificates repealed, but he'd wanted to try as a matter of principle. It was an exorbitant fee, deliberately high, to exclude poorer immigrants from citizenship. And why? Because the poor almost always voted Republican. Then there was the Blount impeachment trial. His Federalist colleagues were eagerly looking forward to it. What a splendid political opportunity it was, they all thought, to see a Republican Senator convicted of treason. The more Jacob researched the question, however, the more certain he was that Senators were not really subject to impeachment. How they would love him, he thought grimly, when he told them that impeaching Blount was unconstitutional.

He tried to slip away the moment the session was over, but Senators Tracy and Sedgwick followed him.

"So much for giving you the benefit of the doubt," Senator Sedgwick confronted him. "It's obvious that you're nothing but Jefferson's lackey."

"Now look here, Senator," Jacob began, but Senator Tracy quickly interrupted.

"Don't take offense, Senator Martin. I'm sure he didn't mean it exactly like it sounded." He gave Sedgwick a warning look, but Sedgwick merely glared back at him.

"I meant exactly what I said," he said firmly.

"It looks odd to see you and Mr. Jefferson on such friendly terms, you must see that," Senator Tracy added reasonably, "and then there's the way you've been voting. I don't believe what they say about southerners always sticking together, but if I were you, I'd take greater care to make the right impression."

The message delivered, Senators Tracy and Sedgwick walked away. Jacob hardly got much further, however, before he was accosted once again, this time by James Mathers.

"Senator Martin, a moment if you will. I've something for you."

"You have a letter?" Jacob asked hopefully. His sister hadn't written in such a very long time. Had there been some problem, too terrible even to tell him? Then too, there was the sale of his rice. The last letter he'd received merely reported that the ship had sailed. Since then he hadn't heard anything.

"No letter, I'm sorry to say," Mathers replied, "but I've some other news you'll surely be interested in. That Bridget LeClair certainly managed to get around. It wasn't just Senator Blount she was friendly with. She also knew Mr. James Callender."

"An affair with Callender? That weaselly little man? Surely you're joking."

"Oh no, that's not what I meant at all. Her and James Callender, what a picture." Mathers chucked. "No, it's his wife she was friendly with. James Callender lives near her father-in-law, and Bridget used to go there. Helped her with the children and so forth."

"That's interesting, I must confess. What did Mrs. Callender have to say about it?"

"I haven't talked to her yet," Mathers admitted. "The last time I tried, she ran away. I'll keep trying though. I've a feeling she knows something she doesn't want to tell me."

∞ 17 ∞

Abigail was particularly annoyed at Jefferson's late arrival. How could she plan the President's welcoming reception for the start of Congress, when the actual starting date was so entirely uncertain? Added to which, she'd much prefer that her reception take place when the fewest possible Members of Congress were in town. The fewer there were, the less it would cost her. She was still grumbling about her Fourth of July party last summer. Usually it was a small, quiet affair, but thanks to her husband's having called the extra session that kept people around, nearly all of the Congress attended. Oh, the cost of it!

Her husband, however, had insisted that Jefferson should be at the opening reception. So now the guest list was very long and growing longer. She had economized as much as was reasonably possible. There was punch, some syllabub, some cake, a few sweetmeats, and that was all. For a Presidential reception it was positively skimpy.

Abigail knew that people would compare her hospitality unfavorably with the Washingtons'. She didn't care (or if she did, she'd never admit it). Martha Washington had money and George knew how to spend it. Abigail and John, on the other hand, were only middling country farmers. And therefore, she told herself, they had to mind their expenses.

Lavish or cheap, it was still a Presidential reception. The guests knew how to make it an elegant affair, even if the First Lady didn't. The rooms might be plain and the food and drink might be scanty, but the members of Congress, the Cabinet Secretaries and their underlings, and the prominent social and diplomatic personages and their wives all looked splendid, adorning the President's house with sparkling jewels and the latest fashions.

The footman met the guests at the door and ushered them to the receiving line, where they would wait to be formally introduced and greeted. The hallway in which they mostly stood was half the width of the house, with a stairway at the back and, on the right side, a sort of open corridor, separated from the rest of the room by a colonnade of floor-to-ceiling arches.

Slowly the guests made their way through the hall and into the State Dining Room, where John and Abigail stood before the great bowed window. The President wore his suit of matching plain drab broadcloth, as usual, and his greetings tended to be short and snappish. Abigail wore her crimson silk gown with her finest lace neckerchief, and tried her best to be polite to everyone.

After enduring the receiving line, the guests were free to mingle. Most of them made their way first to the refreshments. Soon the entire first floor was crowded with guests drinking the punch and syllabubs, nibbling their cake, and chatting. It was a cheerful hubbub of politics interspersed with gossip, with the occasional arch comment about Abigail's penny-pinching.

Nancy Bingham, Senator Bingham's wife and Elizabeth Powel's niece, was clearly the queen of the gathering. Tall, handsome, and graciously self-confident, she had been presented at court and held her own among European royalty. No one ever complained about the parties that she gave in Philadelphia. They were spectacular to the point of decadence. Even Abigail rather liked her.

She didn't need to circulate, as people were drawn to her. At the moment she was surrounded by wives of foreign diplomats, prominently including Mrs. Henrietta Liston, the wife of the British Minister Sir Robert Liston.

"A pity we won't have dancing this evening, don't you think?" Henrietta was very fond of dancing. "I think the ladies in Philadelphia dance so well."

"You shall have dancing at our house, next time you come," Nancy assured her. "You may dance all night if you've a mind to."

"A pity the President Washington, he is gone." Agnes de Freire, the wife of the Portuguese Minister, sighed elegantly. She was an educated and amiable woman, heavily laden with a considerable array of diamond jewelry. Her hair was impeccably arranged and her gown was made of the finest embroidered muslin. She was perfect in every respect except her command of the English language.

"Of course, the President Washington – I confess," she whispered, with a quick look around to see who was listening, "to me he is still the President – well, did he not love the dance himself? I suppose, with the President Adams, the dancing is no more."

"Just be glad that Mr. Jefferson wasn't elected," Henrietta observed tartly. "He never goes to balls, or even theaters or concerts. He is, by all accounts, a most unsociable man."

"Speaking of Mr. Jefferson, have you heard the dreadful rumors?" Rebecca Pickering, Secretary of State Pickering's wife, sounded gleeful. In keeping with the even more vehement views of her husband, she thought that Jefferson was a devil in human form. "Did you read the stories about him murdering that housemaid?"

"It's just pure malicious slander without a feather's-weight of truth," Nancy informed them all sternly. When Jefferson had written to her after Cobbett's initial accusations, she'd assured him that she didn't believe a word of it and would do what she could to help him. "Surely you should know from your own experience not to believe what they print in the newspapers, least of all William Cobbett."

Nancy gave Rebecca a pointed look. Need she say more? Everyone knew how Cobbett had attacked Secretary Pickering quite unmercifully just months before, accusing him of trying to murder Thomas Jefferson.

"The Philadelphia press is quite astonishing indeed," Henrietta agreed most emphatically. "They print the most wicked, disgraceful lies to sell their papers. In Britain it would never be allowed."

"Perhaps that's why all your journalists have fled to America," Rebecca noted wisely, if somewhat tactlessly. "When you look at some of them, like that despicable Mr. Callender, we can't help but wish that you'd kept them."

"But who is performing the investigating?" Agnes changed the subject diplomatically. "Is it anyone? I have heard of no officially investigating, yes? Just these stories one reads in the newspapers."

"That's a good question," Nancy said approvingly. "I haven't heard of an official investigation either. I wish Senator Martin would get involved, like he did before. I'm sure that he'd sort things out and remove this terrible cloud over Mr. Jefferson."

Then, looking across the room, she saw her husband's unmistakable signal.

"Ladies, you must excuse me. Mr. Bingham informs me that it's time to go home." She gave a small curtsy in the group's general direction and left them to join her husband.

Abigail, released at last from the receiving line, came up to join them.

"Thank heavens that's over," Abigail greeted them with obvious relief. "It's such a chore sometimes, having your husband as President. I'm sorry to interrupt; please do go on. Did Mrs. Bingham say that Senator Martin is investigating these charges against Mr. Jefferson?"

"Ah yes," Agnes advised her, "Mrs. Bingham was speaking of the Senator Martin investigating. And to prove Mr. Jefferson the innocent."

"What Mrs. Bingham said," Mrs. Liston began, meaning to clarify Mme de Freire's remark, but she was interrupted by President Adams's arrival.

"My dear Abigail," he broke in, with hardly a glance at the other ladies, "you simply must do something about the servants immediately. The punch is low, and the cake needs replenishing. The footman's been drinking the wine for the syllabub too, and the cook's about to bash his head in with the bottle."

He swept Abigail away and the others continued their conversation.

The next morning, Abigail reported to her husband the tidbits of news and gossip that she had gleaned at the reception. She was a careful listener with a good memory, so her report was detailed and accurate. Accurate, that is, with one significant exception. She'd understood from Agnes de Freire's poorly phrased remark that Senator Martin was now investigating the housemaid's murder, with the goal of clearing Mr. Jefferson from the charges that he did the deed.

"Can you imagine, my dear," Abigail told her husband with some amazement, "Senator Martin is once again working for Mr. Jefferson."

"Jefferson?"

"It's that housemaid, you know? The one that Mr. Cobbett says he murdered?"

"Senator Martin?" Adams was skeptical. "Are you sure? I would think he'd have the sense not to get involved in it."

"I'm surprised as well," Abigail agreed, "but Nancy Bingham said it herself, according to the wife of the Portuguese Minister. I suppose that Nancy heard it directly from Mr. Jefferson, since they're still close. Senator Martin must be trying to keep it a secret, and no wonder. He's risking everything, and for what? To save your chief Republican rival."

"Then more fool he," Adams grunted disgustedly. "I thought all this talk about his being a secret Republican was just empty gossip, but it seems I must revise my opinion of the man. Or perhaps he's suffering from vainglorious pride? Solving that other business last summer may have gone to his head and given him inflated ideas of his abilities. Whereas in truth it was a near-run thing, as close as can be to a total disaster."

"I do wonder who did murder the girl, I must say." Abigail looked thoughtful. "I don't rule out Mr. Jefferson, but the more I think on it, the more I think Alexander Hamilton's a more likely suspect."

"Hamilton?" Adams echoed her, blinking in surprise. "Alexander Hamilton?"

"Yes, Alexander Hamilton. It's not such a wild idea." Abigail's view of Hamilton was even worse than her view of Jefferson. "I'm sure it would have occurred to you as well, were you not so preoccupied with being President. Mr. Hamilton has a roving eye as well, but he can hardly afford another scandal. Not after his affair with Mary Reynolds. And what about those accusations of corrupt and illegal speculations when he was Secretary of Treasury?"

"That old scandal? To be sure, Hamilton's behavior was extraordinary. I can't imagine a stranger way to defend yourself. 'Oh no,' he says, 'it's not what you think. I wasn't engaged in any illegal financial dealings with James Reynolds. I was having an affair with his wife and he found out. That's why I gave him money.' What a defense, can you imagine? His explanation was so outrageous that most people thought it must be true."

"I'm not at all surprised," Abigail rejoined. "To disgrace himself and dishonor his wife, or to lose his chance at position and power? There's no question which he cares about more. It's hardly even a choice for him."

"I'll grant you that." Adams' feelings about Hamilton were if anything more vehement than Abigail's. "That bastard brat of a Scotch peddler is capable of anything. I wouldn't be surprised if he had the affair and took the money too. It's hardly the only affair he's had, either. I remember his debaucheries in New York. Even so, his affair with Mrs. Reynolds was years ago. I would have thought it dead and buried by now, surely?"

"It wasn't public knowledge, until now, my dear. You knew, and a few people in government. It's only just this summer that it became public, when Mr. Callender published his *History of the United States* and included all the sordid details."

"James Callender." Adams pronounced the name with evident distaste. "That man is a menace. He fancies himself some sort of hero, I imagine, for spewing out that poisonous, spiteful venom. If he turned up murdered himself, I wouldn't be at all surprised."

"Nonetheless, as you yourself have pointed out, he does manage to touch on the truth from time to time, despite his malicious motives. I hear he's working on a second book, with even more damaging revelations. So what if Mr. Hamilton had debauched this unfortunate young girl and she'd learned some secret in the process? To my certain knowledge, he has assaulted the virtue of the purest ladies in New York," Abigail said primly. "So he would hardly shrink from seducing a housemaid."

"It's possible, I'll grant you that," Adams conceded, "but I should think he'd find housemaids enough in New York, if he wanted to debauch one."

"I wonder if Senator Martin could actually be working for Hamilton instead of Jefferson," Abigail mused, looking at her husband quizzically. "He's another one for working through others, behind the scenes. So many others seem to be secretly doing his bidding."

Adams's anger rose again and his face turned an unhealthy shade of purple.

"Martin? Working for Hamilton? If he is, I'll make sure he regrets it to his dying day. Working for Jefferson's bad enough, but working for Hamilton is intolerable."

"I'll find out; just leave it to me." Abigail patted her husband's shoulder fondly. "Mrs. Powel is quite close to Senator Martin, from what I hear. She must know what he's doing and who he's really working for. I'll ask her to tea and interrogate her."

～ 18 ～

The boy brought the note in the early afternoon. Seeing who it was from, Lydia ran up the stairs to bring it to Elizabeth.

Elizabeth took the small folded packet from Lydia's outstretched hand and looked to see who the sender was.

"Hmm, what is this? A note from Mrs. Adams?" she said, surprised. She carefully broke the seal, opened the note, and read it. "How very curious indeed. She's inviting me to tea, and she says that it will be just the two of us." She looked at the letter quizzically with a wry smile. "I wonder why she's invited me."

"It's about time she invited you, I would say," Lydia interjected her own opinion boldly. "Aren't you an important woman in Philadelphia and a friend of President Washington's too? Why didn't she invite you long before, is what I'm wondering."

Elizabeth smiled at Lydia's innocence.

"Mrs. Adams is a wholly political creature, my dear, and as you say, she has never asked me to tea before, much less anything so intimate as just the two of us. She has something particular in mind, you may be sure of it."

Elizabeth folded the letter back together and tucked it carefully away in one of her desk's many pigeonholes. Then she penned a quick but formal note of reply.

"Is the messenger waiting?" she asked, and Lydia nodded. "Then you may give him this response. I shall of course accept with pleasure."

Two days later, just before teatime, Elizabeth donned a stylish long-sleeved gown of rose-colored satin and her new pink satin slippers. She'd chosen fashionable but relatively plain and modest attire, as she knew Mrs. Adams disapproved of the showier, more revealing fashions. After a moment's further thought, she picked out a thick woolen shawl. It was late November, after all, and most likely the President's house would be cold. Abigail had a reputation for skimping on expenses.

In the street, her coach was already waiting. It was an elegant, high-wheeled vehicle, maroon and black with gilded edging. She intended to make the short journey to the President's house in style. It was President Washington's carriage and his horses too. She'd bought it from him when he left Philadelphia.

Abigail was waiting for her in the yellow drawing room on the second floor, with the tea things already set out. There were two plain ladder-back chairs facing each other across the little table.

Elizabeth had come to this house often for tea when George Washington was still President. It was the first time, however, that she had been in the house since the Washingtons had left. Glancing around the room discretely, she was rather surprised to see that how plain it looked, even shabby. Gone were the yellow damask curtains and the matching sofas, arm chairs, and side chairs. Gone were the piano forte and the extravagant display of china whimsically called "the Pagoda." There was a good rug still, decent curtains, and the walls were still papered, but the room hardly seemed fit for the President.

"My dear Mrs. Adams," Elizabeth greeted Abigail sweetly, "how very kind of you to invite me."

"And so kind of you to accept," Abigail responded with equal courtesy. "You look splendid as usual. Come sit down. Would you have some tea? Or if you prefer, I can send for coffee or chocolate."

Elizabeth opted for the tea. She looked at the tea service admiringly. It was surely the most elegant and expensive thing in the room, white porcelain edged with gold and decorated with small blue cornflowers.

As she poured the tea and offered Elizabeth a plate of almond macaroons, Abigail noticed Elizabeth's appraising look and guessed what she was thinking.

"It's quite nice china, don't you think? My husband purchased it ages ago, when he was first sent to Versailles. I'm afraid we haven't been able to do as much with the house as a whole. We can't all be heiresses like your friend Mrs. Washington."

"But of course," Elizabeth said politely. She'd heard rumors, nonetheless, that Abigail had amassed a tidy sum from various investments. According to what was whispered among those in the know, Abigail had made various shrewd speculations over the years. Just after the Revolutionary war, when John was Minister to London, she'd had him send her scarce luxuries like gauze handkerchiefs and English pins and sold them. More recently, it was said, Abigail had started making somewhat questionable investments in depreciated government bonds. No one, not even her husband, really knew the extent of her secret savings.

"Such a big house," Elizabeth continued, "and so much entertaining. It must be such a trial, not at all what you're used to."

"Yes, a President's wife has many demands on her." Abigail poured herself a cup of tea as well. "Sometimes I wonder how I keep up with it. Still, I'm quite remiss in not inviting you over before now. I understand you are quite well informed about politics. They say that President Washington valued your advice. That's quite a compliment."

"I'm sure that whatever you heard was greatly exaggerated," Elizabeth said modestly. "I do try to keep myself informed, however. It has been much easier, of course, since Congress moved to Philadelphia."

That led to a lively discussion of current political goings-on, since both of them were close observers. When that had run its course, Abigail turned to the subject of the permanent United States capital.

"The new Federal City of Washington seems a desolate place," Abigail sighed, "so unhealthy and so undeveloped. If, God willing, my husband wins the next election, we'll have to move there. I suppose one does what one has to do, when one's husband is President."

"My sister lives in Virginia, did you know?" Elizabeth's sister had married one of the Byrds, one of Virginia's most prominent families. There had been misgivings at the time and the marriage had ended in tragedy when her husband, a heavy gambler and unrepentant Loyalist, took his own life. "I'm afraid the Federal City itself must be rather grim, but I've heard the Virginia countryside is very lovely."

"That's comforting to hear, but still it's southern. I've never lived anywhere where owning slaves was considered so acceptable."

"It's a dreadful thing," Elizabeth agreed. She, like most Philadelphians, supported abolition. "I'll never understand how otherwise fine and moral men can stand to regard other human beings as property."

"The sin of slavery is still not washed away," Abigail said sadly. "I'm afraid that someday our country will pay for it dearly. I suppose you know that the Quaker petition against slavery was debated in the House of Representatives the other day?"

"Yes. From what I have heard, the debates were quite heated."

"It was the southerners against the northerners, as one might expect." Abigail had gotten a full report of the proceedings from her husband. "The southern Federalists were as bad as the southern Republicans. Mr. Rutledge from South Carolina even said the Quakers should be censured for daring to submit it – can you imagine? That it was a deliberate effort to incite people to violence and destroy the country."

"He's right to say the issue might tear us apart," Elizabeth said thoughtfully, "as much as I hate to say it. The division of opinion is so very great and our union is so very fragile."

It was gratifying to talk with someone of similar views, but Elizabeth knew that discussing the Anti-Slavery Petition was not why Abigail had invited her. As she sipped her tea (a fragrant Pekoe, no scrimping there) and nibbled on the tasty almond macaroons, she wondered when Abigail would reveal her true agenda.

"Speaking of threats to our union," Abigail moved her opening pawn, "I never did have a chance to thank you for all you did last spring to help uncover Jefferson's would-be murderer. I'm sure that without your help Senator Martin could never have solved it. Had the crisis gone on much longer, the whole country would have been gravely harmed, to say nothing of my husband's Presidency."

"You flatter me, but I must give Senator Martin the full credit. I merely listened, from time to time."

"You are too modest," Abigail informed her firmly. "I'm sure that your help was invaluable. Do I understand correctly that he has undertaken to solve a murder yet again? I should have thought that the last one would have been enough for him."

"Oh yes? Pray tell me more." Elizabeth's tone bespoke only casual interest, but her thoughts and feelings were in tumult. She had pleaded with Jacob to get involved and he'd coldly refused. Had he now changed his mind without the courtesy of even telling her? It seemed a callous and insulting thing to do, but Abigail Adams usually had the most impeccable sources.

Abigail frowned. This wasn't the script they were supposed to be following. She had meant to gather information, not to give it away. Surely Mrs. Powel must know all about it, if she and Senator Martin were as close as the rumors had it. Why was she pretending ignorance?

"I'm surprised he hasn't told you," she remarked, with just the hint of suggestion that she didn't in the least believe it. "It concerns a girl this time, a maid I gather. The one that Cobbett accuses Jefferson of murdering. The papers have been full of it for days. Surely you have heard of it?"

Elizabeth merely nodded.

"I wouldn't be surprised if he did murder the girl," Abigail went on. "He's the very worst sort of scoundrel. Just look at the way he has treated former President Washington, after all that

Washington did for him. I know how you feel about him, my dear, Mr. Jefferson, I mean. I must say, I entirely agree with you."

She gave Elizabeth a companionable and sympathetic smile. Mrs. Powel might not be a source of information at the moment, but she could be a useful ally in the future.

"It's a curious thing, though, for I gather that Senator Martin is investigating at the request of Mr. Jefferson, of all people. I gather he's undertaken to prove Mr. Jefferson innocent."

"He has? Are you sure?"

"According to Mme de Freire, your niece Mrs. Bingham said it herself. Just the other night at the reception."

Elizabeth was so shocked that words entirely failed her. So Jacob had refused her pleas but when Jefferson asked him, he agreed to do it?

"There must be some special tie between them," Abigail mused, "though what it is, I can't imagine. Perhaps Senator Martin has in mind to profit by it, if Thomas Jefferson wins the Presidency in the next election?"

"Heaven forbid!" On this point, Elizabeth and Abigail were in total agreement.

"It could also be Mr. Hamilton, of course," Abigail mused. "He was in town, did you know, about the same time. It was supposed to be a secret, I imagine, but Mrs. Pickering let it slip at the reception."

"Really? Alexander Hamilton?" Elizabeth looked at Abigail quizzically, once more in control of herself. "It seems more like Mr. Jefferson's style to me. Did you know that the murdered girl was a cousin of my housemaid, Lydia?"

"How terrible for you." Abigail's eyes flashed with a spark of satisfaction. Her invitation was going to be fruitful, after all. "Do tell me all about it."

"It was Doctor Dobell, really, who started things. He thought her illness quite unusual, according to Doctor Rush, for a supposed case of yellow fever. He made some notes, just before he died of the yellow fever himself, and Doctor Rush ended up with his journal. Apparently, Doctor Dobell wrote that the symptoms were not like yellow fever at all. He said it seemed more like a case of tainted food or even poison."

"I wonder how the newspapers came to suspect Mr. Jefferson of the crime," remarked Abigail temptingly. Elizabeth, however, ignored the remark and continued.

"Poor Lydia, she is quite distraught. First the tragic death and now the scandal."

There was a momentary pause as each woman considered how best to probe the other, delicately of course, for more information. Just then, however, the clock struck the hour. It was later than either one of them had realized.

"Five o'clock already." Elizabeth put down her teacup and readjusted her shawl about her shoulders. "I'm afraid I've stayed too long. You must have so many other things to attend to. I do thank you for inviting me to tea. The tea was splendid, the macaroons were perfection itself, and it has been a most interesting conversation."

"We must have tea again," Abigail said brightly. "We have so many things in common, our love of almond macaroons and, most of all" – she paused for emphasis with a meaningful look – "our views of Mr. Jefferson."

"It has certainly been a most interesting afternoon." Elizabeth's tone made it clear that she understood completely. "I'd be quite delighted to talk with you again. Our conversation has been quite informative."

❧ 19 ❧

J acob sat down at his Senate desk and rubbed his temples, trying to relieve the intense, throbbing pain that ran from the base of his skull to his forehead. He was having a lot of headaches these days, a sure sign that his worries were even deeper than he acknowledged.

Maybe it was just too many troublesome things at once, he told himself. His children, for one. There was still no letter from his sister. It could be that her letter had simply gone astray, left with the mailbag in some tavern. Given the sorry state of the private carriers who transported the mails, it was a frequent enough occurrence. Or it might be that something was very wrong, so wrong that she couldn't bring herself to tell him.

Then there was the loan coming due, from the bank in London. He could pay it if, and only if, his last shipment of rice was sold. Every day that went by without news, however, he wondered if the privateers had seized the ship his rice was on, along with all of its cargo, and he'd lost it all.

What troubled him most of all, however, were thoughts of Elizabeth. Their last meeting had ended so very badly. Admittedly, he'd been a bit sharp with her at the end, but surely that wasn't sufficient reason. She shouldn't hold it against him as much as that, after all that had happened between them. He'd expected that when she had time for her temper to cool, she'd come to understand and appreciate his position. But day after day had gone by, and still he hadn't heard from her.

He tried to make his headache go away by sheer force of will, focusing his mind on the day's upcoming business. With any luck, it would be fairly routine. Chances were, it would be something involving money: approving the budget of the Department of War, enacting an amendment to the duties on whiskey, considering customs duties on imports, making relief payments to various individuals.

"Damnation!" A voice from a desk nearby took him away from his headache and his thoughts. He looked over to see the cause of it. Senator Mason, Republican from Virginia, was handing a newspaper to his Virginia colleague Senator Tazewell.

"Did you see this?" Mason stabbed a finger at the offending article. "The *Gazette* says that France has declared war on us. We send over a diplomatic mission and what do they do? They declare war before our envoys hardly even get there."

Other Senators crowded around, but Senator Tazewell calmly waved them away.

"Gentlemen, gentlemen, hold your fire. They're just reprinting some ignorant rumor. Look at the heading. It was published in New York a week ago. I can assure you that there's nothing to it. The French Consul Citizen Letombe told Vice President

Jefferson last week that our envoys will be 'well received.' Don't you remember? Those were his very words exactly."

"How reassuring." Senator Sedgwick's words were heavy with sarcasm. "If all was going well, we should have heard from them by now. Either the Jacobin terrorists have changed their minds or else Citizen Letomb was lying in the first place. Are they languishing in jail, or have French spies intercepted their letters? You don't even care. The French Government tells you what they want you to believe, and you Republicans simply believe it. Or do you believe it? Maybe you're just playing their game. Maybe you're more loyal to France than to your own country."

Senator Tazewell stood up, a dangerous glint in his eye. Since he was normally an affable, charming fellow, his fury was all the more striking.

"I beg your pardon, Sir. I must have misheard you," he said soberly. "Who was it, exactly, you were referring to?"

"Bah." Senator Sedgwick glowered back at him. "You heard me right. I've said it before and I'll say it again, show me a man who loves the Jacobins, and I'll show you a fool – or a traitor. Maybe Senator Blount isn't the only one we should be impeaching."

"Strange words, coming from someone who'd rather see us still be a British colony." Senator Tazewell's voice was low and dangerous. "Speaking of traitors."

Their hostility was so intense that the other Senators were backing away from them. Soon a watching circle was formed, with Sedgwick and Tazewell just inches apart, face to face in the center. Some of the Senators seemed to be afraid that it would come to blows. Others seemed to be hoping for it.

"Good day, Gentlemen." Vice President Jefferson chose that moment to arrive. It was, in Jacob's opinion, almost providential. "Is something going on? Is there something I should be aware of?"

Senator Tazewell was the first to reply. He seemed to have recovered his equanimity.

"It's nothing – and no one – to bother about. The *Gazette*'s managed to print a malicious lie and our Federalist colleagues are ignorant enough to believe it. The way they kiss the British posterior, you wonder if they were ever Patriots."

He took his seat, once again looking wholly at ease as if nothing had happened at all. Sedgwick looked at him with murder in his eyes, but said nothing.

"Very well, then." Jefferson nodded at them both and took his place on the President's dais. He picked up the ivory gavel and rapped it on the desk three times. "The meeting will now come to order."

After that, Jacob presented a petition from the Charleston merchants. They had paid for the docks and wharves for weighing and assessing customs duties on incoming goods in good faith, he explained, but then the government had changed the rules, and they were never reimbursed by a share of the customs duties. As he talked, he could see the hostile looks not only (as expected) from the Republicans but also from his Federalist colleagues. So soon it begins, he thought miserably. The Charleston merchants are paying the price of my supposed "disloyalty."

After that and a peaceful interlude of routine business, Senator Sedgwick rose to speak. The atmosphere in the room was immediately filled with tension.

"President Washington was right," Sedgwick began, "when he warned about the growth of the political factions. As we see how a certain faction behaves" – he looked meaningfully at the Republican Senators – "we see how right he was in this, as in everything. One has only to look at the evils he said would come – foreign influence, corruption, and even riot and insurrection. Isn't that exactly what's happening? And one needn't look far to see who's to blame. The French are out to conquer the world, and they have agents, here in this very Senate, in their plan to conquer America."

"Point of order!" Senator Mason shouted, but Sedgwick only raised his voice even louder.

"I have named no names," he thundered. "I can't help it if the shoe fits and you choose to wear it. The French, I say, are seeking to destroy us and the Republicans are their agents and allies. First they organized riots in 1793, trying to force Washington to declare war on the British or else to get rid of him. Then there was the Whiskey Rebellion in '94, organized by 'Citizen' Genet's so-called 'Democratical Societies.' And then there was rioting again the next year, when the Jay Treaty with the British was ratified."

"Senator Sedgwick, you're out of order!" It was Jefferson who spoke up this time, but he got no further than Senator Mason.

"It's the truth and you know it," Sedgwick snapped. "I'm almost done. You can stand it a minute longer. Whenever there's rebellion and violence, I say, whenever there's a danger to the Constitution, it's always the same. It's the French and the certain faction that supports them. Even now they have secret societies at work throughout the country, plotting to undermine the elected government. Thirty thousand or more, according to some reports, just waiting for the right moment to rise up and launch a violent revolution. Some of this august body, I'm sorry to say, are a danger to the nation."

The session went quickly downhill from there. Senator Tazewell managed a fairly eloquent response, but soon the Senators were merely trading insults. Jefferson tried to bring the meeting back in line, but finally gave up and merely sat there in dignified detachment.

Jacob's headache returned with double force. What on earth were things coming to? The country was so bitterly divided that it was tearing itself apart, with no help from France or anyone.

Finally Jacob couldn't stand it anymore. He got up and he left the Chamber.

As he passed the Chamber of the House of Representatives on the floor below, he heard angry voices. They were so loud, the sound penetrated even the closed wooden door. It sounded like quite a commotion.

He paused a moment in the hall, trying to listen in, when the House Chamber door swung open. Out came Congressman Harrison Gray Otis, Samuel Otis's son, looking furious.

"Damned Republicans, they'll be the end of us."

"What's going on in there?" Jacob asked. "There seems to a lot of shouting."

Otis quickly recovered his composure and bowed.

"My apologies, Senator Martin. I should have greeted you more civilly. It's a battleground in there and I'm afraid my temper is rather heated. The confounded Republicans won't let us defend our ships from the privateers, but they won't let the ships defend themselves either."

"How well I know," Jacob said heartily, thinking how his own shipment of rice was in danger.

"It's fortunate that I've run into you," Otis declared, "as I've been meaning to ask you. There are some curious rumors going around. What's all this about you and Jefferson?"

"Nothing at all," Jacob answered sharply. "Just the usual ignorant gossip."

"Well, that's as may be, but people are inclined to believe what they hear," Otis cautioned him, "and I must say, you haven't done very much to disabuse them. Don't follow the example of your father. Just because you think you're right, doesn't mean you can ignore what other people think. Not in life, not in society, and especially not in politics. There are plenty of people in Philadelphia who didn't think being a British colony was all that bad and weren't all that keen on Independence. They kept their own counsel, though, and changed with the times, and now they call themselves Patriots. Now don't get offended –" he added quickly, seeing Jacob's dark look, "I only mean it as a friendly warning."

With that, Otis bowed and left the building, leaving Jacob standing there fuming in the hallway.

It was a low blow, to mention his father, but all the same, was the comparison really a false one? He saw himself as dedicated to the truth, unwilling to sacrifice his integrity, but was it only self-delusion? Was he really just like his father underneath, too stubborn to change his ways, too proud to join the crowd, too set in his opinions?

"Damn them all," he muttered angrily. Maybe he was stubborn, or proud, or set in his ways, but there was one thing he knew for certain – he'd about had his fill of "friendly warnings." If they were going to damn him no matter what he did, then maybe he should do something to deserve it?

∽ 20 ∽

As Jacob climbed the stairs to Elizabeth's withdrawing room once again, his usual feelings of glad anticipation were mixed with doubt and disquiet. She'd finally invited him once again to tea, but the invitation had been an oddly formal one.

He'd been thinking about her night after night, in the early morning hours when he should have been sleeping. He still didn't really understand why it was, but she'd obviously been more upset by the death of Lydia's cousin than he'd realized. If he told her that he was beginning to change his mind – that perhaps he really would look into Bridget's death – would that help things? The way he was feeling now, it wouldn't take much to tip the balance. He was disgusted with his colleagues, who seemed to care more for their bitter partisanship and petty politics than for the survival of the country, and he was fed up beyond measure with being doubted, attacked, and given "friendly warnings." He was just about ready to say to hell with them all Sedgwick, Otis, and even Senator Bingham and all the rest of them.

At first, the visit went reasonably well. There was the same cozy fire, the same plentiful array of food and drink, and the same interesting conversation. She was perhaps more reserved than usual, but unwisely he missed its significance. As he recounted all that Mathers had learned, he began to relax and even to enjoy himself.

Elizabeth, on the other hand, was biding her time, waiting for the right moment to confront him. Ever since her tea with Abigail, the thought of Jacob's working for Jefferson had been plaguing her. She'd found it hard to believe at first, but then she'd found it was common knowledge. Jefferson had even thanked Senator Martin for his efforts quite publicly on the floor of the Senate. Everyone seemed to know it but her.

It was all she could do not to raise the subject right away, but first she wanted to learn all she could about Lydia's cousin's murder. As the conversation went on, though, they slipped back, little by little, into the comfortable, easy companionship that they'd had before. The question of his relationship with Jefferson receded from her mind.

"Mathers hasn't managed to speak with Mrs. Callender yet," Jacob reported, as he neared the end of what he had to tell her. "It seems that she's avoiding him. Quite possibly she knows something bearing on Bridget's death, but she doesn't want to tell us. James Callender being what he is, it's easy to imagine that Bridget could have learned some scandalous tidbit that Callender had unearthed. Something that that someone would want to be sure never came to light, especially in a newspaper. If so, Mrs. Callender might very well know what it might be, but she's trying to protect her husband's secrets."

"Bridget certainly was a magnet for scandal." Somewhere along the way, Elizabeth had become fully engrossed in Jacob's tale and trying to puzzle out who could be the murderer. The more she learned of Bridget's life, the more amazed she was. Who would have though it of a simple housemaid? "I must say, there seem to be no end of suspects. Have you read Mr. Bache's piece in the latest *Aurora*?" she asked curiously. "He's accusing Alexander Hamilton of murdering her."

"I read it, but I don't credit it," Jacob said easily. His earlier apprehension had wholly disappeared as Elizabeth had warmed to him. "Benjamin Bache hates Alexander Hamilton with a burning passion. I imagine he'd do anything to destroy him. What do you think?"

"Perhaps you're right. Mr. Hamilton did have the opportunity, however," she added, remembering what Abigail had told her. "Did you know that he was in Philadelphia around the time that Bridget died? Mrs. Adams heard it from Mrs. Pickering. I imagine he met with Mr. Pickering, since they're so close. I suppose that's how she knows. Still, it doesn't really make sense," she added dubiously. "Why would Bridget be a threat to anyone, if it's something Mr. Callender already knows? Surely Callender himself would be in the greatest danger?"

"You're right, of course." Jacob nodded. "If that's what it was all about, why would he kill Bridget instead of Callender? Unless somehow Bridget was killed by mistake and Callender was supposed to be the victim? Given what we know, however, I don't see how that could be the case."

Elizabeth weighed her next words very carefully. Remembering what Abigail said about Alexander Hamilton brought back the memory of their whole conversation. Was Jacob

Martin now working for Jefferson? Looking back over Jacob's report, it seemed clear to her that, contrary to what he'd told her before, he'd become deeply involved in the investigation. He was so familiar with every detail and he'd clearly spent a lot of time thinking about it. To work for Jefferson was bad enough, but lying to her about it was even worse. And yet, it was still so hard to believe that he could really be so false with her.

"You seem to be now more involved in this investigation than the last time we spoke about it," she said pointedly. "I gather you changed your mind about looking into it?"

"It's interesting that you should ask me that." Entirely oblivious, Jacob felt gratified. Here was his chance. "I haven't yet, but I'm certainly thinking about it. Right now, it seems no one cares who really murdered her. It's all just politics. Bache accuses Hamilton, just as Cobbett accused Jefferson, when there's actually no evidence against him."

Elizabeth's heart sank. Clearly, he meant to go on with the charade, though it was obvious he was committed to defending Jefferson.

"I thought you were concerned about losing political support if you got involved?"

"True enough, but there are other considerations." Jacob thought back to his confrontation with Harrison Gray Otis and felt his anger flare up yet again. Damn them all, he thought furiously.

"There certainly must be," Elizabeth tartly observed, "since it seems to me that you are deeply involved in it already. I must say however, looking at it from the outside, your calculations seem to me very mysterious. I'm sure that Mr. Jefferson finds it gratifying that you are on his side, but doesn't this cost you a great deal with your Federalist colleagues?"

"I am not 'on Jefferson's side" as you put it," Jacob said harshly, stung by her accusation. She didn't believe him either? She was one of his attackers as well? It was almost the last straw for his badly fraying temper. "I haven't even been investigating either," he added coldly, "and I must say, I'm getting very tired of being accused of it."

"I have it on good authority, I'm sorry to say." Angry at his continued deceit, Elizabeth's tone was chilly also. "And I've heard it from the most impeccable sources. Even Jefferson himself has said so, from what I hear. It seems that I'm the only one who didn't know it. If it isn't true, then why is everyone saying so? What have they to gain, and why have you done nothing to disabuse them?"

Hearing her echo Harrison Gray Otis's very words, Jacob lost the last vestige of self-control.

"Representative Otis said the very same thing to me, just the other day," he said heatedly, "but I'm shocked to hear you say it also. Are you like all the rest, believing all the rumors and outright lies? I thought that you were more intelligent, knowing politics as you do. I thought that you of all people knew me better."

Elizabeth's eyes flashed with indignation.

"I do not pretend any great intelligence in political matters," she said icily. "I'm sure you have good reasons for what you're doing, though I can't imagine what they are. As for what I should and shouldn't know about you, I think you are being quite presumptuous. We've known each other for how long? A few months, if I'm not mistaken. I do not know your family, your life in South Carolina, or your friends. All in all, I would say that ours is a rather slight acquaintance."

∽ **21** ∽

In order to speed up work on Volume Eighteen of her employer's *Encyclopaedia*, Rachel McAllister was now regularly working double, tending the book and stationery shop during the day and setting type for the *Encyclopaedia* in the evenings. For hours now, she had been bending over the boxes of typeface and the galley trays, carefully arranging the letters for page after page. It was tedious, careful work, arranging the individual letters one by one into words and sentences, and it all had to be set in backwards.

"selgna eerht, sedis eerht fo erugif a, yrtemoeg ni, ELGNAIRT," read the line before her now, but the printing process would transpose it mirror-fashion so it was readable. "TRIANGLE, in geometry, a figure of three sides, three angles." She double- and triple-checked the order, and then she carefully moved the last line of type into the galley tray, tied it up with twine, and set it into the printing press. There it was, another page finally finished. That was enough for tonight. It must be well past midnight.

She gently massaged the small of her back, straightening up with difficulty. Her vision was bleary after focusing so long just a few inches in front of her by candlelight.

What to do now, to relax and recover from her labors? She didn't feel like going back to her room to sit by the fire alone. She considered several possibilities and quickly discarded them. It was too dangerous to take a walk for walking's sake, too late to go visiting. There were taverns by her lodgings, but they were not the place for a woman alone at this time of night, except for women of "easy virtue."

She decided to go to the Man Full of Troubles, since Martha Smallwood, the owner and proprietress, was a friend of hers. It was a bit out of the way, but Martha would protect her from any unwelcome attentions. Martha might even let her stay in one of the rooms for the night instead of having to walk home again.

Mindful of the night-time dangers, Rachel made her way briskly to the corner of Dock and Spruce Streets, warily alert for any possible source of danger. When she was almost to the tavern though, only a few steps away, she heard the running footsteps of someone rushing up from behind her.

She said a little prayer, took a small knife from her pocket, and readied herself for trouble. To her great relief, the young man – for it was a young man – ran straight on by. He didn't even seem to notice her. When he reached the Man Full of Troubles, he stopped abruptly and went up the step. Only then did he look around. Seeing Rachel, he stood there politely and held open the door, gesturing for her to go in before him. Rachel smiled in relief and bemusement.

Once inside, the young lad went quickly across the room, weaving his way through the tables and chairs and disappearing through a doorway. Rachel herself stood for a moment just inside the door, surveying the scene and looking for Martha Smallwood.

The room was small but its furnishings were a cut above average. There were three red-painted pine trestle tables, with a mix of Windsor chairs, various mismatched rush-bottom chairs, and two ancient arm chairs with threadbare upholstery. The walls were plain white plaster, but decorated with inexpensive copies of popular engravings – romantic Italian ruins, picturesque English landscapes, and full-sailed ships gliding across vast ocean waters. The whole was dimly lit by the fire and the glow of a few tallow candles.

The Man Full of Troubles was a waterfront tavern of a middling sort and the patrons by and large reflected it. They were amiable, ordinary folk, neither rich nor especially poor, neither morosely nursing their beers nor drunkenly loud and boisterous. For the most part, the clientele consisted of a usual group of men (and some women) who lived around the neighborhood, men who fancied a pint or two and a quick and ready supper before they went home.

Two men sat by the fire, smoking their long clay pipes and nursing their drinks in pewter tankards. Three men in the corner were playing a spirited game of cards, sitting at a small mahogany table with betting chips in little piles before them. Martha herself was seated at the smallest pine table, trying to work on her ledger by the light of a single candle.

Martha Smallwood was a plain woman with an open face and welcoming smile. Her one extravagance was her wardrobe. Tonight she was wearing a high-waisted gown of cream-colored cotton printed with delicate green leaves and multi-colored red flowers, an expensive fabric imported from India.

Hearing someone enter, she took off her spectacles and looked up to see who it was.

"Rachel, how good to see you," she greeted her warmly. "I've worn my eyes out on these miserable ledgers long enough. Come here and sit with me." Closing the ledger and setting it aside, she drew back an empty chair beside her at the table.

"Would you like something to eat? I've a nice lot of oysters, some good cheese, and fresh bread and butter. There's a porter from Robert Hare, just arrived. I had a taste of it earlier and it's very good. If you want some, I'll join you."

Rachel's smile was sufficient answer, and soon she was tucking in to her modest feast with gusto.

"Who was that young fellow who came in with me?" Rachel ventured between mouthfuls. "He almost knocked me down, there in the street, but then he held the door for me very mannerly."

"Oh, that's Jimmy. Jimmy Tucker," Martha replied. "That's him all right, him all over. One minute he's as sharp and polite as he can be, the next minute he's heedless and distracted. I found him one night sleeping outside by the back door. He came up from the country, he said, to make his way in Philadelphia. I let him sleep upstairs and in return he does odd jobs for me."

"You always were soft-hearted." Rachel smiled at her friend affectionately. "He's lucky that you found him. The times are still pretty hard, I'd say, for all that they're said to be improving. Even a wealthy man can be ruined in an instant. Just look at Robert Morris. He was the richest man in Philadelphia not long ago, and now he's hiding out to avoid being tossed in the debtor's prison."

"Jimmy won't ruin me," Martha said with a laugh, "it's little enough that I'm doing. Just a corner of the attic to stay in and a bit of bread and cheese for breakfast. At the moment, though," she went on in a more somber tone, "I'm afraid he's struggling. He needs to find some other work for the winter. I wish I could offer him something myself, but I have all the help I need. I can't afford to be supporting stray lads for charity."

After their conversation, Martha's concerns about Jimmy lingered on in Rachel's mind. She had taken a liking to Jimmy, even on such a slight and unpromising acquaintance. Was there some way to help him find a living, at least to see him through the winter? Her employer Thomas Dobson, like Martha, had no need of any further employees, but something might turn up. She resolved that she would keep an eye out.

A few days later, a chance remark by a customer at Dobson's shop provided the answer.

"The Senate buys its supplies here, I've heard," a young man observed to Derrick, as he was counting out the coins to pay for his purchase. He was only buying a few pennies' worth of paper, but it must have seemed like a lot of money to him, given how he was taking his time about it.

"That it does," Derrick agreed. "We see their Doorman pretty regularly."

"What's he like, the Doorman?" The fellow's tone was deliberately casual, but his look was intensely interested. "Have you heard they're looking to hire him an assistant?"

"An Assistant Doorkeeper?" Derrick shook his head. "No, haven't heard. The Doorkeeper, though, he's all right, I'd say. You fancy working for him?"

The young man nodded.

"Seems worth looking into."

As he took up his parcel and left the shop, Rachel felt her burden of concern was suddenly lifted. Jimmy as Assistant Doorkeeper – wouldn't that be just the thing. Here was something she could do, or try to do, to help him.

From what she could tell, the job seemed pretty much what Jimmy had already been doing, running errands and such, and Martha said he was bright, lively, and reliable. She resolved to raise it with Mr. Mathers at the first opportunity. He must have some influence over who was hired. After all, it was his assistant they were looking for. It was surely a grand idea, she told herself. She'd be doing both of them a favor, the lad Jimmy and Mr. Mathers also.

She didn't have long to wait. His appearances at Dobson's shop were frequent and habitual. He always came up with some more or less flimsy excuse, but his true motives were pretty obvious.

"It's good to see you again, Mr. Mathers," she greeted him when he next appeared, with a smile that was warm and friendly. "I haven't seen you for a while. You must be very busy at the Senate."

Noting her smile and concern for his well-being, Mathers's mood brightened up immediately.

"Terrible busy it is, that's for sure. It's not only the Senate, though that's busy enough, but I'm also investigating the girl Bridget's death, like I promised you."

"I heard they were thinking to hire someone to help you there at the Senate," she asked sweetly. "Is it true?"

"Yes, finally." He'd been throwing out not-so-subtle hints for months and was gratified that the Senators had finally responded. "Someone to run errands when the Senate is in session, to muck out the stables and help take care of the horses, to tend to the fires, and so forth."

"How does one apply for the position?

"I suppose they'd be coming to me first, being as how they'd be my assistant. But did you have someone in mind?"

"I do know someone who might be good," Rachel admitted cheerfully. "He's a likely young man and he needs a job quite badly."

"A young man, you say?" Mathers's good mood instantly vanished. A "likely young man," was it now? Here she was, all smiling and friendly, but it wasn't for him at all. It was only to get a job for some other fellow. She must really fancy this fellow, he thought sadly, to be asking me so bold and plain as that. She must surely know how I feel about her.

"Your young man should start by coming to see me." A sudden reserve marked Mathers's attitude. "He should come in the morning if he can, before the session starts, so I can explain what's wanted and see if he's up to it."

He turned away quickly and headed toward the door. He wasn't mad at her, only at himself. Whatever had he been thinking of? Naturally she would fancy some handsome young fellow more than his ancient self. Why did he ever think he had a chance to begin with? It was a good thing he'd been so shy and hadn't too obviously pursued her. He hadn't made a fool of himself at least, trying to woo her.

"I'll do that then. That's very kind," Rachel began, but already he was gone. She was taken aback by his sudden departure. Had she said something to upset him, she wondered anxiously? Replaying the conversation in her mind, she remembered how he'd said "your young man." There was something about the way he'd said it. Was that it, she wondered? Did he think she was taking advantage of him, trading on their relationship, such as it was, to beg a favor for some friend of hers?

She stewed all through the afternoon, torn between guilt and annoyance. By the time evening came, however, she was far too busy to spend more time worrying about it. She was setting type from the moment the shop was closed until far into the night. A meat pasty from a street vendor, nibbled on as she worked, was her supper. A few candles were her only light, and a single small fire her only warmth and companion.

By the time she was done, it was so late and she was so tired that she didn't even have enough energy to go home again. She took her cloak and wrapped herself up in it, made a pillow of rags, and slept curled up on the floor by the presses. The next several nights were much the same, with only a little time off to scurry home and back again. It was therefore several days before she went to the Man Full of Troubles tavern to tell Jimmy about her conversation with Mr. Mathers.

❧ 22 ❧

Jimmy's reaction to Rachel's kind intervention, like James Mathers's, both surprised and annoyed her. Jimmy agreed that the job sounded perfect but, nevertheless, he seemed strangely unwilling to pursue it. Rachel shrugged her shoulders and let it be. After she was gone, however, Martha Smallwood bore down upon him.

"You've no other choice," she said flatly. "You have to do it. You need a job and there's nothing else to hand. I'll not be clothing and feeding you."

In the end, he reluctantly surrendered.

The next day he rose early, ate his breakfast quickly, and made off for Congress Hall. As he knocked on the great white double door of the entrance, he felt deeply apprehensive. It was true that he desperately needed a job, and here was something that seemed to suit him. All the same, the thought of seeing Mr. Mathers again made him strangely afraid. He couldn't understand the reason for it. Was it just that he'd almost run the man down, that time on the street? Still, they seemed on friendly enough terms when they parted.

He waited anxiously for someone to open the door, wondering if he'd come too early. Then he heard footsteps coming closer and closer, the handle turned, and suddenly, James Mathers himself was looking down at him. He seemed even larger than Jimmy remembered.

When Mathers saw who it was, he frowned.

"You again?" This was the boy who'd almost run him down. Why had he come to Congress Hall, and at this hour of the morning? He didn't have any idea that this was Rachel's "young man." Ever since that day, he hadn't been to see her. "What are you doing here?"

"Please, Sir," Jimmy said earnestly, "I hear that you're wanting an Assistant Doorkeeper. I'd like to be considered."

"Hmmph." Mathers looked the boy up and down, thinking of their last encounter. Then he relented. "Well, we'll see. You can come in then."

Once settled in the Doorkeeper's Lodge – Mathers in his chair and Jimmy standing respectfully at attention – Jimmy tried his best to give a good account of himself. He mentioned every virtue and ability he possessed, hoped to possess, or might hope (given half a chance) to develop in the future. He talked hurriedly and at length, desperately trying to sound like the best possible candidate.

All the while, Mathers was studying the boy, only half listening. He found it difficult not to stare at Jimmy's face. The boy's resemblance to his dear Catherine was disconcerting. As he listened, he fiddled absently with the penknife he used for sharpening quills, turning it over and over in his hand. Distracted, at last he dropped it on the floor. Jimmy bent over to pick it up for him.

As he did, the leather necklace with the gold and ruby ring peeked out through the slit at the neck of his shirt.

Mathers stared it with horrified fascination.

"What's that?"

"What's what, Sir?" Jimmy responded, confused.

"That necklace – that ring." Mathers forced himself to sound casual. "It seems an interesting design. May I see it?"

Reluctantly, Jimmy took the leather thong from his neck and handed it over. Then, still preoccupied with securing the job, he continued his monologue.

"And if there's anything I don't know, if you please, Sir, I'm sure that I could quickly learn it. There's nothing much doing on the docks, Sir. If I may say so, I'd give anything for a chance. If only you would hire me, I'm sure you wouldn't be sorry. I'd do my very best for you."

"Hmm, well, yes, that's quite impressive," Mathers said at last, though he'd hardly heard a word of it. "Tell me a little more about yourself. You said that your mother had died, the last time we ran into each other."

"That's right."

"And you didn't know your father?"

"That's right, Sir."

"Your mother, was Tucker her family name?"

Jimmy looked at Mathers curiously.

"No, it was her married name. Not my father, but my stepfather. Her family name was O'Brian."

Catherine O'Brian. Mathers paled. And the ring was the ring that he'd given her.

"Well lad, I think you might be suitable," he managed to say at last, with a semblance of self-control. "There's other candidates,

I have to say, and it's the Senators who make the final decision. Your chances are good though. Very good indeed," he added gruffly, "if I have anything to say about it. How can I get ahold of you? I expect I may know something in a week or so."

Jimmy nodded, not trusting himself to speak. He was feeling light-headed and shaky. The way Mathers reacted when he saw the ring – surely he'd seen it before. And then the way he looked when he heard the name Catherine O'Brian. Could it be? Could it possibly be? Jimmy looked at the doorman searchingly.

"You can leave a message at the Man Full of Troubles," Jimmy finally managed to say, his voice rough and unsteady with sudden realization. "Mrs. Smallwood will see that it gets to me."

"All right then. I'll let you know. Now be off with you, lad," Mathers said brusquely. "I've work to do, to get ready for the session."

As Mathers escorted Jimmy back down the stairs and out the door, he wondered how much influence he really had with the Senators. Enough to get the boy the job? He'd certainly try his damndest.

It was too bad for Rachel's young man, whoever he was, but anyway he'd never shown up to ask for it. It's just as well, he consoled himself, that she's interested in some other man. I never could explain to her about Catherine, how I loved her and left her pregnant with my child. Her young lover, whoever he may be, has saved me no end of trouble. Likely he's some sly boots with a handsome face – a negligent sort of fellow, all flash and shine. Well, if that's the kind she fancied, she deserved him.

∞ 23 ∞

"**G**ood day to you, Mr. Mathers," Jacob called out as usual as he passed by the door on his way to the Senate Chamber. "And to you too, Jimmy," he added.

For Jimmy had indeed been hired, thanks to Mathers's strong recommendation. If the Senators had noticed Jimmy's strong resemblance to Mathers himself or their unusually close relationship, it didn't appear to bother them. Only Samuel Otis, the Secretary of the Senate, was annoyed. For him, it was yet another of Mathers's many offenses. It was bad enough that the doorkeeper lacked the proper attitude of subservience and respect, without also having to suffer the presence of this boy, who was obviously, from the looks of him, Mathers's bastard son.

Mathers intercepted Jacob before he could continue down the hall.

"I've a need to talk to you soon, Senator Martin, if you can spare the time." He'd gotten into the habit of reporting to Jacob on what he'd learned, even though Jacob didn't really want to hear it. Talking to someone helped him sort things out, and sometimes Jacob made a useful comment or suggestion.

"If you must. After the session then," Jacob conceded grudgingly. "I can meet you at the Bull's Head, in Strawberry Alley."

"Not the Indian Queen? It's much closer."

Jacob shook his head.

"That's just the point. I'd rather we were somewhere further away from the Senate. I'm in enough trouble with my colleagues as it is, thanks to Vice-President Jefferson. I'm a secret Republican, is the common view, though I can't only blame Thomas Jefferson. It's my fault too. I keep getting into trouble by voting my conscience. It's so bad that I'm beginning to wonder myself if I really belong with the Federalists."

"The Bull's Head it is, then," Mathers agreed. "And I'm wishing you luck for the session. There's a vote to repeal the naturalization tax coming up soon, if I'm not mistaken?"

"Not much luck there, I'm afraid," Jacob said gloomily. Last session they'd passed a law, after heated partisan debates, imposing a twenty dollar tax on naturalization certificates. The arguments for and against it made the purpose very clear – to keep the Irish and other poorer immigrants from becoming citizens by making it too expensive. "I was hoping to persuade my colleagues to lower the tax at least, but I'm afraid that I've lost any influence with my colleagues."

Mathers knew the prejudice against the Irish all too well from his own experience. Harrison Gray Otis had accused him of shielding a murderer just months before, for no better reason than they both were Irish. According to Otis, the Irish and other "immigrant hordes" were violent, lawless and degraded men, unfit to live in civilized society. They also tended to vote Republican.

"I'll see you after the session, then," were Mathers's parting words, as Jacob headed off toward the Chamber. "'Tis a great pity, though, that you can't be helping me," he added to himself, once Jacob was out of earshot. "Talking at a tavern is all very well, but I could really use more help than just talking."

Jimmy had been listening closely to this exchange, standing off to the side and silent.

"I can help you with your investigating, if you like," he ventured timidly. "I know that area down by the river. That's where I've been living and working."

"Don't you even think of it!" Mathers cursed himself for not realizing that Jimmy was listening. "It's not a game, you know. Chasing after a murderer is deadly dangerous. Don't you know, once someone brings themselves to murder the first time, they find it easier and easier to go on doing it."

Jimmy should have taken the warning to heart, but it made very little impression. He was full of the heedless confidence of youth and his desire to help his father (for the more he thought about it, the more he was sure that's who Mathers was, though neither of them had come right out and said it) was far stronger than his sense of caution.

So the first day he was free from his Senate duties, he woke even earlier than usual, downed a quick bite of bread and cheese, and headed off toward Front and Water Streets. His idea was to drop in here and there and ask about Bridget LeClair. He was bound to find out something useful.

When it came to actually doing it, however, it was harder than he thought. He couldn't bring himself to just knock on doors and start asking questions of total strangers. So he went to the shops and the taverns instead, all up and down the waterfront. The Harp and Crown, the Boatswain and Call, the Crooked Billet, the Cross Keys, the Pewter Platter – he stopped at them all, and many others.

As the day wore on and he worked his way further north, the neighborhoods became seedier and more dangerous. North of Arch Street was the worst of all, where the very dregs of Philadelphia clustered – the criminals, alcoholics and the insane, the escaped servants and slaves, the criminals and prostitutes. All the same, he carried on. He even screwed up his courage and braved the notorious Three Jolly Irishmen.

By afternoon he was beginning to despair. No one took him seriously, and why should they? To them, he was just one of the many young men who hung about the docks, being nosy when he should be working. Dispirited, he was making his way back to the Man Full of Troubles tavern, when a voice he knew well called out to him.

"Jimmy, my lad, I'm glad to see you." Stephen Girard was at the door of his counting house, looking worried. "I have an urgent errand to run, can you do it? I need Doctor La Roche to come to the house as quickly as he can. Tell him that Polly is ill and I'd be greatly obliged if he could come right away and see her."

Jimmy sped off and soon returned, with Doctor La Roche huffing and puffing behind him. The doctor went up to examine Polly while Jimmy, drawn by his hunger and the tantalizing smells, ended up eating leftover roast goose and potatoes in the kitchen. He was just finishing up when Doctor La Roche came down again. Girard was still at his desk and Jimmy could hear them through the open door between the hallway and the counting house.

"I'm afraid she has the pleurisy," La Roche reported to Girard. He had a rich, deep voice that inspired confidence, a good thing in a doctor. "I bled her, but I will need to bleed her more. I'll come back tomorrow after dinner. In the meantime, keep her in bed and give her light things to eat and drink, like barley water and honey. She's young and strong and the case seems to be mild. I think she'll recover quickly."

"That's good news, very good news." Girard looked at him gratefully.

Doctor La Roche bit his lip, as if he was debating whether to say more but hadn't decided.

"Is there more?" Girard asked, suddenly worried.

"Oh, it's nothing to do with Polly," Doctor La Roche reassured him. "It's another matter entirely. Would you mind if I asked you for some advice?"

"Ask what you will," Girard said encouragingly.

"You recall that girl, Bridget LeClair, the one who was murdered?"

Girard nodded, and the doctor went on.

"It's a curious thing. As it happens, she came to me for treatment before she died, complaining of recurrent nausea. I've never know the like," he added, shaking his head in wonderment. "Can you imagine, she was pregnant. She hadn't realized it at all. I'm not even sure she understood how such things happened."

"Pregnant." Remembering his barber's concern about sharing confidences, Girard did his best to look as if he didn't already know. "How very curious."

"I saw her at nearly the end of September," the doctor continued, "and from what I hear, she died quite shortly afterwards.

She hadn't been pregnant long, I think. It was just beginning to affect her."

"Did she tell you who the father was?"

"Not a word, but I wouldn't expect it. They seldom do you know. The odd thing was, the diagnosis seemed to cheer her up considerably. For an unmarried girl I must say, that is not the usual reaction."

"She may have been glad that it wasn't something worse," Girard suggested, "considering the yellow fever had just come back again. But wasn't she already ill at the time? From the fever, or whatever it was that killed her?"

"Not that I could see. Of course, I only saw her once very briefly and my focus of attention was her pregnancy. There may have been some other problem that didn't show itself. Still, apart from being pregnant, she seemed entirely healthy.

"The question is," La Roche continued, "what shall I do about it? A doctor should not talk about his clients, that's understood. She's dead, however, and there are these terrible charges being made – Vice President Jefferson, and all that. You understand me?"

Girard was silent for a moment, considering.

"Yes, you are right to wonder. It might be important information, but then again, perhaps it has nothing whatsoever to do with her dying. I wonder if it would help or hurt things? It might only make things worse, to add yet another ground for wild accusations."

"You understand me," La Roche observed. "It would be a terrible pity if this should add to Mr. Jefferson's troubles. You understand these things better than I, so may I leave it in your hands? I trust entirely to your judgment and discretion."

With that, the doctor was content. He went off to go back home, and Girard left the counting house to go upstairs to see Polly. Jimmy, unnoticed in the kitchen, felt a thrill of triumph. His investigating had been successful after all. Now he had something to tell his father.

∞ 24 ∞

"Pregnant! Is that what you're telling me?"

Suddenly sensing that someone was in the hall, Mathers looked out to see who might have overheard. He was relieved to see it was only Jacob.

"Who's pregnant?" Looking in through the door, Jacob regarded Mathers and Jimmy with curiosity.

"Bridget LeClair was pregnant. I learned it from Mr. Girard," Jimmy proudly repeated for Jacob's benefit. "He heard it himself from the doctor who saw her. It was just before she was poisoned."

"I should have thought of it myself," Mathers added ruefully. "Especially with all that Annie was saying about her spreading her favors around."

"That's why he murdered her," Jimmy added excitedly.

"Now don't go leaping ahead of yourself," Mathers cautioned. "The graveyards would be much fuller than they are, if every wayward servant girl was to turn up murdered."

"Still, it's common enough," Jacob noted, "where there's a question of jealousy or pride, especially. Some young fellow who thinks she's his alone, but then he finds out he's been cuckolded, and another man's child in the bargain. With all the men she seems to have had in her life, do you think that one of them might have thought she was his exclusively?"

Mathers scratched the back of his neck, considering.

"I don't see how anyone could, with her reputation. But you never know. Some men believe what they want to believe, especially when a pretty girl tells them. Then he finds out he's been had. 'That wanton slut,' he thinks, and he's furious. But then would he take his time to plan on poisoning the girl? Wouldn't he just beat her to death or strangle her?"

"I suppose you're right," Jacob conceded. "Poisoning's a different sort of crime, more cool and calculating. Are we back to secrets again? Someone who doesn't want the relationship to be discovered? Would Senator Blount care, I wonder, if he was the father?"

"It wouldn't be Senator Blount, from what Jimmy says. The timing's against it. The doctor saw her in September, he says, and Senator Blount left at the beginning of July, just as soon as he knew he was in trouble. I'll tell you what though, speaking of secrets. Annie never said a word about Bridget being pregnant. Not even a hint, but she must surely have known. I'm thinking it's about time for another little talk with her."

He wasted no time getting in touch and Annie was happy to accept his invitation. They met as before at the Kouli Khan, at the very same table and ordering the same supper of pea soup, London ale, and roast mutton.

The atmosphere, however, was entirely different.

"It's good of you, Mr. Mathers, to be seeing me," Annie began, giving him her second-best smile. (She saved her best one for expensive presents.)

He scowled at her.

"You may not be thanking me, Miss Dawson, when you hear what I have to say to you."

"Whatever do you mean?" She sounded genuinely surprised. Her face was a perfect picture of astonishment.

"You've been holding out on me, my girl, and I'm not best pleased. You didn't tell me that Bridget was in an increasing way. You must have known about it."

"Yes, I knew." She didn't sound the least bit guilty. "I'm sorry if you're upset I didn't tell you, but it's a delicate thing. It's a hard thing to talk about to a man you hardly know – not as well as you'd like to know him." She gave him a fetching look and pouted prettily. "And then, afterwards, well, it didn't seem so important any more, and I thought I'd said enough bad things about her already. I would have told you, if you'd asked me straight out. I didn't lie to you."

"Come now, Annie," he chided her, still suspicious and annoyed, "don't be playing me for a fool. Not saying anything was as good as a lie. How would I know enough to ask you?"

"Well, if you put it like that, I suppose you're right. I'm sorry, I really am." She lowered her gaze, all modesty and contrition. "But honestly, I didn't think it had anything to do with her murder. I didn't know right away, mind you, but only later on, when she came to ask me about it. She told me she was feeling sick every morning, and asked me what might be wrong."

"She didn't know?"

"She was that innocent, that she didn't know what had happened to her. She didn't really believe it until the doctor confirmed it."

"Did the Walns know? Is that why they sent her away, and not her illness?

Annie shook her head.

"I was the only one what knew. That wasn't the reason."

"How do you know?"

"Mrs. Waln would have said that was why she was sending Bridget away, as a lesson to the rest of us."

That sounded reasonable, Mathers thought, but then again, he hadn't talked to the Walns, had he? To tell the truth, he didn't know how to approach them. Since he was really just looking into things on his own, a man as rich and famous as that likely wouldn't even talk to him.

"Who was the father, do you know? Or can you guess it?"

"I wish I could tell you, but I can't." Annie shrugged. "She never said who it was. I did ask her, couldn't they just get married, but she told me he never would. I think it must have been someone already married or someone far above her station."

"Apart from Senator Blount, what about the other men she was friendly with?"

"I don't know of anyone specific." Annie seemed sincere. "Don't think I haven't thought about it. Like I said before, she called them by made-up names, so I don't know who they were exactly. So now I've told you all I know, I really have." She looked at him imploringly. "I'm truly sorry about before. Will you forgive me?"

Mathers regarded her thoughtfully. She was an attractive wench, to be sure. He was coming to enjoy her company more and more. She was lively and bright, easy on the eye as well as his spirits, and strangely enough, she seemed to fancy him.

True enough, she couldn't hold a candle to Rachel. But what was Rachel to him now? She had already given her heart to another. His chances, if he'd ever had any, were gone. It was time to let go of her.

"You're a treat, that you are," he said sincerely. "If you promise you'll never do it again, I'll forgive you. If you think of anything more, anything you overlooked or forgot to mention, you will tell me, won't you?"

He reached across the table and patted her hand, in a gesture that might have been fatherly but wasn't.

"I promise I'll tell you everything." She gave his hand a little squeeze and smiled at him broadly. "So will you see me again, Mr. Mathers, and next time not about Bridget?"

"Yes, my girl," he said warmly, "I'll see you again and next time not about Bridget."

They stared at each other for a long, lingering moment, still holding hands across the table.

"Oh, look who's here," Annie exclaimed, her attention drawn to a group of people coming in the doorway. "Isn't that Rachel McAllister, the one who works in Dobson's shop? I don't really know her myself, but Lydia told me a lot about her."

He turned to look and saw Derrick, Rachel, and a handful of other Dobson employees, heading straight over to their table. Suddenly realizing that he and Annie were still holding hands, he quickly withdrew his and picked up his tankard. Blast it, he told himself, Rachel was the one who jilted him. So why did he feel so guilty?

"Well, who have we here? Mr. Mathers and a very lovely lady." Derrick said it in his usual jovial tone, but his expression was surprised and disapproving.

"Yes, indeed," Rachel added with a frozen smile. "Won't you introduce us to your charming companion?"

∽ 25 ∽

James Mathers told Jimmy yet again, this time even more firmly, that he had to stop going around the waterfront asking questions. With all the criminals and desperate men who hung out there, it was a risky enough area to begin with. It was the very worst place to go around stirring up trouble.

This warning, however, made as little impression as the first one. Hadn't he been the one, thought Jimmy, to find out about Bridget's being pregnant? They would never have known, he told himself, if he hadn't been going around asking questions. (That it was entirely an accident that he'd overheard Girard talking with Doctor La Roche was a fact he'd conveniently forgotten.)

"You're getting a reputation, you know," Martha Smallwood warned Jimmy as well, one evening as he sat at a tavern table eating his supper. "Everyone knows you're looking for the man who killed that girl. Don't you know how dangerous that is? What if you get too close? Whoever it is, he has killed already. What if he goes after you?" She looked at James Forten, a regular patron sitting nearby, for confirmation.

"You'd best listen to the lady," Forten chimed in. A fourth-generation freeborn African-American, he was a sail maker who worked for one of the most successful sail makers in the city. Rumor had it, the man would soon retire and he'd own the shop himself. "She knows what she's talking about."

"I can take care of myself," Jimmy told them stubbornly. "I'm just trying to help out. I'm not doing anything to get into trouble. I know this area pretty well, after all, much better than Mr. Mathers does. Wasn't it me that learned she was pregnant?"

After his supper, he set out again.

In the daytime, the area by the docks is a beehive of honest industry. At night, there's a very different sort of business. Prostitutes and overly-sharp young men in stained and second-hand finery rule the streets, while the vagrants, the thieves, and the drunks lay claim to the shadows and the corners. A wise man passes by, if he must pass by at all, as quickly as he can, always alert for the sound of following footsteps.

Jimmy, however, was used to it all. Being too young to matter and too obviously poor to hustle or rob, he could usually slip through the streets without attracting much attention. It was a skill that would keep him safe now, was what he figured.

Where should he go and what should he look for, that was the question. He had a vague idea of looking around, but no real plan. He chose a tavern at random and entered. It was the Ship Aground, one of the better-known and more respectable of the drinking establishments along the waterfront.

Standing just inside the door, he peered into the murky, smoky darkness. In the subdued hubbub of the crowded room, his eyes were drawn to a little group huddled at a small table in the corner. It was a group of boys that lived, as he had lived, by doing odd jobs for the merchants. He knew them.

They saw him too and one called out.

"Well come on over, then. Or have you forgotten us already?" Tim, the speaker, gestured to an empty place on a rough wooden bench and Jimmy was soon seated amongst them.

"Haven't seen you for a while. I hear you've come got yourself a government job," a scrawny lad called Pat greeted him enviously. "You're a rich man now, so I expect as you'll be treating us to a drink or two," he added pointedly.

"I'll be back here soon enough," Jimmy responded amiably. "It only pays for a few months when Congress is meeting. Since they're meeting now though, I expect I could stand you to a bowl of punch."

There were cheers around the table.

The serving girl, duly summoned, soon brought forth the punch in a large china bowl. It was chipped, to be sure, but the serving was generous and it smelled wonderfully of lemon, rum, and nutmeg. The lads toasted Jimmy and drank it down, and then wolfed down their dinners of bread, salt beef, and cabbage.

The table was quiet, except for the clink of knives and the occasional belch or fart, until the plates were cleaned and the conversation began again.

"Seriously, it's good to see you," said Henry. Of all of them, he'd been Jimmy's closest companion. "What's it like, working for the government?"

Jimmy scratched his head, trying to think how to explain it.

"It's a lot like working here, only different. Mostly it's a lot of errands, running around here and there to get this and deliver that. And standing in the Public Gallery sometimes when the Doorkeeper's busy, minding the people who come to watch."

"Maybe we'll come sometime and join them," said Tim mischievously. "We'll cause a ruckus and see how you do."

"You just do that," Jimmy dared him. "Mr. Mathers – he's the doorkeeper – is bigger than two of you. Though I expect you'd just fall asleep before you had a chance to cause any trouble. When they get going, those Senators can talk you to a living death, I swear it."

"I'd like to come watch Mr. Jefferson," Henry said seriously. "I've never seen him in person, you know."

"Yes, Mr. Jefferson's a topping fellow," Pat chimed in. "I'm thinking he'll be President next time, instead of that sorry old Mr. Adams."

"I hope it's not true what they're saying," Jimmy ventured, thinking to take advantage of this opening, "about him murdering that girl Bridget."

His friends all nodded sagely. No one was more interested in keeping up to date on all the latest gossip and scandal than they were.

"You should know," said Pat. "Isn't the Doorkeeper the one who's looking into it? Him and one of the Senators?"

"Senator Martin, you mean. I don't know as he is, to be honest, but Mr. Mathers is. It would stand me in good stead if I could help him. You could count on me to be grateful," Jimmy added with a meaningful glance at the empty punchbowl, "if you knew something useful."

The hint was well understood. A deep silence fell on the table, as they all tried to think if they knew anything that would gain them another round of punch.

At last Tim spoke up.

"I used to see that Bridget at the taverns from time to time, on her own or with some gentleman or other. I never paid much attention, for the most part. One time, though, she was with someone you'd never think to see with a girl like her." He looked around the table at his comrades one by one, relishing their full attention.

"It was someone you'd all recognize," he hinted temptingly. "His wharves is just nearby and you've all run errands for him." He paused and smiled, seemingly enjoying tantalizing them. "It was Old Square Toes, that's who."

This was greeted with a chorus of disbelief.

"Thomas Willing?"

"What was you drinking?"

"Not on your life!"

"Thomas Willing himself," Tim answered firmly, "and Bridget LeClair. They was sitting as near as there –" he pointed at a nearby table, "and as close to each other as that," he held up two fingers close together, "and they wasn't just discussing how things was going at the Bank of the United States, I'll bet you anything."

"Come to think of it, I think I saw them too," Henry spoke up hesitantly. "I think it was them, anyway. It's hard to be sure, given how it was some time ago."

By the time Jimmy left his friends, it was well past midnight and he was more than a little bit tipsy. There wasn't any moon and the night seemed especially black and cold. The main streets were lit well enough by the gaslights, but it was shadowed and dark in the alleys. Jimmy knew them all by heart, however, so he turned into one of the alleys between Front and Second Street, hurrying toward Dock Street and the Man Full of Troubles.

There were patches of snow and ice on the ground, so the going was tricky. He was looking down to watch where he walked, so at first he sensed more than saw that he wasn't alone. Looking up, he saw two shadowy figures materializing out of the gloom just ahead of him. He hoped they would pass him by, but they stood their ground.

"Have I the pleasure of encountering Mr. Jimmy Tucker?" said the taller one. His studied politeness was dark with menace.

Sudden fear made Jimmy suddenly quite sober.

"That's me. Who are you?"

The other one came forward, grabbed Jimmy's arm, and spun him around, with his arm bent up painfully behind his back. The tall fellow moved in beside him.

"It's no concern of yours who we are," he whispered in Jimmy's ear. "We're just here to give you a message. You'd better leave off meddling in things as don't concern you."

Jimmy felt the prick of the knife at his throat.

"Just some friendly advice. Do you understand me?"

"Yes," Jimmy stammered, his knees weak and his legs trembling. "Yes, I do."

"That's good. To be sure you don't forget, though, I think we'll give you something to remember us by."

The knife traced a circuit along his neck, very lightly. Then up to his ear, his cheek, his eye, and back down to his ear again.

Jimmy closed his eyes and said a silent prayer.

"Let him go!"

A pistol shot accompanied the words, as loud as a cannon in the narrow alleyway. It was deliberately aimed high, however, to miss them.

Jimmy opened his eyes and saw James Forten standing at the corner, reloading his pistol. Another man stood beside him, holding up a lantern with one hand and brandishing a stout walking stick in the other.

"Let the boy go," Forten commanded. "The first shot was a warning but the second will surely hit you."

Jimmy felt his arm suddenly free of the painful grip he'd been held in, and heard the rapid footsteps of his assailants as they disappeared into the darkness. The tall one, however, had left a parting token. Jimmy was too scared to feel it at the time, but his scalp was nicked and bleeding freely. When Forten led the shaken boy out of the dark alley and back into the streetlight, he immediately saw it.

Forten led him back to his sail making loft, cleaned off the blood, and inspected the injury.

"It isn't deep," he pronounced. "You're very lucky."

He went over to a small mahogany chest, opened it, and removed a bottle of rum. Then he poured a generous dose into a glass and put it in Jimmy's hand.

"Rum," he said. "Drink it down."

As Jimmy drank, Forten poured some of the rum on his handkerchief and dabbed at the wound with it. Then he covered the wound with a bit of sticking plaster, frowning mightily.

"I hope you realize now that Mrs. Smallwood was right," he said grimly. "If I hadn't just happened to come by, you could be bleeding to death there in the alley."

Still terrified, Jimmy nodded.

"No more investigating, then? And even so, they may still be looking for you, so you'd better not be wandering around in the dead of night."

Jimmy nodded again, and Forten led him back to the Man Full of Troubles tavern.

Martha Smallwood lectured him again before she let him go up to bed, and Jimmy meekly promised her to stop investigating also. As he lay there on his straw mattress, however, gradually his fear gave way to a sense of triumph. He had done it again. He'd found another important clue to Bridget's killing. He hoped that his father would be proud of him.

When he got to the Senate the next day, Jimmy only reported what he had learned from his friends, making no mention of his encounter with the ruffians in the alley. Mathers didn't miss seeing the plaster on his scalp, however, and then the whole story came out.

"I should kill you myself, you idiot boy, and save those damned ruffians the trouble." Mathers roared. He was furious and he didn't care who heard him.

"I only wanted to help," Jimmy said miserably. "You said you need help and so I helped you, that's all. And I did learn something important."

"What's all this?" Jacob paused at the door, shocked by the extraordinary commotion.

"That numbskull nearly got himself killed," Mathers snapped. "He heard me complain that I had to investigate all on my own, so he decided to help me."

Looking at Jimmy, Jacob felt a wave of remorse rush over him. This was all his fault for not helping Mathers himself. Damn it all, what was he thinking? Had he become like the bloody French revolutionaries? Did he think his political goals were so important that it didn't matter if people died for them?

"I'm sorry," he said simply.

Mathers looked at him for a long moment, and then he shook his head.

"It's the boy's own fault, not yours. We all warned him, but hasn't any more sense than would fill a thimble."

"I'm still sorry," Jacob said again. "I should be helping, and I'm going to."

"Do you mean it?" Mathers's spirits immediately brightened.

"I might as well prove Senator Sedgwick and the others right," Jacob said with a wry smile. "It won't matter much, I suppose, since everyone thinks I've been doing it anyway. Even Mrs. Powel," he added bitterly.

So after the session was over, they went off to the Indian Queen tavern. They sat for a very long time in one of the private rooms, talking and nursing their ciders. Mathers reviewed what he had learned in greater detail, with Jacob asking the occasional question. Mathers finished up with what Jimmy had learned the night before.

Jacob could hardly believe what he was hearing.

"Thomas Willing? Maybe he had a bastard child by a servant girl and then maybe he killed her? Hang it all, Mathers, I thought this was a terrible mess before, but it just gets worse and worse the more you tell me. The Republicans will make trouble from that like you can't imagine. It might even give them what they need to bring down the entire Bank of the United States. How can Jimmy be so sure that Willing even knows the girl? What if these fellows made it all up to get the punch he promised them?"

"In truth, I have a hard time believing it myself," Mathers admitted, "but Jimmy says he knows the boy and he vouches for him. And it fits with what Mrs. Finch hinted before, and Bridget's talking about her 'Mr. Fancy Merchant.' Poor Mrs. Powel." He gave Jacob a questioning look. "Are you going to tell her?"

Since their last unhappy meeting, Jacob hadn't heard from her at all. He couldn't think of a worse way to try to restart their relationship.

"Will I tell her that her brother might have fathered a bastard child? That he might be a suspect for Bridget's murder? No, I don't think I will. She's bound to hear it sooner or later, though. You know how news of scandal travels."

∞ 26 ∞

Even before she woke, Elizabeth felt a sense of impending doom. She had dreamt she was lost in a dark, tangled maze, surrounded by menacing, ghost-like figures. Even when she forced herself awake, her sense of fear remained. Was it only a dream, she wondered, or a premonition?

What was she doing in the maze at all? It seemed to have something to do with Senator Martin. Ever since that day at tea, she'd regretted that she'd ever met him. She'd been contented in solitude, leaving the turmoil and heartache of love far behind, but now she'd almost allowed herself to care again. She'd thought Jacob was different, a truly honest man, only to find that she was sadly mistaken.

Lydia soon arrived with the morning cup of tea and the newspapers. Elizabeth took a sip of tea and winced. It was as cold as the room, bitterly strong, and unsugared.

"Are you quite all right, Lydia?" It was the mildest of reproofs, but Lydia looked at her mournfully.

"I'm so sorry, Mrs. Powel," she said miserably, "but I just can't help it. It's preying on my mind, it is. I keep trying to forget about it, but it's just plain impossible."

"And what is 'it,' pray tell?" Elizabeth asked gently.

"I saw her last night, in my dreams. I saw Bridget." Lydia stared wide-eyed into space, as if seeing once again this apparition. "She was dressed all in white, and calling my name, with the ghost of her poor dead child beside her."

"Her child?" Without Jacob to keep her informed, Elizabeth knew only what she read in the newspapers. And the newspapers, she knew, couldn't be believed at all.

"Oh, Mrs. Powel, it's terrible," Lydia wailed. "Bridget was pregnant when she died. Annie told me about it, just yesterday. And who was the father? That's what I'd like to know. Mightn't he be the one what killed her?"

"Does Mr. Mathers know about this?" Despite Jacob's betrayal, Elizabeth still had high regard for the doorman. "Surely he's looking into it?"

"I don't even know," Lydia answered piteously. "It's been ages and ages since I saw him. Most often when I used to run into him, it was on account of Rachel. I used to think they were quite the pair, but lately he doesn't come to see her. I think she's more upset than she lets on, but she's never told me the reason."

When Lydia left the room, Elizabeth idly picked up the latest issue of the *Aurora*. She read it regularly, though sometimes she felt guilty about favoring Benjamin Bache with the price of a subscription. It was the very antithesis of her own political views but she found it refreshing, and even educational once in a while, to challenge her own opinions.

As she glanced through the items, her attention was drawn to a name she knew all too well – Thomas Willing, her brother. She read the story with growing horror, though in truth it could have been much worse, considering it was in the *Aurora*.

It didn't come right out and accuse Thomas Willing of getting Bridget pregnant and murdering her to keep it quiet. It was only full of dark hints, innuendo, and implications.

Reading it was like a physical blow. For a moment Elizabeth actually had trouble breathing. Then she lectured herself firmly. It was Benjamin Bache's paper, after all. Obviously he'd invented the story. It was just a way to discredit the Bank of the United States, her brother, and most of all, the Federalists.

All the same, perhaps it was time to find out what was really going on. She certainly couldn't ask Senator Martin. He'd sat at her very own table, drinking her tea, and lied to her about his working for Mr. Jefferson. A man who would lie like that might do anything at all. He might even have something to do, she thought suddenly, with concocting this awful story.

She reached for her quill pen and paper and composed a short note to Mr. James Mathers, Senate Doorkeeper. Could he do her the favor of coming by? She'd be most grateful if he could come soon, even today or at latest tomorrow.

Lydia, once informed of Elizabeth's plan, embraced it with grateful enthusiasm. She assured her that she'd deliver the invitation herself, handing it over to him in person. True to her word, she ran all the way to Congress Hall. It wasn't even an hour before she returned again, announcing happily that he'd accepted.

At just after the stroke of four the next day, James Mathers arrived at Elizabeth's doorstep. Lydia herself let him in and

Elizabeth received him in the first floor front parlor. Once upon a time, it had been her late husband's study and office.

"Thank you for coming," she welcomed him graciously. "Would you like some tea? Or some other refreshment?"

He looked at his large hands, rough from his life and his labors. He could heft a heavy load of firewood easily enough, but he couldn't see himself elegantly sipping his tea from a fine, fragile teacup.

"Some cider would be fine, if you happened to have some." Then he was silent, waiting for her to tell him why she'd summoned him.

"I hope you don't mind my asking you here," she began, once Lydia had brought the cider and left again, "but I hope you will excuse a womanly curiosity. Lydia and I have been wondering whether any progress has been made in finding out who killed Lydia's cousin Bridget and I thought you might be able to enlighten us."

He was surprised that she asked him instead of Senator Martin, but he knew better than to ask her why.

"Was there anything in particular you'd be asking about?"

"Lydia's gotten some rather surprising news from Annie," Elizabeth said evenly. "Perhaps you know more?"

"I'm not sure as to what you mean," Mathers said uneasily. He felt a coward for saying it, but he didn't want to be the bearer of bad news. How much did she know? Had she heard about her brother's relationship with Bridget?

"Annie mentioned something to Lydia about Bridget's condition, if you understand me?"

"That I do," he conceded. "Yes, the girl was in a family way, at least that's my understanding."

"And the father?"

"Oh, the father." Mathers braced himself. "It seems she had a number of gentlemen friends. Senator Blount, for one."

"And the others? I read the *Aurora* this morning," she added helpfully, guessing that he felt squeamish talking about such sordid affairs to a lady. Surely he'd tell her the story about her brother was nothing but a malicious lie, she thought confidently.

"It was Jimmy who heard it," Mathers said miserably.

She turned pale.

"You can't mean it's true? It can't be true. My brother is not a murderer."

"Of course not." Mathers tried to sound reassuring. "The story in the *Aurora* is ever so much worse than what Jimmy heard about him."

"What exactly did this boy Jimmy hear?" she asked sharply. "And who is he?"

Mathers took a deep breath, and then explained.

"Jimmy Tucker, the Assistant Doorkeeper is who he is. He's the one who found out about it. I never meant him to get involved in this, but he took it on himself. Trying to help me, he was. And I have to say, he does know that area pretty well, Dock Creek and so forth, where Bridget used to go. That was where he used to work before."

"Before he came to work for the Senate, you mean?"

"Yes, he was one of the errand boys, working odd jobs. Running messages for the merchants, packing, unpacking, hauling, whatever they needed done. And he lives in that area as well, at the Man Full of Troubles tavern. So he went poking around, asking questions. And then he ran into some of the others, his friends. It was one of them, what told him. About your brother, I mean."

He looked at Elizabeth anxiously, but she only nodded.

"This friend of his," he went quickly on, "said he'd seen Bridget with Mr. Willing, sitting together in some tavern. He said they was, well, how should I say – well, they was close, is what he tells me. There was another one too, who thought he saw them."

Elizabeth braced herself for worse to come.

"Go on, pray do. Don't spare me the details."

"That's all there is," Mathers said simply. "It seems they knew each other, maybe pretty well. The rest of it – the story you read – it's all just Mr. Bache's speculation."

"So that's all there is, the word of some dockside urchins?" Elizabeth's anxious fear had turned in an instant to haughty indignation.

"My son Jimmy's one of those 'dockside urchins' I'll have you know." In his anger, Mathers blurted it out unthinkingly.

"Your son?"

Wishing heartily that he could take back his words, Mathers cursed himself for his all-too-ready temper.

"His mother was a woman I knew before the war," he explained apologetically. "I cared for her, I really did. But what with the war and all, well, I lost track of her. I didn't know before, that Jimmy even existed. I only just found out about it. I never knew it, not all these years," he repeated softly. "She moved away, his mother did, before I came back from fighting. I looked for her, but never found her again. Maybe I should have looked for her harder."

"It's nice that you found each other at last." Thinking of her own two sons, dead in infancy, Elizabeth felt a bit tearful. "About my brother though, does it all boil down to this – that someone saw them together at a tavern?"

"You might say that," Mathers answered carefully. "The story was, they was cozy together too, though that's as may be."

"Well, whatever men she was involved with," Elizabeth said primly, "my brother was certainly not one of them. And if it's just some gossip that this boy told your son, how did Bache ever get the story?"

"I don't know, but it wasn't my son," Mathers said defensively. "As Senator Martin said himself, scandal gets around in Philadelphia."

It gets around indeed, Elizabeth fumed, especially if you help it. If Jimmy wasn't the one, then it must be Senator Martin himself who told Bache. Or maybe he told Jefferson and Jefferson told Bache. It's just the sort of thing that Jefferson would do, to point the finger away from himself and towards another man, especially if the other man is a prominent Federalist.

"It weren't Senator Martin neither," Mathers added, sensing how her thoughts were trending. "You can ask him yourself, if you doubt me."

"As if anyone would admit such a thing." Elizabeth disbelief was obvious.

"Senator Martin's the most honest man I know," Mathers countered staunchly, "and many a time he's paid the price for it. He'd do better to 'go along to get along' sometimes, like Senator Bingham told him, if you'll pardon my saying so."

"Well, Mr. Bache got it somehow, however it was." Elizabeth was unconvinced but there wasn't any point in arguing. The Doorman was loyal to Senator Martin, that much was clear, but he couldn't really know how the story started.

With that, Mathers took his leave. Lydia escorted him out, giving no hint that she'd been listening at the door and overheard the entire conversation. So Jimmy was Mr. Mathers's son. Did Rachel know? Was that why they'd stopped seeing each other?

∽ 27 ∽

To her lasting regret, Mrs. Callender opened the door when Mathers came to call. It wasn't really her fault, however. The one small window that looked out on the stoop was tightly shuttered and she couldn't see who was standing there.

She opened the door just a crack and tried to shut it again as soon as she saw him. By then, however, it was too late. He was pushing back and holding the door open. Not for nothing was he the Senate Doorman. He was nearly twice as big as she was and at least thirty times stronger.

"I need to talk to you," he said firmly. "Shall I shout at you from outside? Do you want all the neighbors to hear me?"

Reluctantly, she let him in. She was so slight that she almost disappeared in the darkened room, and she had a dull, hollow look that made Mathers think she was desperately hungry. She led him to the small, dark front room just off the hallway, the one where the window was blocked by the heavy shutters. Without natural light, it was lit only by a meager fire and a single tallow candle.

She offered him the only chair and herself remained standing, frightened and anxious, near the doorway.

"What do you want with me?" she asked plaintively.

"Just a few questions, that's all. I don't mean you any harm, nor your husband either," he said encouragingly. He wanted to put her at ease, now that he held her effectively captive. "I understand that Bridget LeClair used to come here, from time to time?"

"I'm so sorry she died." Mrs. Callender did look deeply sorrowful. "She was a good girl, no matter what Mr. LeClair says. She was always kind and helpful."

"It's a pity, her dying like that," Mathers said sympathetically. "Was she here very often?"

Mrs. Callender looked at him warily.

"Sometimes she was, sometimes she wasn't. But I'll not be talking about it, nor Mr. Jefferson neither, so you can save your breath from asking."

"Mr. Jefferson? What about him? Does he come here also?"

"I didn't say so, did I?" She sounded frightened. "I just know what they're saying in the newspapers."

"Then you know they're saying she was murdered?" She nodded numbly. "If someone killed her then," he said gently, "wouldn't you like to help find out who did it?"

"It doesn't matter. It will never bring her back," she answered miserably.

Mathers's heart went out to the woman, seeing her standing there so dejected and beaten down. Bridget must have been one of the few bright spots in her life.

"You cared a lot for her, didn't you?"

She started to cry. Tears streamed down her face and she didn't even wipe them away. It was like she didn't even notice them.

"I loved her like a daughter. We was that close, and she didn't have anyone. I even went to see her at the hospital."

"Weren't you afraid you might get yellow fever too?"

"I lived through it the last time," she answered simply, "so I figured as I'd live through it again. I didn't tell my husband, though. He'd forbidden me to go anywhere near there."

This, more than anything, convinced Mathers how much she cared for Bridget LeClair. It would take a powerful emotion for her to do something her husband had forbidden her to do, that was obvious.

"But I went anyway," she added, with a sudden burst of spirit animating her face, "and I took her his candied oranges."

"His candied oranges?" Mathers echoed dumbly.

Realizing she'd just given something away, she looked at him in consternation.

"You won't tell him? My husband, I mean? He'd be so angry. They were for him, and they were so fine. We could never afford sweetmeats like that."

"Didn't he notice then, that you gave them away?" Looking around at the barren room, Mathers couldn't imagine how a treat like candied oranges could disappear without being missed. Mrs. Callender saw his look and understood it.

"He didn't know they was here. I don't think he was even expecting them. One day, I just found them at the door, a little paper bag with a few nice little pieces of candied oranges. The note said 'For Mr. Callender, with thanks.' He never saw them and I never told him."

"Where did they come from then? Who left them?"

"I don't know. There was just the note, like I told you."

He took a minute to absorb her revelation, amazed. This could change things entirely. What if it was the candied oranges that were poisoned? What if someone meant to kill James Callender and Bridget was killed mistakenly? It certainly made sense. Callender surely had more enemies than Bridget did.

"Did you try them yourself?"

"Oh, no." She couldn't have been more horrified if he'd suggested she steal the candlesticks right off the church altar. "I'd never take sweets from my husband for myself. But there was sweet little Bridget, sick and dying, and I didn't have anything for her. And then there it was, just the thing to cheer her up, a little paper bag with some nice little pieces of candied oranges on my doorstep."

"Couldn't have been better," Mathers agreed, hoping she couldn't read his mind. "When did you give them to her?"

"When was it? Let me think now." Mrs. Callender dutifully thought back. "Why, now that you ask me, I guess it must have been the day she died. Isn't that a coincidence!"

"A coincidence indeed," Mathers echoed grimly.

As he stood in the Senate Gallery the next day, Mathers's thoughts kept coming back to the mysterious gift of candied oranges. Were they poisoned? Was Bridget killed by mistake? Was the poison really intended for James Callender?

He thought about it as he walked to Congress Hall. He thought about it as he trimmed the candles on the Senators' desks and filled the Senate fireplaces with firewood. He puzzled it over as he stood there through endless Senate debates, keeping a wary eye on the spectators in the public gallery. Bridget ate the candied oranges the day she died. It couldn't be just a coincidence.

How hard would it be to poison candied oranges? He couldn't begin to imagine it. He'd eaten candied oranges once or twice but he hadn't the faintest idea how to make them. He was no cook, to say the very least of it.

He decided he needed to talk to Samuel Richardet, the famous caterer and proprietor of the City Tavern. He'd met Richardet last March, when he was investigating the other murder. It was Richardet's food that was poisoned then, so Mathers was pretty sure Richardet's memories of him weren't very fond ones. Richardet was, however, the only professional cook he knew, so off he went to the City Tavern.

Sure enough, when he opened the door and saw it was Mathers come to call, Richardet almost shut the door again.

"Why are you come to cause me the trouble again? What you have already done, is it not enough?" he greeted Mathers accusingly.

"Don't worry," Mathers reassured him, "It's nothing to do with you this time. I'm only wondering about what's in candied oranges, and I didn't know who else to ask. You know I'm not much for cooking."

Richardet wasn't exactly pleased, but he knew the man could be stubborn. Answering his question, he decided, was the quickest way to get rid of him.

"All right then. I write it out for you, if you wait a moment. But not here," he added quickly. "I don't want the merchants to see you and think something's wrong. Go wait in the kitchen."

So Mathers went to the kitchen and waited. He occupied his time by looking around. The preparations for the mid-day meal were in progress. A steady fire burned in the massive fireplace, with four heavy iron pots hanging on the crane just over it. Three reflector ovens were set on the hearth, facing toward the fire, surrounded by covered iron pots and smaller pans on three-legged stands and other things that were (to Mathers at least) quite mysterious.

Watching the cook James German, Mathers was fascinated. He had two younger fellows who helped, chopping things and lifting things and hauling firewood, but German was responsible for it all. He was constantly busy. He tasted this dish and stirred another, added ingredients and adjusted spices. He lifted lids and peered inside, called for the pots to be raised or lowered over the fire, and had the younger men put fresh coals here and there, around the iron pots and on their iron covers.

"What are you cooking?" Mathers asked when German glanced his way. The kitchen was full of appetizing smells and Mathers's stomach was rumbling.

"Roast beef, roast mutton, scotch barley soup, and a stewed beef with turnips and carrots, plus a winter salad, mashed potatoes, and carrot pudding. There's also leftover egg and onion pie." Unlike his employer Richardet, German was well disposed to the Doorkeeper. It was his nephew who'd been killed by mistake instead of Jefferson and he was grateful to Mathers for finding the murderer.

"What's in the covered pots?"

"The carrot pudding." German smiled. "Stay 'till things are done and I'll give you a taste of anything you want."

Just then, Richardet came in, obviously still unhappy.

"There's your receipt," he said impatiently, handing Mathers a piece of paper. "Now go away and stop bothering me."

Notwithstanding Richardet's command, Mathers accepted German's offer of something to eat. The stewed beef went down very well and the rich carrot pudding, spiced with nutmeg and thickened with butter, eggs, and cream, was practically sinful. As he ate, German picked up the receipt and read it out loud.

To Candy Oranges. Make a high Candy of double refin'd Sugar, wet with Water; take preserv'd Oranges, and draw them through the Candy, and lay them on a Hurdle and stove them.

"Why did you want this?" German asked. "To make candied oranges, you don't need a receipt from a famous caterer like Richardet. It's the easiest thing imaginable. Any housewife could do it."

"Easy for you, maybe." To Mathers the directions were totally incomprehensible. "To me, it might as well be Greek. What does it say, pray tell, in plain English?"

The cook chuckled.

"Richardet once said as how you probably couldn't boil water. Now I see what he was talking about. Why are you so interested in how to make candied oranges, anyway?"

"I'm wondering if they could be poisoned and how," he explained, scraping his bowl for one last bite of carrot pudding. "That girl Bridget LeClair, the one they're saying Jefferson killed, she died the same day she ate some candied oranges."

"Ah." German looked at the receipt again. "All right, then, I'll explain it. A 'high candy' is a sugar syrup – that's sugar and water boiled to the right temperature, so it makes a candy coating when it cools. You dip the oranges in the coating, and then you put them by the stove to dry." He looked at Mathers, to see if he understood. Satisfied that he did, he continued.

"Now if you wanted to add some poison," he said thoughtfully, "I guess there are several ways you could do it. First, it could be in the oranges to begin with, when they were first preserved. Or else it could be in the sugar coating. It would have to be something that wouldn't keep the coating from setting up right. Like if you added something liquid after it boiled, chances are it wouldn't harden properly. Or the easiest thing, I suppose, would be to take the oranges already made and put some poison inside them. If they were candied in quarters, or even whole oranges, it would be easy enough to do it. Of course, it would have to be something without a strong taste, or else you'd notice it."

"So the poisoner wouldn't have to be a cook or confectioner? It wouldn't take any special skill?"

"Even you could do it," German said with a grin, "if you had a mind to. But are you sure it's the candied oranges that were poisoned? There's lots of different ways to put poison in someone's food. What do they eat out there at the Wigwam Hospital?"

"I haven't talked to them yet," Mathers admitted guiltily. As brave as he was in a fight or a battlefield where he could see his opponent, he was afraid of invisible enemies. The pestilent airs that could deliver a fatal blow and you didn't even know it until afterward. "I'm not keen to go out there, to tell the truth, but I suppose there's no avoiding it."

So the next day he screwed up his courage and went. He interviewed the Superintendent and even the head cook himself, but he could have saved himself the trouble.

It was easy enough to find the hospital cook. He was in the kitchen. The Wigwam's cook was a thin, wiry man, quite the opposite type from the big, beefy James German. Ironically for a cook, he seemed almost undernourished.

"What does they eat?" The cook echoed the Doorman's question. "We serve 'em whatever we happen to have. It's not so bad, mind you. Some of them isn't allowed to eat much, according to the doctors. Thin barley gruel for some, or even just the barley waters. But for the rest, there's many in the city that would envy it. There's oysters of course, but not so's they'd be sick of them. There's fish too, and meats as well, at least some of it, pretty regular. They gets food from outside too, some of them, though the doctors don't like it."

"And to drink?"

"Milk, coffee, tea. Even rum sometimes, for some of them." The cook looked at Mathers with curiosity. "But why's you asking?"

"It's about a patient who was here, some time ago. The doctor who saw her seemed to think she might have been poisoned."

Immediately the cook's attitude became hostile.

"You've got some nerve," he said angrily, "coming here, accusing me of poisoning."

"I didn't say anything of the sort," Mathers began, but the cook wasn't done with his tirade.

"Have you got beans for brains? That's the stupidest idea I ever heard of. How could I poison just one patient, I'd like to know, just one poor soul in the entire hospital? There isn't anything I cook that any of 'em eats, that isn't eaten by all the others."

"Calm down, man. I'm not saying it was you," Mathers repeated patiently. "If I thought you'd done it, would I be coming here asking you? I'm only trying to understand how something like that could happen."

"Don't ask me," the cook grumbled, somewhat mollified but still unhappy. "I only cook it. All I can say is, there wasn't no poison added here. If you think I'm not minding my own kitchen, you couldn't be more wrong. Now get out of here."

Mathers headed off to the main part of the hospital, considering. The cook's logic was pretty convincing, it seemed to him. If the poison was added in the kitchen, it would be hard to make sure that only Bridget was poisoned and not some other patients also. It was a different story though, it seemed to him, once the food came out of the kitchen. One of the staff could add poison easily enough, or even maybe some visiting stranger. He needed to talk to the nurses and maids who might have served the food or tended Bridget, he decided. He soon learned, though, that wasn't so easy

"They come and go, I'm afraid." Peter Helm, a friend of Stephen Girard's, was the current Superintendent. "And they're not assigned only to specific patients. At the time you're asking about, we were overwhelmed with the sick and the dying. I doubt that any of them can even remember which ones they were taking care of. Even if you found the right nurses or maids and they remembered, I don't expect that you'd learn anything of use to you. All they do is serve the food. Unless the patient needs special help, they leave it there beside them. They don't sit around and watch them eat it."

In addition to which, Mathers learned, the patients often had food from outside, brought or sent by friends or relatives. So something could have been added to the food when it was out of the kitchen, on the way to being served, or afterwards when it was lying about waiting to be eaten. Or it could have been in some other food or drink brought in from the outside – the candied oranges, maybe, or something else that someone brought to Bridget, something that he hadn't discovered yet.

So, Mathers reflected unhappily, he'd risked his life coming here, and for what? He couldn't rule out much of anything. Not knowing what the poison was, whether it was fast- or slow-acting, he couldn't even be sure of the timing. The upshot was, James German had put it exactly right. There were any number of different ways that Bridget could have been poisoned.

❦ 28 ❧

The Earl of Gloucester, holding the fatal letter in his hand, speaks to his treacherous son Edmund. Little does he know how cruelly he has been deceived, nor what betrayal and doom awaited him.

"We have seen the best of our time:
machinations, hollowness, treachery, and all
ruinous disorders, follow us disquietly to our
graves. Find out this villain, Edmund; it shall
lose thee nothing. Do it carefully. And the
noble and true-hearted Kent banished, his
offence, honesty! 'Tis strange, strange."

With that, the actor grandly exited stage left, while the audience clapped and shouted like crazy.

Elizabeth liked the theater, especially Shakespeare's plays. She had been very glad when it was legalized. The quality had certainly improved now that they had a proper theater and it was all honest and above board, not having to pretend the play wasn't really a play, nor having to travel outside the city limits. All the same, she regretted that she had come to the theater on this particular night. The choice of play was particularly unfortunate.

She should have known better than to see *King Lear*. It was all too relevant to what she was trying to escape from.

Cordelia, the only one of King Lear's daughters who actually loves him, is disinherited and exiled because she insists on being honest. The deceitful lies of her sisters, more extravagant and elegantly phrased, sound sweeter to the King's foolish ears than the truth spoken by Cordelia. In the end, the King's realizes that Cordelia was right, but by then it is far too late to mend things.

Is that how Senator Martin feels, Elizabeth wondered guiltily? Had she wronged him, just like King Lear? From Shakespeare's time to the present time, she knew, the nature of politics was unchanging. In politics, even the politics within a royal family, honesty wasn't necessarily the best policy. "He should go along to get along sometimes," wasn't that what Mr. Mathers said? That was the prudent course. Wasn't that what her very own brother-in-law had told him?

No, she told herself, he was obviously just playing a part, like Cordelia's sisters, hiding his true ambitions. He was just like Thomas Jefferson and no surprise there, for wasn't Thomas Jefferson Jacob's patron? The evidence for that was overwhelming. Abigail Adams herself had even invited her to tea, just to tell her that he was. She'd heard how Jefferson had greeted Senator Martin like a long-lost friend and thanked him for all his efforts.

She'd thought they were friends. She'd trusted him. Then he'd slandered her brother, just to divert attention away from Thomas Jefferson.

But why had they picked on her brother? Why him and not someone more prominent, with a reputation for chasing the ladies, like Senator Blount or Alexander Hamilton? Was there something between Thomas and Bridget, anything at all? Could there possibly be any truth in these terrible rumors?

For the rest of the first act, through round after round of deceit and deception, she couldn't escape her troubled thoughts. The play was stirring up everything she'd hoped to forget for a while. It was a relief when the intermission came. She seriously wondered if she could stand to suffer through to the end.

She rose from her seat and made her way to the box tier lobby, wondering if she should just leave and go home again. Then looking up, she saw her brother Thomas standing there, only a few steps in front of her. What an ill-fated evening this was.

He was looking the other way and apparently hadn't seen her. He would surely notice, however, if she passed him by, and it would be most extraordinary if she didn't greet him.

"Thomas, my dear." Putting on a brave smile, she greeted him as cheerfully as she was capable of.

He turned, saw her, and executed a most graceful bow.

"My dear Elizabeth, how lovely to see you. How are you enjoying the play?"

"It's rather a grim story, is it not?" she replied unhappily. "To be frank, I'm wondering whether to stay for the rest of it. With all that's going on just now, I'm finding it rather too dismaying."

Thomas looked at her shrewdly.

"Is there anything in particular that is troubling you? What they're saying about me, for example?"

"How can you be so calm about it? The things they're saying are so terrible."

Her brother patted her arm reassuringly.

"You shouldn't take it so seriously. I don't. I'm quite used to it. These days, being slandered and publicly attacked seems to be quite the normal way of things, if you happen to be politically prominent. Did you know that I'm part of a vast, secret conspiracy to sell the country to British investors? Or so the Republicans tell me. At least I'm selling it, say I. They'd just give the country to the French, if we'd let them."

"That's all very well, Thomas," she said stiffly, recovering her composure with some difficulty, "but being accused of murder is a different sort of thing entirely."

"You really mustn't worry so much." Her brother smiled encouragingly. "I'm quite secure given my position. Even the Mayor, Republican that he is, can scarcely accuse me of any crime, especially when there's nothing to it."

Having gone this far, Elizabeth couldn't help but go on. His words were intended to be comforting, no doubt, but he wasn't really answering her question.

"Is there anything to it, anything at all? Anything they can get ahold of?"

He gave her a long, appraising look, as if trying to decide how much she knew and how much to tell her.

"I knew the girl slightly, if that's what you mean. I've employed her father-in-law as a translator. I ran into her once near his house and happened to take her to some nearby tavern, the Man Full of Troubles I think it was, and bought her a cider. It was just a sudden impulse. She seemed so downcast that I felt sorry for her. She was such a simple girl, so innocent despite it all, and widowed when she was barely married. Her father-in-law pretends she wouldn't come to live with him but really it was the other way around. After his son died, he refused to have anything much to do with her."

"And that's all there is to it?" She studied his face, uncertain. She'd known him all her life. It seemed to her there was more to it than he was telling her.

"You can't really believe I had anything to do with the girl's death." He said it with a curt finality that told her the conversation was over.

"Of course I know you couldn't possibly have killed her." Elizabeth's eyes filled with tears and she willed them back. What would people think of her – and worse yet, of her brother – if she started crying in public, in the theater. "It's just that it's all so awful, what they're saying, that I can't help but be worried. It's become so political, with that dreadful Mr. Jefferson, and Senator Martin's even working for him."

Elizabeth's tears seemed to upset her brother far more than the stories about him.

"Shall I take you home, my dear?" he asked anxiously. "My carriage should be nearby waiting for me."

Elizabeth nodded, so he escorted her down the stairs and out of the theater. Once they were inside his carriage, he began again.

"You shouldn't worry about me, Elizabeth. I really mean it. I don't have any secrets worth killing for. And perhaps you're being unfair to Senator Martin. In the play, Cordelia is vindicated in the end, but even so she is defeated in battle and executed. It wouldn't be wise of anyone to follow her example. I don't credit these stories about him working for Jefferson, but even if he is, I'm sure he has his reasons. It's all in the nature of politics."

"Bridget was Lydia's cousin, you know," Elizabeth said stiffly. "I asked him to look into it, but he wouldn't."

"So that's it, is it? I'm very sorry. If it's of interest to you, I've heard that Bridget may not have been the intended victim. There's a rumor going around that the murderer really wanted to kill James Callender."

"James Callender the journalist?" This was news. Mathers's discovery about the candied oranges was one of the very few details – true or not – that hadn't made its way into the papers.

"The very same. Personally, I wouldn't be at all surprised if Callender's somehow involved. I'm sure he has things to hide himself, things that might land him in jail or get him prosecuted for libel. From some of the things I've heard, some of the secrets might even be about Thomas Jefferson."

Elizabeth perked up immediately.

"About Jefferson? What have you heard? People often hint that the man has secrets, but no one seems to really know what they are."

"Jefferson's secrets – where shall I begin?" By now they'd reached Elizabeth's house. Willing paused while he got out and helped her down from the carriage. "There's the question of his religion, for one thing. He's hardly a Christian as he claims, to say the least of it. He tries to hide his true beliefs, and no wonder. I wouldn't be surprised if he had some secret altar to a pagan Goddess of Reason, like some French Revolutionary, hidden away in his home. After what happened in France, with the guillotine and all, no one wants a godless revolutionary for President."

"Not sufficient motive for murder, I should think? Not unless someone had definite proof of it?"

"All right, since I know that you'll never rest until you have it all, I'll be entirely frank with you. I have also heard it suggested," he went on, lowering his voice so not even the coachman could overhear, "very indirectly, I must say, that the man has a mistress. Not an ordinary mistress, mind you, but one of his slaves. I've heard it said that this slave and his dead wife have a lot in common."

Elizabeth's eyebrows shot up high. She wasn't shocked, not exactly. She'd heard stories before about southern plantation owners and their slaves – but for Jefferson, a man who was desperate to be President, that was surely a motive for murder. However much such things might be tolerated in the south, in the northern states it would surely be a scandal.

"As impoverished and disreputable as James Callender is," her brother observed, "he might even have stooped to blackmail. Then again, what they're saying could be true, that Jefferson was involved with Senator Blount's conspiracy and Bridget learned about it. Rumor has it, Jefferson was meeting secretly with General Wilkinson and Blount at the very time they were planning their treason. Jefferson might have innocent reasons to meet with another Republican Senator, of course, but why would he be meeting secretly with General Wilkinson?"

"Why indeed." Elizabeth wasn't at all surprised that it all came back to Thomas Jefferson. She wondered if Senator Martin knew about the secret meeting or the secret mistress. Well, she'd make sure he knew and in a way that he couldn't deny or overlook it. As soon as she got home, she penned a note to Mr. Mathers giving him all the details and had Lydia deliver it the next morning in person.

❧ 29 ❧

Walking into the Senate Chamber these days, Jacob felt like he was walking into a lion's den. His days as a Senator must surely be numbered. Nearly all his Federalist colleagues were now on Senator Sedgwick's side, thinking him a secret Republican spy and a traitor to the Federalist Party.

As he'd foreseen and feared, he'd lost any last few shreds of political influence that he'd ever had with his Federalist colleagues. The Republicans, meanwhile, suspected he was playing some deep and devious game. As a consequence, he was virtually isolated. If he supported a proposal, everyone else had second thoughts, even if it was something trivial and politically neutral. The proposal to lower the exorbitant twenty-dollar tax on naturalization certificates that kept the poor from becoming citizens went down in flames, unsurprisingly.

Just wait till he told them what he thought about impeachment, he thought bleakly. With the impeachment proceedings coming up, he'd been doing a lot of Constitutional research. The more he read, the more certain he was that impeachment wasn't something you could do to members of Congress. When his Federalist colleagues heard that he thought Blount couldn't be impeached, they'd tar and feather him.

Even Senator Bingham, one of the few who still treated Jacob civilly, harbored doubts about Jacob's true allegiances.

"What does Jefferson have to say for himself?" he kept asking him. "Don't tell me that you haven't confronted him. You two are as tight as two thieves. It's clear from the way he treats you."

"I don't know what Jefferson's game is," Jacob finally responded angrily, "but his great show of friendliness is only a bit of theater. I haven't talked to him about the murder at all. Contrary to what everyone believes, I've been spending my time on Senate business. I haven't been investigating. Things are about to change, though, and you'd best believe I mean to talk to him."

That, however, was easier said than done. Jefferson was studiously avoiding him. He was full of friendly smiles and hearty encouragement for Jacob's efforts to "save him," as he put it. Most regretfully, however, whatever day or time Jacob suggested for them to meet, Jefferson was too busy to talk to him.

"You know yourself from being President *pro tem*," he smoothly explained, "how hard it is to preside over the Senate and keep up with everything else in addition. I'm the President of the American Philosophical Society too, you know, and then there's my correspondence, and trying to oversee things at Monticello. You must know how hard it is to run a plantation from afar. Then there's a fellow from Baltimore who's attacking me viciously in public, saying a story I published in my *Notes on the State of Virginia* is libelous. To top it off, I'm working on a manual of procedural rules to govern the Senate. When Adams presided, he ran things however he pleased, like a little King of the Senate."

"That's all very well, but I really must insist." Jacob was at the end of his patience. "Cobbett was asking me the other day what I thought of you as a suspect. I put him off, but I can't put him off much longer. If I don't tell him something soon, I'll be the one he's going after. Shall I tell him that you seem to have something to hide, since you refuse to talk to me? I'm sure he'd be happy to speculate in print as to what your secrets might be. I'm sure you can imagine what he'll make of it."

The threat was effective.

"I suppose I could give you a few minutes today," Jefferson conceded at last, with little effort to disguise his annoyance. "You may join me in my rooms after the session is ended."

Jefferson's rooms were only a little over a block away, at John Francis's house next to the Indian Queen tavern on Fourth Street. Once there, Jefferson offered Jacob his most uncomfortable chair, making no offer of wine or other refreshment. Knowing his opportunity was limited, Jacob got straight to the point.

"The girl who was murdered, Bridget LeClair, did you know her?"

"Why do you say she was murdered?" Jefferson sidestepped the question by challenging it. "Isn't that only speculation? Do you have any proof?"

"It seems to be the general medical opinion," Jacob said mildly, "but we can call it an assumption – a hypothesis – if you like. The question remains the same, however. Did you know her?"

Jefferson hesitated, seemingly calculating how to respond. His answer, however, was unequivocal.

"No, I didn't know her at all. A simple kitchen maid? Why would I?"

"But you do know James Callender, if I'm not mistaken."

"After a fashion, I suppose." Jefferson's look was cagey. "What does that have to do with anything?"

"It seems that Bridget was rather close to the Callenders, is why I ask." Jacob was surprised at Jefferson's response to the mention of James Callender. "She helped Mrs. Callender with the children and so forth, spending time at their house. And James Callender is – well, you know what he is. Let's just say that if there's a nasty secret hidden anywhere, he likes to find it."

As he explained the connection between Bridget and the Callenders, Jacob carefully studied Jefferson's reaction. Jefferson didn't seem surprised by the news, but he also didn't give any sign that he already knew it.

"That's a rather negative way to describe the man," Jefferson chided him. "You might better say that James Callender is a patriot, an idealist who wants the truth to be known, a man who shines light in the hidden corners."

"Have it your way," Jacob responded calmly, "but the point is this – he was a man who knew secrets. And perhaps, when she was spending time there, Bridget learned what one of those secrets was and she couldn't be trusted to keep it."

"I suppose it's possible," Jefferson said lightly, "but your theory seems quite far-fetched to me. As far as motives go, there are surely better ones. If what I read in the newspapers is accurate, the girl was with child when she died. So why go chasing mythical secrets? Wasn't it more likely one of her lovers who killed her? Like Senator Blount, for example? Or what about Alexander Hamilton? Yes, Hamilton," Jefferson repeated with enthusiasm, obviously warming to the idea. "He's a lecher, he's corrupt, and he has secrets to hide. You've surely read what Callender has published about him."

"His supposed corrupt dealings as Secretary of the Treasury? I could hardly have missed it. The entire Congress has undoubtedly read Callender's charges as well as Hamilton's self-defense, which I must say is quite extraordinary."

"Exactly my point." Jefferson smiled at Jacob condescendingly, as if he were an especially promising pupil. "If after all that, a servant girl turns up with his bastard child, he would be ruined. He couldn't afford another such blow to his reputation. As for his rebuttal of the charges of corruption, I don't believe it at all. He was surely speculating on the side, arranging deals with the public debt to line his own pocket. So there are two separate secrets he might kill for. And here's a third – his role in creating the so-called Whiskey Rebellion."

"Hamilton starting the Whiskey Rebellion?" Jacob looked at Jefferson with blatant disbelief. "Surely you can't be serious. Hamilton's the one who put it down."

"It was a brilliant job of public deception," Jefferson explained patiently. "There actually was no rebellion at all. As the *Aurora* said, when they came to put the so-called rebellion down, did Washington's army find a single rebel? They did not. It was all a ruse cooked up by Hamilton. I'll grant you, the whiskey taxes may have sparked a small riot or two, a spontaneous outpouring of local outrage. The vast conspiracy against the government and Constitution, however, was a fantasy created by Hamilton. He wanted to intimidate and discredit the republican societies and the poor, honest farmers, and he succeeded."

Jacob shook his head.

"You think everyone's as devious as you are, and it seems to have addled your reason. Even if I thought Hamilton would lie about there being a rebellion, I'd never believe it of Washington.

I agree with you, though, that the other things – the corruption and the child – those could be motive enough for murder. Still, what's the connection to Bridget LeClair? If Hamilton's to blame, why kill her and not James Callender?"

Of course, thought Jacob, Callender might very well have been the intended victim, given what Mathers had learned about the candied oranges. Would Jefferson give any hint, Jacob wondered, that he knew it too? Might he betray his own guilty knowledge to build a case against Hamilton?

"Callender might keep it to himself if he didn't have enough proof, I suppose," Jefferson said dubiously. Even he seemed to realize this wasn't a very convincing scenario. "You're right though, it's more likely Hamilton was having an affair with the girl and killed her in order to hide it."

"I'll grant you, what you say is not impossible," Jacob conceded, remembering what Elizabeth had told him about Hamilton's being in Philadelphia. "Still, there's no indication so far that Hamilton even knew Bridget LeClair, much less had a relationship with her. You say you believe the corruption charges against him, but you're his worst political enemy. Senators Muhlenberg and Venable, who are relatively independent, say they're satisfied he's innocent. Who should I believe?"

"Well if you don't believe me, why seek my opinion at all?" Jefferson said peevishly.

"I'm compelled to ask you about your relationship with Senator Blount, is why. I would hardly expect you to admit anything, but I'm compelled to ask. You must know what they're saying, that you were part of his conspiracy. You were seen together, I'm told, dining with Senator Blount and General Wilkinson, when they were hatching their plans. You've reason to meet with Blount, no doubt, but what were you doing with Wilkinson?"

"Federalist lies and slander," Jefferson responded coldly. "I think this discussion has run its course. You've done what you came for."

Jefferson stood up to show him the door, but Jacob remained calmly seated.

"I'm not quite finished, thank you. I'm still interested in Bridget and Callender. You know Callender rather well, from what I hear." Jacob raised one eyebrow questioningly. "You give him money, for example."

Jefferson dismissed the question with a wave of his hand.

"I'd hardly call him a friend. He writes things that are politically useful. Like exposing Alexander Hamilton for the dog he is. I believe that his writings should be supported and spread around, so in a small way I support his publications."

Methinks thou doth protest too much, Jacob thought to himself, with a bow to Shakespeare. Jefferson was clearly uncomfortable at the mention of Callender. What was going on there? Was it true, what Elizabeth had written to Mathers? Was Callender blackmailing Jefferson because one of Jefferson's slaves was his mistress?

"My dear Sir." Jefferson leaned forward, suddenly shifting to the attack. "I think it's time this little talk was ended, before you go too far. Your questions are becoming quite offensive."

"All I'm doing is trying to find the truth." Jacob felt certain that Jefferson's show of anger was a deliberate tactic. "Is it the truth that makes you so uneasy? These days, in politics at least, trying to find out the truth of things doesn't seem to make you very popular."

"You should know by now that there are many truths in politics." Jefferson was more comfortable now, smoothly adopting the role of elder statesman. "There's your truth, my truth, and the truth of public opinion. What really matters is the end result, in my own considered opinion."

It was the first truly honest thing he'd said, Jacob thought, in their entire conversation.

Jacob made his way slowly down the stairs and out to the street, wondering what was really going on between Thomas Jefferson and James Callender. He didn't notice Lydia coming out of a shop nearby. Lydia noticed him, however.

"Do you know who I saw today?" she reported to Elizabeth Powel when she got home. "I saw Senator Martin coming out of Mr. Francis's house. He must have been visiting Thomas Jefferson."

∾ 30 ∾

Lydia wasn't a deep thinker, to say the least. She acted mainly on impulse. So she didn't think very long or very hard about whether to tell Rachel what Mr. Mathers told Mrs. Powel. To her mind, it was just the sort of thing Rachel would naturally want to know, if she didn't already. Rachel had been worried about Jimmy before, saying good things about him, so wouldn't she like to know he was Mr. Mathers's son?

Cook told her she ought to think twice, but Lydia didn't take her warning to heart. She could hardly wait to see Rachel again, to tell her.

Lydia hadn't seen Rachel for a while, not to really talk to. Rachel was working night and day, she'd explained, between the shop and the *Encyclopaedia*. Finally one Sunday they were able to get together.

"What shall we do?" Rachel had been working so hard for so long, she'd almost forgotten how to amuse herself.

"What about a sleigh ride?" Lydia suggested.

Rachel looked at the sky where dark clouds were gathering.

"I don't think today's the day for it. It looks like it maybe will storm."

"Then let's go see the dwarf." Lydia had lots of ideas at the ready. She'd been saving them.

"The dwarf?"

"You know, he's at Mr. McPhail's house. It costs a whole quarter to see him, but I've never seen a dwarf before. Then we can go see your friend who runs the tavern and have a cider."

It wouldn't have been Rachel's choice, but she went along with it. They walked off toward Mr. McPhail's.

"I learned something the other day," Lydia ventured as they walked along, with just a touch of smugness, "something pretty interesting."

"Oh yes? Then I can't wait to hear."

"Mrs. Powel was talking the other day to your Mr. Mathers —" Lydia began.

"He's not 'my' Mr. Mathers, Lydia," Rachel interrupted crossly. "I wish you wouldn't call him that. He's a customer of Mr. Dobson's, that's all. I couldn't care less about him."

Lydia felt a small stab of worry that Cook might be right. Rachel sounded almost angry. But it was obvious to Lydia that Rachel cared a great deal about the man, notwithstanding what she said.

"Anyway," Lydia pressed on, "Mrs. Powel invited him over the other day to tell her what he had learned about Bridget's murder. There was that terrible story about Mrs. Powel's brother, you know, and she couldn't ask Senator Martin. I'm not sure why," she added, "but they haven't seen each other for quite a while."

"So, what did Mr. Mathers have to say?" Rachel was full of curiosity.

"Can you believe it? The *Aurora* was right. There was something between Bridget and her brother. Mrs. Powel's brother, I mean, Mr. Willing. Can you imagine it? "

Rachel tried, but failed.

"No, I really can't. Mr. Willing and a girl like Bridget? With him as proper as he is? Are you sure you heard it right? I have to say, it seems awfully unlikely."

"They were seen together, Mr. Mathers says, going out together to a tavern. Someone saw them there, sitting together. Close together, if you know what I mean."

"Poor Mrs. Powel." Rachel was fond of Elizabeth Powel, just as Elizabeth was fond of Rachel. "If it's really true, how dreadful."

"Worse than you know," Lydia added darkly. "Did you know that Bridget was going to have a baby? And it looks like her brother Mr. Willing is the father."

"But how does Mr. Mathers know? Did he see them?"

"No, it was one of the boys that works down by the docks. It was Jimmy what found out about it. Jimmy Tucker, do you know him?"

"Yes, I know Jimmy."

Lydia should have been warned by the look on Rachel's face, but she was too intent on her own design to be mindful of any distractions.

"And did you also know that Jimmy was Mr. Mathers's son? From some woman he knew, named Catherine?"

Rachel turned suddenly so deathly pale that Lydia feared she would faint right there on the sidewalk.

"I'm so sorry," Lydia said sheepishly. "I should never have said it like that. I meant to tell you more gently. It's true, though. He told Mrs. Powel himself. With my own ears, I heard him."

"All this time, he had a son?" Rachel's head was spinning. "And this woman – are they married?"

"Oh no. He only just learned about Jimmy himself. It was someone he knew before the Revolution."

"He never told me, he never did." Rachel shook her head, stunned by Lydia's revelation. "He never told me, but I'd bet he told Derrick. That time they went off together, I bet it was then, and then Derrick told all the others. I expect they all knew except for me. They all knew and nobody told me."

Too late, Lydia realized she'd miscalculated. She'd expected Rachel to be surprised, or curious, or excited, but she hadn't expected her to get so mad.

They had reached Mr. McPhail's house, so there the conversation ended. They handed over their quarters and were escorted to the room where the dwarf could be found. He was very small and very young.

"Have you come to see me?" he greeted them when they entered. "My name is Calvin Phillips. I'm seven years old, twenty-six inches high, and I weigh twelve pounds. Who do I have the pleasure of addressing?"

Rachel and Lydia introduced themselves and then the boy entertained them with a monologue. He seemed quite a smart boy for his age. He told the story of his life and his travels, all the while walking about the room and striking various elegant poses.

"I don't think it's very nice," Rachel said afterwards, as they headed for the Man Full of Troubles for a cider, "being on display like that."

"In a way though, he's a lucky one," Lydia said shrewdly. "He's got a job and it's not too hard, and he can go on like that forever.

There's some others with no job at all, or working for someone mean, beaten regularly and always hungry."

When they were settled with their ciders at the Man Full of Troubles, Lydia resumed their earlier talk, forgetting about her earlier qualms that maybe it was a rather dangerous subject.

"You shouldn't be too hard on Derrick for not telling you," she counseled Rachel. "That's how men are. They're brave enough when it comes to some physical danger, but they're scared as mice when it comes to us women. It explains things though, doesn't it, knowing that Jimmy is Mr. Mathers's son? Doesn't it make things better, knowing what was going on?"

"Better? Are you serious?" Rachel looked at Lydia in astonishment. "It just shows me how mistaken I was about him. If he didn't tell me that, what else didn't he tell me? He's not a mouse, he's a sly and cunning fox, and he's treated me most shamefully. And to think, when I said he might hire Jimmy as Assistant Doorkeeper, he acted like I'd said something wrong. I was even feeling guilty."

"Maybe he –" Lydia began, but Rachel cut her off.

"And that isn't all. It isn't just that he was courting me when he had a wife already and he left her. Two women aren't enough for him, he wants three. You should have seen him with your friend Miss Annie Dawson."

"Is that it? Is that what you're worrying about?" Lydia brightened. "I'm sure that's nothing to be upset about. It's just part of his investigating. What else would it be?"

"What else, indeed," Rachel fumed. "It was pretty clear to me, what else it was, and you'd know it too, if you had seen them. They were sitting there together at the Kouli Khan, and he was holding her hand. Is that what you call 'investigating'? Men are all alike," she added heatedly, "fickle and inconstant by nature. And to think that I almost – well, never mind."

Scowling mightily, Rachel downed the last of her cider and slammed the mug down hard on the table.

"I suppose it's just as well," she continued after a pause, her tone more philosophical. "What would I be wanting with Mr. Mathers, anyway, as old as he is and with a son? And who knows what else he hasn't told me?"

"I'm sorry to be the one to tell you, and so sudden like that," Lydia apologized again. "Maybe Cook was right that I shouldn't have said anything."

Rachel was belatedly aware of Lydia's feelings.

"Don't feel bad, Lydia. It was right of you to tell me. Otherwise, I'd be the only one who didn't know. I'll have a word or two for Derrick about that, believe me."

∽ 31 ∽

Elizabeth made her way slowly along the winding grav-
el path in the garden of State House Yard. Overnight,
the rain had turned to snow and the path was extremely
slippery. She should have stayed home, but she was feeling restless and lonely. It was only the terrible stories about her brother
that were getting her down, she told herself sternly. It couldn't be
that she was missing Senator Martin. She just needed a change of
scenery and some fresh air.

She'd decided to visit Mr. Peale's Museum. It had been a
while since she'd been there. She could stroll about in the garden
outside and there'd surely be something new to see. The museum,
once a small collection on display in Mr. Peale's home, was now
one of the wonders of Philadelphia, maybe the entire country.
He'd begun by gratifying the public (for a small fee) with a chance
to view cunningly crafted waxworks, rare and exotic natural cu-
riosities, and his own portraits of heroes of the Revolution. Word
spread, and the collection expanded with gifts from everywhere
one could imagine.

Now he had a huge collection of exotic objects and even animals, including a hyena from Bengal (still alive), a feather helmet from Hawaii, the birds' nests that the Chinese make into soup, Mammoth's teeth, a giant buffalo, tomahawks, rattlesnakes, and Birds of Paradise. His house was too small to house it all, so in 1794 he leased most of Philosophical Hall from the American Philosophical Society. Not only had he filled the space inside, but there was even a little zoo of live animals outside, at the edge of the garden behind the Statehouse.

Elizabeth lingered a moment outside looking at the animals. The sight of the helpless creatures taken away from their homes to live in such little cages made her sad. With a soft sigh, she made her way up the stairs of Philosophical Hall and into the main gallery.

She hadn't been to the museum in months and much had changed. She was immediately captivated at the sight of so many new exhibits. Most dramatic was the waxwork exhibit of the different races of mankind, meant to commemorate an incident that happened the prior December. Two rival Indian tribes, traditional enemies, had each been visiting the museum and had by chance run into each other. This chance encounter had led to talks between them, culminating in a peace agreement.

Mr. Peale had fashioned a full length waxwork figure of the Shawnee chief Blue Jacket and his friend Red Pole, both in full regalia. Then he'd added eight additional figures. There were natives of Guyana, the Sandwich Islands, Tahiti, the far northwest of the American Continent, north-eastern Russia, and the Gold Coast of Africa, along with a Chinese laborer and a mandarin. The theme was "Harmony among Man as in Nature."

It was another new exhibit, however, which struck her most forcefully. It was a model of a Chinese lady's foot, bound, crushed, and deformed into the tiny "lotus foot" that the Chinese deemed so attractive. It was accompanied by an actual miniature shoe, just four inches long, that such a pitiful appendage would fit into. With such feet, a woman could not even walk. She could only totter a few steps and even that most painfully.

Such was the way that women were imprisoned, she thought, just like the poor beasts outside in their cages. With only this difference – that the women embraced their imprisonment voluntarily, even gladly, and taught their daughters to do the same.

"Are we so different, I wonder?" asked a voice beside her.

Elizabeth turned toward the sound with a start, abruptly torn from her reflections. It was Rachel McAllister.

"Compared to the woman who wore this shoe, we are certainly fortunate, I think," Elizabeth responded, surprised to realize how glad she was to see her. Here was someone she could really talk to about the serious subjects that were on her mind. It had been too long since she'd enjoyed such companionship.

"You and I are fortunate," Rachel said thoughtfully, "but then we have means enough, we are free, and we are widows. We can do what we want, within reason, and the law recognizes our independent personality. What about the women who are indentured or enslaved, or who don't exist at all except as dependents of their fathers or their husbands?"

"I don't know," Elizabeth said honestly. "Men are enslaved and indentured as well. In comparison, I wouldn't say it was so bad being married. It does take some delicate management, especially for a woman who is intelligent and strong-minded. Men do not always appreciate competition from the gentler sex."

As she said it, she couldn't help but think of her many conversations with Senator Martin. He was one of the rare exceptions – or at least, she used to think so.

"I miss my husband a lot sometimes," Rachel said wistfully, "but now that you're on your own, don't you enjoy the freedom? When I was married, I had little time for myself, between one thing and another. Now I can do what I want, when I want to do it. I can read by the candlelight until morning, if I choose to. When I'm not working, that is."

Elizabeth smiled at her fondly.

"I was lucky with Mr. Powel. We had a good life together and he indulged me. I didn't realize how good it was until he was gone. But once is enough. Losing him was just too painful."

"I'll never marry anyone again, ever," Rachel declared with great conviction. "Men are nothing but trouble. Even when they say they care about you, they're still like little children. They want what they want, when they want it, and they're fickle and inconstant."

"I suppose you're right. You think you know them, but then you find you don't understand them at all." Elizabeth sighed, thinking of Senator Martin and Jefferson. And what of her brother Thomas and Bridget LeClair? She thought she understood him too, but did she really? What was really going on between him and Bridget?

Rachel heard the depth of the sigh and looked at Elizabeth with concern.

"You seem distressed," she said anxiously. "I'm so sorry, Mrs. Powel. Did I say something to upset you? I didn't mean to. It was thoughtless of me, I'm sure."

"Please don't blame yourself. It's only that this conversation made me think of something I've been worrying about."

Elizabeth paused. Normally, she'd never discuss worrisome family matters with anyone but the closest friend or relative, but wasn't it likely that Rachel had already heard the worst of it? All of Philadelphia was already talking about her brother, no doubt, thanks to the *Aurora*, and the stories surely were very much worse than the reality. Rachel might even know more than she did. People would talk more freely to her.

"May I talk to you candidly?" Elizabeth asked hesitantly. "May I trust to your discretion?"

Rachel didn't hesitate.

"Of course you can."

Elizabeth looked around the room. There weren't many visitors at the museum today, but one never knew when someone might come by.

"Perhaps we could go for a walk in the park? Is it too cold for you?"

"That would be fine," Rachel agreed. So they went back down the stairs to the garden.

"It concerns something I heard about my brother," Elizabeth began, and then stopped abruptly. It was harder to talk about it all than she had thought it would be. Did she need to explain who her brother was? Surely Rachel already knew? She took a deep breath and continued. "Well, this boy Jimmy," she continued. "I think he's the son of Mr. Mathers the Senate Doorman –"

Rachel winced and Elizabeth immediately noticed.

"Is something wrong?"

"It's nothing." Rachel forced herself to look politely interested. "Please do go on. You were talking about Jimmy. I know who you mean."

"This boy Jimmy took it into his head apparently to do some investigating on his own, of Bridget LeClair's murder that is. If you know of him, you may know this also – he used to work for the merchants, doing odd jobs. So he's familiar with the docks area."

"I'd heard that, yes. I heard it from a friend of mine, Mrs. Smallwood. He lives there at her tavern."

"He does? How very interesting. I didn't know." Then again, Elizabeth realized, what did she know of the boy? Or the world he lived in for that matter. "What is he like, this lad?"

Rachel considered how best to respond. According to Lydia, Jimmy was the one who found out about her brother and Bridget LeClair, so it wasn't hard to guess why Elizabeth wanted to know about him.

"He's a bright young fellow," Rachel said carefully choosing her words, "a bit rash, certainly, he's quite young, after all, but sincere and good-hearted. I like him, actually." She did like him, she realized, but she was surprised to hear herself say it.

"I gather he went around asking questions about Bridget," Elizabeth continued, "to help his father. Some friend of his said he'd seen my brother, Mr. Willing that is, together with this Bridget. According to this other boy, they were quite – quite –"

"It's all right," Rachel rescued her, "I know what you mean. I've heard it too."

"I suppose it's common knowledge," Elizabeth said miserably. "I gather that Bridget was – well, you know."

"I'm sure your brother has done nothing wrong. Perhaps this friend of Jimmy's just has too much imagination. Young men, I have to say, aren't always the best judge of things. Have you spoken to your brother?"

Elizabeth thought back to the night of the play and sighed again. "I talked to him and he tried to reassure me that he'd done nothing wrong, but somehow I still feel uneasy. He did tell me some other interesting things, though, that point back to Vice-President Jefferson again. Have you heard that James Callender, not Bridget, may have been the intended victim?"

"James Callender the journalist?"

"So my brother said. Mr. Jefferson's said to have a mistress who's one of his slaves, and it's possible Mr. Callender was blackmailing him. Then too, the story of Jefferson and Blount could be true. Apparently he was meeting secretly with the main people involved when they were planning it. He's got much better reasons to kill the girl, it seems to me. They're only attacking my brother to distract attention."

Elizabeth could feel her emotions rise again. How could Senator Martin do this to her?

"You say that Mrs. Smallwood is a friend of yours?" she continued after a pause.

"Yes, we've known each other for ages. Why do you ask?"

"She runs the Man Full of Troubles tavern, I think? Apparently they were there together, Bridget and my brother. Maybe you could ask her what actually happened?"

"I can talk to her," Rachel said cautiously, "but are you sure that you really want me to? Even if she knows something, it's still only second-hand. You still wouldn't know the truth of it, not really."

"I understand, but I'd feel better if I knew the details. I thought it was all just a malicious lie, but perhaps there's more to it. Perhaps I've been gravely mistaken." It wasn't just her brother she might be mistaken about, she thought, with a sudden stab of guilt. It might also be Senator Martin.

∞ 32 ∞

For a long time now, James Mathers had been itching to talk to Mr. and Mrs. Waln, Bridget's former (and Annie's current) employers. As a mere doorkeeper with no official status, though, he didn't think he could just barge in there and expect them to talk to him. With Senator Martin involved, however, it wasn't a problem at all. Jacob shared his view that they needed to find out what the Walns had to say about it all, so at last they were going to talk to them.

Like so many merchants, Mr. Waln lived close to the river, close to his ships, his wharf, and his counting house. He had a solid, well-built house with a double-wide front, on a large lot that stretched from Second to Front Street.

This visit had been carefully arranged in advance and it was the Walns themselves who greeted them. Though only in his thirties, Robert Waln looked older. His brown eyes sparkled behind his spectacles with intelligence and habitual good humor. His wife, who looked younger than he, had a calm self-possession and classically handsome face that reminded Jacob of a wealthy Roman matron.

The Walns were generally said to be Quakers of the old school, conservative in matters of doctrine. Clearly though, thought Jacob with an inward smile, they were of more liberal views when it came to their household furnishings. The first-floor rooms, so far as he could see, were uncommonly well-appointed.

In addition to the usual furnishings of wealthy Philadelphia homes – thick, richly-colored Belgian rugs, oil paintings of ships and landscapes, window curtains of shimmering silk and taffeta – the furniture and objects on display clearly proclaimed that Mr. Waln was engaged in the China trade. There were carved rosewood chairs in the Chinese style, with richly-colored brocade upholstery, lacquered tables displaying brisé fans, gaming counters made of mother of pearl, delicate porcelain figurines, and puzzle boxes elaborately carved in ivory.

Robert Waln led Jacob off to his study, while Mrs. Waln talked to Mathers for a moment in the hall before he went off to talk to the servants.

"Poor Bridget. I was afraid she'd come to no good end," Mrs. Waln began with a heavy sigh. "Not that it was her fault entirely," she added charitably. "As simple-minded as she was, she could hardly help herself."

"Did you know about her 'condition'?" Mathers asked delicately, hoping that he needn't say more. Mrs. Waln's answering look made clear that she understood him.

"No, I never knew it," she answered plainly. "To tell thee the truth of it, I'm not sure what we would have done if we had known it."

"Might you have kept her on, despite the fever?"

She looked at him with puzzlement.

"Despite the fever? That's not why we sent her away. Didst thou think it?"

"Well, yes. Wasn't that the reason?"

"Oh no, not at all." She looked chagrined. "Whatever dost thou think of us? It was on account of her thieving that we let her go. If she hadn't been so ill, she'd have gone to the goal instead of the hospital."

"She stole something?" Mathers cursed Annie silently. First it was the pregnancy, and now a theft. What was she up to, not telling him these things?

"Yes, I'm afraid so. She took a pair of my earrings. They were French and very fine. There were a number of diamonds set in gold, very valuable. And to make things worse, when we found out that she took them, she lied and said she didn't. I was sorely put out, I must say. I could hardly believe it of her."

"How did you know that she took them, if she didn't confess to it?"

"She was always the most likely one, I'm sorry to say. She loved bright, shiny objects, like a child. When I wore them, she couldn't take her eyes off them. We considered all the possibilities, of course, and we looked everywhere. We found the empty box hidden amongst Bridget's possessions."

"But the earrings weren't in it?"

"I suppose that she put them somewhere else, or lost them, perhaps. She was sometimes quite absent-minded. It would be harder to hide the box, though. It was rather a large one, made just to hold the earrings, lined in white silk and covered in red leather."

"Wouldn't she know it gave her away, that she still had the box in her possession?"

"Thou wouldst think it, but she wasn't a cunning one. She often overlooked things that were fairly obvious. She'd be thinking only of the earrings, perhaps, since that's what everyone was talking about.

"After we found the case," Mrs. Waln went on, "I confronted Annie as well, since she and Bridget were so close. Annie confessed that she'd seen Bridget hiding something. I was that cross with Annie, that I almost sent her away as well, but in the end I decided to take the path of mercy. I suppose she wanted to protect Bridget, but she saw in the end that it was wrong to do so. One must always be truthful, no matter what the consequences, dost thou not agree?" She looked at Mathers earnestly.

"Yes, Ma'am. I suppose so." It can be a pretty hard thing to do, though, Mathers thought guiltily. Fear could easily lead a person to lie or keep silent. He hadn't been honest with Rachel, had he? "Tell me about Annie Dawson. Has she been with you long? What is her background?"

"Annie has been here for a long time. She's such a good girl, so reliable. She's clean, too. Thou'd be surprised, the lice they have on some of them."

"Where did she work before?"

"I think this was her first time in service. She had no friend or family connections to start her out and she hadn't any references. I didn't even want to take her on at first, but it seemed an act of charity. Everyone has to start somewhere. Dost thou not think so?" Mrs. Waln turned and headed off down the hall. "Come now, and thou can talk to the other servants."

Meanwhile, Jacob and Mr. Waln were chatting comfortably in the study. A servant brought them biscuits and tea and they talked for a while of politics and trade. The French privateers and exorbitant insurance rates gravely troubled both of them. At last, with the biscuits eaten and the tea half-gone, Jacob turned the conversation around to Bridget.

"I'm surprised thou art looking into a murder again," Mr. Waln observed, "and this one involving Thomas Jefferson especially. Does it not cause thee trouble?"

"You're right there," Jacob agreed ruefully. "I wanted to stay out of it this time, but my conscience wouldn't let me." He looked at Mr. Waln intently. "You've a strong reputation for fairness yourself, so maybe you can understand. Even if it's just a servant girl, it's just no good, letting a murder get away with it."

"But what about the authorities?"

"That's what I was hoping for, but they didn't seem very interested in really getting to the bottom of it. Maybe it's because Jefferson was accused. As you know, the Mayor's a fellow Republican and great supporter of Jefferson. Anyway, I went so far as to ask them about their plans, but their enthusiasm was distinctly lacking."

"I do understand as a matter of fact." Waln nodded gravely. "I thought it was something like that. In thy position, I'd probably do the same. I never did believe the stories about thee and Thomas Jefferson."

"I thank you for saying that," Jacob said warmly. "I can't tell you how much it means to me, to find someone who understands and believes what I say. That's getting to be pretty uncommon these days."

He couldn't help but think of Elizabeth then and a heartfelt sigh escaped him. If only she could have believed him, like Robert Waln – but no, there was no use thinking of things that might have been.

"Since Bridget worked for you," Jacob went on, "I'm wondering if you know anything that might help figure out who killed her. Did she have any enemies that you know of? Or any particular friends, even?"

"I know very little about the servants, I'm afraid," Mr. Waln said candidly. "That's my wife's domain and the housekeeper. I've heard the stories about Bridget and William Blount, of course, but surely thou dost not think that he murdered her?"

"As a matter of fact, I don't. The timing is against it. He left Philadelphia as soon as he realized he was in trouble. I don't think he would have dared to come back after that, even secretly."

"I've read the accusations against Thomas Jefferson," Waln continued thoughtfully, "and those against Thomas Willing too, though in his case it's preposterous. I've heard some even say James Callender was supposed to be the victim. But it seems that the newspapers all know more than I do. I paid very little attention to Bridget, really. Not until she stole the earrings."

"Bridget stole a pair of earrings?" Jacob's face clearly registered his astonishment.

"Thou hasn't heard?" Robert Waln was even more surprised than Jacob. "Bridget stole a pair of diamond earrings, rather valuable ones, too."

"That's odd," Jacob said with obvious puzzlement. "James Mathers, our Doorman, has spoken to Annie Dawson several times, yet she never mentioned it."

"Didn't she? Well, it was all very painful and unpleasant for everyone. And now since Bridget is dead, perhaps she didn't want to speak ill of her. *De mortuis nil nisis bonum*, as they say, speak no ill of the departed. A common opinion, though not always a correct one."

"When did this theft happen?"

"It was some time after the epidemic had started. I don't recall the date exactly, but I can look it up for thee."

Waln went to his desk and thumbed through a small pocket almanac, the sort that had empty space for daily notes as well as providing the dates, the phases of the moon, rates of exchange for foreign money, and other useful information. He thumbed through a few pages, and then found what he was looking for.

"It was early in September when the theft was discovered – the thirteenth day to be precise. The yellow fever had broken out and we were packing to leave the city. We'd left it rather late, I'm afraid. I was waiting for one of my ships to arrive. It was a few days more before we found out that Bridget was the one who had taken them."

"How do you know she was the one who took them?"

"No one saw her steal them, but it had always been obvious that she was fascinated by them. It would have been easy enough for her to take them unobserved. Between the yellow fever and the packing, the house was in an uproar. We found the case among Bridget's things and finally Annie admitted that she knew, or suspected at least, that Bridget was hiding something."

"Where were the earrings kept?" Jacob was trying to develop a mental picture.

"Normally my wife kept them locked in the cupboard in her bedroom. At the time we were packing, however, as I said before. So the cupboards weren't always locked and things weren't always where they should be. Or maybe the cupboard was locked, but the keys were handy. My wife usually wore the keys at her waist, but in all the confusion, she might have left them lying about."

"Did Bridget go into your wife's room?" Jacob probed further. "I thought she was a kitchen maid?"

"Yes, Annie was the one who helped my wife dress, cleaned the room, and such, but Bridget was the one who usually brought my wife tea, nearly every morning."

"When she was bringing the tea, wouldn't Mrs. Waln be in her room also?"

"I suppose that's so." Mr. Waln looked as if this thought hadn't occurred to him, but then he dismissed it. "But Bridget is the one who comes again later to take the cup away again. My wife might have just stepped out for a moment. It wouldn't take long. The household was in such disarray at the time that no one would notice if something was out of the ordinary. The servants are always coming and going. Who can keep track of them?"

"And the earrings, did you ever find them?"

"No, we never did. It was quite a loss, not the money so much, but they were particularly fine ones. Bridget may not have even realized how valuable they were. Here was something bright and pretty, that's probably all she thought of them. Once there was a hue and cry, though, she was clever enough to hide them. We only found the empty case. We never found the earrings."

The rest of the interview yielded nothing more, nor did Mathers learn anything more of interest from talking to the servants. What they had already learned from Mr. and Mrs. Waln, however, was significant enough. They hadn't known about the earrings before. The theft could be of critical importance.

∞ 33 ∞

Discussing it all afterwards at a convenient tavern nearby, Jacob and Mathers agreed that the Walns' views on the matter weren't very satisfying. What was there to prove it was Bridget, after all? There was only an empty box that could have easily been planted among her things and Annie's word for it.

For his part, Mathers was half convinced that Annie was the murderer herself, and wholly convinced that time and again she'd lied to him. He'd believed her excuses the time before, when she'd failed to mention Bridget's being pregnant. Even more, he'd given in to her flirtatious charms. He'd been seeing her pretty regularly of late, and not to gather more information.

He had to admit, they'd had some good times. She was lively, bright, and fun to be with. Her not mentioning the theft of the earrings was inexcusable, however, whatever her explanation or motives. Now he suspected everything she'd said and done before.

"She's a sharp one, that Annie," he said bitterly as he and Jacob shared their thoughts over a pint of Morris's best bitter, "and she's a cold one, cold enough to murder. She had me going, that's for sure, and I fell for it."

"Perhaps, but there are other possible explanations as well." From his long experience with self-deceived or lying witnesses, Jacob was cautious about making final judgments. "From what Mr. Waln described, the house was in a state of chaos. The earrings could have been stolen by almost anyone on the staff. Or anyone else who happened to be around – someone delivering food, or coal or firewood, or coming to take away their trunks and other baggage."

"I was a proper pudding-head, not to see right through her." Mathers couldn't get over how gullible he had been. Surely that was the only reason that she'd ever flirted with him. He was blinded by vanity, to think his aging charms could ever be so attractive to a pretty young thing. It was all just a ruse to distract him, and it had worked out just as she planned it.

"Even if Annie is the thief, it doesn't mean she's a murderer," Jacob noted skeptically. "Aren't you forgetting about the candied oranges? You told me you were pretty sure that's how Bridget was poisoned. So if she was poisoned by the candied oranges, it was Mrs. Callender who killed her."

"Maybe it wasn't the oranges. Maybe I was wrong. I'm sure as can be that Mrs. Callender would never want to kill the girl."

"And if not Mrs. Callender and the candied oranges, what else and who else? There can't have been many visitors, considering the risk of contagion. If you're right about Mrs. Callender's love for Bridget, it seems that the poison must have been intended for her husband. Remember what Mrs. Powel said, that Jefferson had a mistress who was one of his slaves. If that's true, I wouldn't be at all surprised if Callender was blackmailing him.

That would certainly explain Jefferson's strange behavior when I questioned him."

"That it does." Mathers sighed. "It's a complication for certain. All the same, time and again that girl Annie has lied to me. What else did she lie about, I wonder," he added angrily. "Maybe she even lied about Bridget and Senator Blount being lovers."

"Quite a few people have commented on Bridget's loose ways, from what you've told me," Jacob pointed out mildly. "Didn't someone also confirm that she was involved with Senator Blount in particular? Wasn't it that woman at the boarding house?"

"Mrs. Finch. Yes, she did in a way," Mathers conceded, "but it wasn't what I call definite. She did say he was 'interested,' I'll grant you, but wasn't he interested in all the pretty ladies? It was only the way she said it that made it seem like more." Thinking of Mrs. Finch, he remembered his feeling that she was holding something back. He was pretty sure that she knew something she wasn't telling him.

"And anyway, when it comes to Mrs. Finch," he went on, voicing his thoughts, "I wouldn't be so certain about anything. She's another one I wouldn't trust."

"You don't trust what she told you? You didn't mention that before."

"Didn't I?" Mathers seemed surprised. "Well maybe I didn't mention it because I couldn't explain it. It was just a feeling I had and I know you don't like to hear about feelings, lest there's facts to back 'em up. All the same, she was holding something back, I'm sure of it. I wish I knew what it was. Do you think she might be in league with Annie?"

"In league with her how?"

"About the earrings, maybe." Mathers was seeing the picture take shape as he talked and it all made a lot of sense to him. "It would be pretty suspicious for a girl like Annie to go running around with a pair of earrings like that, trying to sell them. Mrs. Finch would be in a better position to do it with no questions asked, maybe saying she was doing it for one of her boarders. Maybe they planned to sell the earrings and split the money. In the meantime, Mrs. Finch could safely hide them."

"It's a plausible theory," Jacob agreed, "but it's all pretty speculative. You don't know it was Annie who took the earrings. Maybe it was Bridget, after all. You've only got 'a feeling' about Mrs. Finch, and even if you're right that she's holding something back, it could be a hundred things besides the earrings."

"It all makes sense, though," Mathers insisted stubbornly. "Annie takes the earrings, and Bridget finds out about it. Annie knows Bridget can't keep a secret, even if she wanted to. So to save herself, Annie has to get rid of her."

"I'll grant you the logic," Jacob countered, "but it's facts we need and we don't have enough of them. We don't even know if Bridget was the intended victim or Callender. Either way, Jefferson seems to have a pretty good motive. Or what about Hamilton? He might have a motive for killing either one of them as well. What if Callender knew something even worse than he's made public so far and Hamilton wanted to kill the man before he published it? Or if he was the father of Bridget's child? Then too, there's a question about her relationship with Thomas Willing, though I hate to say it, and who knows what other lovers.

"Or it could have been someone we don't even know about, someone at the hospital perhaps." Ignoring Mathers's increasingly unhappy looks, Jacob continued on relentlessly. "What if Bridget really did take the earrings and had them with her at the hospital? A pair of diamond earrings would be motive enough for some, if they saw them. They might even have thought that it wasn't so bad to poison someone who was dying anyway. They were only helping her die more quickly."

"I'll grant you there's possibilities enough," Mathers conceded reluctantly, "but I'm still putting my money on Annie. She's a two-faced, lying hussy is what she is, and there isn't any maybe about it. She took the earrings, sure enough, and she's going to be sorry she ever lied to me."

With Mr. Waln's permission, Mathers searched their entire house again quite thoroughly. He asked Jimmy to help him search as well, though he felt some qualms about involving him. A second pair of eyes might help to discover some secret hiding place that he had overlooked, especially if those eyes were much younger. It wasn't like Jimmy was looking around on his own, he told himself. It wouldn't give the lad the wrong idea, surely, just this once to be helping?

He wasn't really surprised that their search was just as unsuccessful as the Walns' search had been. It wasn't as if finding the diamond earrings still in the house was very likely. If Bridget had really taken them, she wouldn't have left them behind when she went to the hospital. If someone else had taken them (like Annie, Mathers thought sourly), they wouldn't have left them in the house if they could help it, not with all the searching going on.

So he looked for the earrings all over town, in the shops where they might have been sold or pawned, including (after some delicate inquiries among his more disreputable friends) the shops which dealt in more "questionable" property. There were a surprising number of jewelers, he found, who would buy a pair of diamond earrings from a servant-girl with no questions asked.

Twice he found earrings that were close enough to the Waln's description that he asked Mr. Waln to take a look at them. They were not Mrs. Waln's.

"I wouldn't spend too much more time searching for the earrings," Jacob advised him finally. "Chances are, they're not even still in Philadelphia. These earrings sound too special, too recognizable, to risk reselling in town. Far better to sell them to some ship's captain who can take them to another city or even to another country. I think we're better off looking for the father of Bridget's baby."

Remembering how his stubborn pursuit of the waiter Fritz had helped him find the murderer before, Mathers carried on. Convinced Annie took the earrings and suspecting Mrs. Finch was involved as well, Mathers returned to the boarding house. This time, when she saw who it was, Mrs. Finch greeted him with considerably less enthusiasm.

"Why are you here again?" she said crossly, her large form blocking the doorway. "Didn't you already bother me enough? I've got nothing more to tell you."

"Ah, Mrs. Finch," he said sweetly, "don't you know you're the woman of my dreams? I couldn't stay away and that's the truth of it."

She smiled at that, though she knew it was nothing but blarney.

"You're a terrible man, you are," she said, but she took a step back and let him enter. "Tell me about your dreams, then."

Mathers thought fast.

"Oh, I couldn't be telling you that," he said, letting a hint of a leer cross his features. "Not with you being such a lady. They were wonderful dreams to me, they were, but they weren't exactly – well, delicate."

He wouldn't have believed it, but he swore that she simpered like a shy young girl. It seemed to be working, so he went on with it shamelessly.

"Your eyes, your fetching cap, your ample figure." He was somewhat surprised with himself, to discover he had such a talent for deception. "And your lovely roast and your delicious chicken."

He'd gone too far, mentioning the food, and the spell was broken. She snorted in disbelief and they both broke down in laughter.

"I'll give you this much," she said, still chuckling, "you had me going for a moment. It's been a long time since anyone's buttered me like that. It's grateful to hear, even if you didn't mean it. So go ahead and ask your questions. Maybe I'll even answer them."

Mathers got straight to the point.

"Do you know anything about a pair of diamond earrings?"

"Earrings? I don't know what you're talking about." She looked at him boldly, as if daring him to contradict her.

"I think you know what I'm talking about. Mrs. Waln had a pair of diamond earrings. According to Mr. and Mrs. Waln, it seems maybe Bridget was the one that stole them. I'm wondering if you ever heard or saw anything, anything at all, about the earrings or her stealing them."

"Just like them rich folks, isn't it, to blame the servants," Mrs. Finch sniffed. "Most likely Mrs. Waln sold them herself to pay some gambling debt, or maybe she lost them. And you're just as bad as them, believing their stories. Slandering Bridget now that she was dead, as if she hadn't had enough troubles in her lifetime.

It's just as Annie said you'd –" she broke off suddenly. Clearly she had said more than she meant to.

"Annie? She talked to you about it? What did she say?"

"Be off with you now." Mrs. Finch said angrily. "You've asked your question and I've answered it."

She moved her great bulk toward the door, pushing Mathers before her.

"You've read what they're saying about Mr. Thomas Willing now. Just as I said. Those rich Federalists, they think they own the world and can do anything they please. That's what you should be looking into. Poor folk like me and Annie, you should leave them be. You're only stirring up trouble."

❦ 34 ❦

The Articles of Impeachment would be finished soon, so the Senate debates began in earnest. How did one actually hold an impeachment trial? The question was wide open. This would be the very first impeachment ever in the land, and nothing, neither the Constitution nor anything else, said a word about how the Senate should do it.

There were myriad questions about the details of the proceedings. Should there be an oath? Who should take it – all the Senators, or only witnesses? What should it say? How would witnesses be called? What would be the order of questioning? Should there be a single "prosecutor" for the Senate or should every Senator be able to ask questions? Should key members of the House be able to attend? What rights did a defendant have – a lawyer? Could he cross-examine witnesses, and how and when should it be conducted? Should the Senate's decision give just the conclusion, or also the reasons and grounds for it? And so forth and so on.

For every question of procedure, there was a question of Constitutional powers – could the Senate decide all these things on its own, or would it have to pass a law, which meant the House of Representatives had to pass it as well and the President had to sign it?

The Senators argued at length about every detail and question. The Republicans threw up every problem they could think of, with Senator Tazewell leading the arguments. Jacob found himself, to his own surprise, taking the lead in arguing against him. His hours of research, it seemed, had come in handy. For a little while, his relations with his Federalist colleagues were, if not actually friendly, at least reasonably civil.

It was after one particularly trying day that Mathers handed Jacob a couple of letters. His long-awaited mail. A quick glance, however, told Jacob that neither was from his sister. One was from his New York agent, and the other was from a legal client of his in Charleston.

As Mathers handed them over, Jacob anxiously wondered what they had to say. Were they good news or bad news? He decided to save them to read later.

When he finally got back to his rooms, he set them down side by side on the desk before him. Which one should he open first? He shut his eyes, shuffled them around, and picked one at random. It was the one from his Charleston client.

"When I first engaged you, I must say," it began, "you were well recommended. You were said to be conservative, steady, and reliable. Now, I must confess, such bizarre stories are circulating about your activities in Philadelphia that I must wonder whether you have changed, or whether your good reputation was sadly mistaken. I hear that you have turned away from the Federalists and are working secretly for Mr. Jefferson. They say you were always (like Charles Pinckney, I must say) a wolf in sheep's clothing. They say you are consorting with criminals in order to avenge a common strumpet's death and you're not even being paid to do it.

"If there is any truth to these rumors, one must wonder if you have lost your reason. I beg you therefore to advise me at your earliest convenience what account you can give of yourself in relation to these matters."

With a heavy heart, Jacob laid the letter back down and picked up the other one.

"Dear Senator Martin," it began, "I regret that I must advise you of a most unfortunate circumstance. Just yesterday, we received the news that the ship which was carrying your rice has been seized by French privateers. As you know, this surely means the loss of ship and cargo. We are endeavoring, rest assured, to become acquainted with the exact particulars and will, as soon as we learn, further advise you. The ship was insured, but it may be some considerable time before the details can be confirmed and the insurance company makes payment."

Jacob poured himself a stiff drink of brandy, fearing to think of the implications. The ship might be insured, but his rice most assuredly wasn't. Was it possible that the ship's insurance might somehow cover him? It seemed very doubtful. And even so, he needed the money from the sale of his rice right away, not in some long-delayed and (at the moment) quite improbable future.

How he wished that he'd stayed in Charleston this time, instead of coming to do his duty in Philadelphia. Nothing had gone right since he'd returned here. All his worst fears were coming to pass, or very nearly. He'd managed to alienate Elizabeth Powel, to say nothing of his Federalist colleagues. Added to which, his rice was lost, his debts were coming due, and he was losing his remaining legal clients. He'd tried to be true to himself, to steer by his own lights, and it wasn't working. Maybe Jefferson and Bingham were right after all? Maybe he should give up and go along with his colleagues?

He'd planned to take supper in his rooms, a bit of bread and cheese and some onion pie that he'd bought on the way home. Now however, he hesitated. If he stayed home all evening he'd only fret and stew. He decided to visit Thomas Dobson's shop, in hopes that a change of scene would distract him. Maybe he could even find something light and entertaining to read, like a traveler's tale of some exotic and foreign land. He seemed to recall that Dobson had published something like that last year that he hadn't read yet.

Downing the last of his brandy, Jacob stood up with a heavy heart and set forth for the Old Stone House on Second Street.

As he walked along Chestnut Street, he was struck once again by how much the neighborhood had changed since he'd first come to Philadelphia. It was 1783 when, with the Revolution nearly won, he first came to attend the Continental Congress. Congress Hall was on the outskirts of the city then, and Chestnut Street beyond it was only a muddy dirt road that ran through mostly fields and meadows. Across the street from Congress Hall was the Half Moon Inn, an old country tavern with a yard full of Chestnut trees, the remnants of the fine old forest. Now the Chestnut trees were gone and the blocks around were filling in with grand new construction. In addition to grand public buildings like Oeller's Hotel, Rickett's Circus, and the New Chestnut Street Theater, there were splendid private residencies, spacious homes with many stories, balconies and piazzas, flights of marble steps leading to their street side doors and elaborate formal gardens behind them. The times had changed so much as well, alas, and not for the better. The innocence, excitement, and hopeful idealism of those early days had been transformed into a poisonous stew of bitterly partisan politics.

Over and over again, Jefferson's parting words kept coming back to him. Were there really "many truths in politics," as he said? Wasn't it just a convenient turn of phrase to cover up ruthless expediency? Or was his own the more dangerous view, to think there was one truth, and one truth only? Wasn't that what the French Revolutionaries believed, when they sent thousands of men, women, and children to the guillotine?

By the time he reached Dobson's shop, Jacob was so depressed that he felt like giving up and going home again. His mood changed, however, the moment he opened the door. He was surely right to have come here. The shelves full of books and stationery, the tables full of books and pamphlets in neatly-stacked piles, the pervading smell of dust, ink, and leather, created a peaceful and soothing atmosphere. Rachel McAllister was at her accustomed place behind the counter, with Derrick standing beside her, counting out a box of quill knives and scissors.

There were two other patrons besides Jacob himself. A gentleman in a brown frock coat was standing by the window, deeply absorbed in paging through a thick tome bound in calfskin. Another customer was at the counter, taking out shiny silver dimes from a small leather wallet. He kept looking at them one by one, as if he wasn't sure what they were exactly. It was no wonder if he still found them strange. After all, the Mint only started making dimes a year ago. American-made coins were only just beginning to replace the foreign currency people still used and were used to.

"Can I help you, Senator Martin?" Derrick was quick to leave off his counting and greet him.

"Yes, if you please. I'm in the mood for someone's tale of their travels, preferably to some exotic foreign land. You published something along those lines last year, if my memory serves me?"

Derrick went over to a shelf and pulled out a slim brown volume.

"George Barrington," he said, handing it over to Jacob. "*A Voyage to New South Wales; with a Description of the Country; the Manners, Customs, &c. of the Natives.*"

As Jacob leafed through the book, Derrick went over to a shelf full of books and extracted another, much thicker volume.

"But here's another one I could recommend. It's a longer and more interesting tale, just published."

Laying down the Barrington, Jacob took the second book and turned to the title page. *A Journey over Land to India, Partly by a Route Never Gone Before by Any European*, by Donald Campbell. He leafed through it quickly, and then looked at the end. It was four hundred thirty pages long. That ought to hold his attention.

"Thank you, Mr. Wilkens. I think this will do very nicely."

As he watched Derrick wrap the book in brown paper and tie it with twine, Jacob felt suddenly content, a feeling which had been exceedingly rare for him lately. Perhaps things weren't as bad as they seemed. He was dwelling on his problems too much and it magnified them. Perhaps he should go next to the City Tavern for supper and treat himself to a nice dessert. Maybe a Shrewsbury cake (or two) or a couple of iced biscuits?

As he counted out the coins for his purchase, he felt a blast of cold air on his back from the opening door. Another customer must have just entered. He turned to see who it was. It was Elizabeth.

He could see from her face that she was as surprised as he was. It was the first time in a very long while that they'd seen each other. After their last meeting, for a while he had cherished hopes that she would invite him back again, but eventually he'd reconciled himself to her absence. Now suddenly, there she was, standing only a few feet away, looking as charming and lovely as ever.

Seeing him, she felt faint, and felt a rush of something very like panic. Jacob Martin, here! For a moment she seriously contemplated running away. Don't be foolish, she told herself. He's the one who should be leaving.

"Good day, Mrs. Powel," he greeted her right away, more eagerly than he'd intended.

"Good day, Senator Martin," she greeted him stiffly. The very last thing she wanted was to make a scene, not in public.

"I hope you are well?" he asked with deep concern, suddenly aware that she was very pale and her hands were ever so slightly trembling. "Is there any way that I can assist you?"

Thus far, she'd managed to maintain her self-control, but the warmth in his words undid her. How dare he greet her as if they were the closest of friends, when he'd treated her so badly?

"I'm surprised you should feel the need to ask." This time, there was no mistaking the chill in her attitude. "I am as you might expect me to be, given these scandalous rumors about my brother."

"Yes of course." Jacob quickly retreated. "It must be terrible for you. I'm very sorry."

"It's rather late to apologize, don't you think?" She glared at him pointedly. "The damage is done, and after all, haven't things gone just as you planned them? The newspapers are full of stories about my brother now. One hardly ever reads about Jefferson."

"Mrs. Powel," he said earnestly, "I have planned nothing at all. Whatever you are thinking, you are mistaken. I'm as sorry about your brother as I can be and I wish to God that I'd never heard of Thomas Jefferson."

"I shouldn't blame you, of course," she added reluctantly, remembering how her brother had said she was being unfair to him. "No doubt you have your reasons and, considering your position, I suppose they're much more important than my own little feelings. As you said before, I should know by now how things are in public life and politics." With an effort, she nodded politely, turned away, and went over to Rachel at the counter.

Rachel of course was listening to the whole exchange, though pretending to be looking something up in the ledger.

"Good day, Mrs. Powel," she greeted her as if nothing had happened at all. "Can I help you?"

"Yes please," Elizabeth answered gratefully. "Can you suggest something for me to read? You know what I like. Have you anything that I haven't read yet?"

"I have several ideas. Please follow me and I'll show you."

As they walked toward a corner of the shop, Rachel leaned closer and whispered softly.

"I'm afraid I haven't any information yet on the other matter we discussed, but I expect to have an opportunity very shortly."

Watching them together, Jacob sighed. He was cursed, he thought miserably. He gave up his thoughts of going to the City Tavern and headed back to his rooms, glumly clutching *A Journey to India.*

❧ 35 ❧

James Mathers hurried back into the Senate Chamber, his face still flushed from running down the stairs and then quickly back up again. The Senators had heard an awful commotion from the House Chamber on the floor below and he'd been sent down to find the cause of it.

He stopped for a moment to catch his breath, wondering how to describe the spectacle he'd witnessed. He decided there was nothing for it but to say it straight out. There wasn't any way to say it diplomatically.

"I regret to inform you," he announced to the Senators in what he hoped was a dignified fashion, "that the noise below is because two of the Congressmen was engaged in fisticuffs on the floor of the House of Representatives."

Of course he couldn't stop there. Everyone wanted to know all the details.

"It's Mr. Griswold from Connecticut and Mr. Lyon from Vermont," he explained. "According to Mr. Condy the clerk, Mr. Griswold struck Mr. Lyon with his cane, so Mr. Lyon grabbed the tongs from beside the fireplace. They was swinging at each other something fierce, and they fell onto the floor, but it didn't stop them. Mr. Lyon, being the younger one, he was gaining the upper hand. He was like to beat Mr. Griswold's head in with the tongs, says Mr. Condy. About then, though, the others managed to grab them and pull them apart. It took a lot of them to do it too, is what he tells me."

Having given his report, Mathers retired to his customary place in the public gallery. No one asked why they were fighting because everyone knew. It had all begun about two weeks ago. Representative Lyon had spit tobacco juice in Representative Griswold's face, after Griswold had grabbed Lyon by the arm and called him a coward. Griswold wanted Lyon expelled, but the motion hadn't passed. Now he'd taken matters into his own hands and it seemed that he'd gotten the worst of it.

Opinions varied as one might expect, depending on whether you were a Federalist or a Republican. At bottom, that was the fatal divide that had brought them to such hostile behavior. Representative Griswold's great-grandfather, coming over from England, had established his family in Connecticut. He was a Yale graduate who'd studied Greek and Latin, a lawyer, and a Federalist. Representative Lyon was an Irish immigrant who'd come to America as an indentured servant and worked his way up, but never lost his rough edges. Needless to say, he was a dyed-in-the-wool Republican.

"Representative Lyon's a madman," Senator Tracy loudly proclaimed. "He's as fanatic as Robespierre, the one who said 'Terror is nothing else than justice.' You can see what it would be like if the Republicans ever seized power. It's an outrage that he wasn't expelled after he spit at Mr. Griswold."

"It was Representative Griswold's fault," Senator Mason retorted angrily. "Representative Lyon was provoked beyond what a man can be expected to put up with. First Griswold calls him a coward during the official debates, in front of everyone. Then, when Mr. Lyon tried to be dignified and ignore it, Griswold assaulted him and repeated it."

"Representative Griswold only spoke the truth." Senator Sedgwick joined in support of his Federalist colleague. "It's a known fact that Representative Lyon was dishonorably discharged from the Revolutionary Army. It's not Griswold's fault if Lyon can't stand to hear it."

Quickly the Senators chose sides, and the next half-hour was given over to impassioned argument. It was just as heated as the fight between Griswold and Lyon themselves, albeit without the added element of actual physical violence. Jacob stood it as long as he could, then he left the Chamber, walked down the stairs, and went out to the park in back of the building. He sat on a bench and smoked a pipeful of tobacco to calm himself.

"Two grown men, grappling on the floor of the House," he muttered disgustedly. "What have we come to? Two duly elected Representatives of the nation, baiting each other, spitting, and beating each other with sticks and fire tongs. A pox on both their houses."

When he came back upstairs, the argument had pretty much exhausted itself. After several unsuccessful efforts to restore order, Jefferson had let things run their course, but now he pounded the gavel to get back to business. The House of Representatives would soon be sending the Articles of Impeachment to the Senate, so they needed to finish deciding what should be the procedure.

They'd already set up one Committee to look into it, with four Federalist Senators and Senator Tazewell the lone Republican. One Republican was one too many, however, so they set up a second Committee consisting only of northern Federalists, with no Republicans or even southerners.

Perhaps it was the Griswold-Lyon fight, or perhaps it was only the result of months of unhappiness and aggravation. Or perhaps he was only tired of endless partisan bickering over trivial things, when real and immediate crises threatened the nation.

As he looked around the Chamber at the other Senators, many of them half-asleep, reading newspapers, whispering to each other, or otherwise not paying the least attention, Jacob realized that he'd made his decision. However many Committees they set up and whatever his colleagues might think of it, he was going to tell them all that he believed the whole impeachment proceeding was unconstitutional.

He spent half the night working it out, making sure his arguments were thorough and persuasive. He submitted his motion the very next day. The wording was plain and straightforward:

"RESOLVED, that the duty or trust imposed by the Constitution of the United States, on a Senator of the United States, is not of such a nature as to render a Senator impeachable."

It's done, he told himself, and he steeled himself for the fury of his colleagues. Apart from the sudden return to chilly relations and hostile looks, however, there was surprisingly little reaction. It was as if he didn't exist, as if he'd never even proposed anything.

His stock had sunk so low it seemed, that no one felt the need to take him seriously.

So the debates went on and on, interminably.

❦ 36 ❧

Mathers had made a big mistake when he asked Jimmy to help search the Waln's house for the earrings. Since the night he was hurt, Jimmy had (more or less) obeyed his father's command to stop looking around on his own, but he took his father's request for help as a sign that he should go back to investigating on his own.

Jimmy had a pretty good idea where things stood. Often enough, he'd overheard his father and Jacob talking. He knew that Mrs. Callender was a likely source of information but she wasn't talking.

"Here's something I could do," he thought to himself. She wouldn't talk to his father, but she'd have less hesitation in talking to an innocent-seeming lad if he approached her properly. What was the right approach? He thought about it long and carefully.

It was Martha Smallwood, in the end, who gave him the idea for it.

"Has the man no scruples at all?" She was reading a piece in the *Aurora*, undoubtedly by James Callender, and she knew the answer to her question perfectly well. "Just listen to this – he's accusing the Secretary of State of asking for bribes to issue passports."

"Bribes? Mr. Pickering?" Of all the Cabinet officers that ever were, the stern, self-righteous Pickering seemed the very least corruptible.

"Some fellow came in for a passport, it says, and he had to give the clerk some money to get it. It's supposed to be free, so Callender says the money must have gone into Mr. Pickering's pocket. Can you imagine saying such a thing about Mr. Pickering, of all people? That Mr. Callender knows no bounds at all. It's no wonder that someone wants to kill him."

Martha knew all about Bridget, the Callenders, and the poisoned oranges, for Jimmy had kept her informed as things went along. In her mind, there was no question that Bridget had died by mistake and James Callender was supposed to be the victim. The oranges were poisoned, she was sure, and it was only chance that Bridget and not Callender had eaten them.

"I feel sorry for his wife," she added, shaking her head sadly. "Someone ought to warn her. From what I hear, she doesn't have any idea how soon she might be a widow."

Mrs. Smallwood was right, Jimmy realized right away. Someone ought to warn Mrs. Callender.

The very next day, he went to her house. She opened the door just a tiny crack, ready to shut it in an instant.

"My husband isn't here," she said, peering out at him warily. "Go try the *Aurora*."

"I'm not looking for Mr. Callender," Jimmy said quickly. "I know about the candied oranges and I came to warn you, for your sake and for the sake of your husband."

"Warn me?" She stared at him anxiously for a very long time. Then she looked up and down the street, motioned him inside, and shut the door quickly behind him. She didn't invite him further in, so they stood there just inside the door, in the hallway.

"What is it then?" She was clearly frightened as well as wary.

Jimmy hesitated. Seeing her standing there so frail and pitiful, he felt guilty. According to his father, the time before she didn't seem to realize that the oranges might have been poisoned. She might be the one who poisoned her dearest friend and he was going to be the one to tell her.

"I heard about the candied oranges," he said at last. "The ones you gave to Bridget."

"Are you going to tell my husband?" She looked so afraid that, once again, Jimmy wondered whether to go on. Then he thought of his father and how long and hard he'd tried to find the killer, and how unhappy and upset he was that he'd failed to find him.

Jimmy steeled himself and continued.

"It isn't that," he said reassuringly. "It's only that – well, some are saying that the oranges might have been poisoned."

"Poisoned?" As she gradually understood the meaning of his words, Mrs. Callender's fear was replaced by a look of anguish. "Are you saying I was the one who poisoned Bridget?"

The blood suddenly left her face and she swayed backward. Fearing that she was going to faint and fall, Jimmy quickly guided her to a chair and settled her gently into it. He looked around the room and saw an earthenware pitcher full of water by the fireside. He poured some into a rusty tin cup and held it out to her.

She took it gratefully but didn't drink it. She just sat there, cradling it in her hands.

"Poison, I never thought – and they was meant for Mr. Callender."

"Yes, that's it. They were a gift for Mr. Callender, weren't they? I'm very sorry to be the one to tell you," he said sincerely, deeply wishing he'd never gotten into this, "but it's best to know, isn't it, if your husband's in danger? What if you get another gift like that? What if next time he eats them?"

Mrs. Callender took a deep breath to steady herself and then nodded weakly.

"Who could have done it, do you think? Does he have any deadly enemies?"

"Enemies?" she repeated shakily.

"People who might want him out of the way. People he's written about, people with secrets?"

"I understand, but I don't know what to tell you." The color was returning to her face and her voice was still soft, but stronger. "He doesn't talk about his work very much."

"What about Mr. Hamilton?" Jimmy prompted. "Mr. Callender was working on something more about him, wasn't he? Something more than what he printed in the History?"

"It could be," Mrs. Callender answered uncertainly. "I know he was trying to. 'Hamilton is a thief,' he'd say, 'and I'll prove it.'"

"What about Vice President Jefferson. I know he and Mr. Callender are friends, but sometimes friends know each other's secrets." Remembering how Senator Martin and his father had said that Callender might be blackmailing Jefferson, Jimmy had asked the question simply on impulse. He was astonished to see Mrs. Callender's instant and horrified reaction.

"You have to go!" she cried pleadingly. "I don't know anything, I swear it. And soon my husband will be coming home. He mustn't see you." She rose from the chair and stood unsteadily, nearly weeping with panic.

Jimmy left her standing there and made his own way out. He felt like a cad entirely. What had he learned, at the price of upsetting the poor woman so cruelly? It seemed true what they said, that Callender was bent on proving Hamilton was a criminal, but they'd pretty much figured that anyway. What was that all about, though, when he mentioned Vice President Jefferson? Why was Mrs. Callender so frightened?

∞ 37 ∞

Tonight was one of the quieter nights at the Man Full of Troubles tavern. Winter was always quieter, to begin with. With the Delaware River frozen shut, the great horde of transient trading ships was absent. Added to which, tonight it was snowing heavily. The handful of regular patrons was clustered mostly by the fire, chatting and sipping their drinks.

Rachel entered the tavern, removed her cape, and brushed off the worst of the snow. She looked around and saw Martha settled in a corner by the fire, chatting with an old, grizzled sailor.

Martha, looking up and, seeing Rachel, greeted her with a friendly smile. Excusing herself from the sailor, she rose and guided Rachel to a quiet table.

"It's good to see you. It has been quite a while. How about some supper? You look hungry."

That sounded good to Rachel. Soon Martha came out with a plate of cold roast chicken and fried potatoes, along with a glass of cider.

"I've been wanting to ask you something," Rachel remarked when Martha arrived with her meal. "I ran into Mrs. Powel at Mr. Peale's museum. She's terribly upset about the story that's going around about Bridget and Mr. Willing. The two of them met here once, she said, so I told her I'd ask you about it."

Martha set down the plate and nodded knowingly.

"I'll tell you what I know about it later on when things calm down."

She headed back to the bar, leaving Rachel to eat her meal in solitude.

Before too long the door opened again and a small, timid face peeked in. It was a woman, so wan and pale that it seemed almost a ghost. Martha Smallwood's eyes were drawn to her immediately.

"Come in my dear," she called out kindly. "Ladies are welcome. You'll be perfectly safe here."

Still the woman stood there, unwilling to leave but uncertain whether to enter.

Rachel got up from her table and went over to her.

"You're Mrs. Callender, aren't you?" Rachel had seen her once before, at Benjamin Bache's print shop. He'd invited some of the other publishers to celebrate his fifth year publishing the *Aurora*. James Callender had been there, sampling liberally of the spirits on offer, and Mrs. Callender had come very late in the night to take him home. That night, she'd shown the same uneasy mixture of timidity and determination.

"Yes," she answered, surprised to be recognized. "And you're . . .?"

"Rachel McAllister. I'm a friend of Mrs. Smallwood's." Rachel inclined her head toward Martha.

Mrs. Callender took a step further into the room, seemingly reassured by Rachel's presence. Rachel helped her take off her thin, threadbare cape and led her over to the table.

"Would you like something to eat? I'm having some chicken. It's very good."

Mrs. Callender looked at Rachel's plate with such obvious hunger that Rachel didn't wait for an answer.

"Mrs. Smallwood," Rachel called over to Martha, "could we perhaps have some more chicken?"

Soon Mrs. Callender was devouring the food like someone on the brink of starvation, which perhaps she was, considering her appearance. In between bites, however, she looked around the room in fascination. To her it obviously seemed strange and mysterious, thought Rachel, though it was an ordinary enough scene for the tavern.

"You had some reason for coming here?" Rachel asked, after Mrs. Callender had finished. "If I had to guess, I'd say that you don't often come to taverns."

Mrs. Callender turned and stared at her, startled into awareness of her presence. She smiled a wan and self-deprecating smile.

"Would you believe it? I've never been in a tavern before. Not all the way inside."

Rachel smiled back at her. She had no trouble at all believing it.

"And how is it, now that you're here?"

Mrs. Callender's smiled again, shyly this time.

"You're very nice. It makes it easier. All the same, I'm feeling like I shouldn't be here. It's just that I'm looking for my husband. Oh no, it isn't that –" she added, seeing Rachel's knowing expression. "It's not like that night at Mr. Bache's. You were there, weren't you? Is that where you saw me?"

Rachel nodded.

"My husband doesn't drink very much these days. We can't afford it." The last part was true, but the first part was true was only hopeful conjecture. "But he isn't home and I expected him. The truth is, I'm afraid for him."

Rachel remembered what Elizabeth had said, that perhaps Bridget's murderer was really trying to kill James Callender.

"Do you think he's in danger? Is that it? Is that what you're worrying about?"

"Yes," Mrs. Callender answered softly, "that's it. That boy, Jimmy, he works here, doesn't he?"

"He helps Mrs. Smallwood, yes. Why do you ask?"

"He came to see me, about Bridget." Talking about Jimmy and Bridget, Mrs. Callender seemed to grow even more anxious. "Bridget LeClair, you knew her?" She looked at Rachel inquiringly.

"I didn't know her, but I know who you mean."

"It was about the candied oranges. He wanted to warn me. You know about the candied oranges?"

"Candied oranges?"

"They were on the doorstep," Mrs. Callender said miserably, "a gift for Mr. Callender." She looked at Rachel in anguish. "God help me, I gave them to Bridget. Were they poisoned? Was I the one who killed her?"

There was nothing Rachel could say to that, so she didn't answer.

"Why did Jimmy come to see you?" she asked instead.

"He said he wanted to warn me. He said they might have been meant for my husband." Mrs. Callender looked around the room again, as if somehow her husband might magically appear. "And now he hasn't come home and I don't know where he is."

"You shouldn't assume the worst," Rachel said reassuringly. "There could be any number of reasons he isn't home yet. Maybe he ran into someone or he had something to do. Does he always come home when he says he will?"

"No, not really." Mrs. Callender brightened. The thought of her husband's chronic unreliability seemed to comfort her. "It could be that, now that you mention it."

She looked wistfully over at the bar cage where Martha now was, pouring out beer and cider.

Rachel saw her look and smiled.

"Would you like a little cider? I'd be happy to get you one." Before Mrs. Callender could say no, Rachel got up and went over and fetched her one.

"Have a good drink of that, you'll feel better."

Mrs. Callender took a tentative sip, then sighed and drank deeply. She looked up guiltily but seemed to relax a bit.

"My husband used to come here, sometimes. It's close to our house. He said it was a good place, you got what you paid for."

"I'm sure of that. Mrs. Smallwood is a friend of mine, as I said. She's the owner. She took it over when her husband died. I'm sure she wouldn't cheat anyone."

"He said you could tell by the clientele. It wasn't just the riff-raff, the sailors and such, but sometimes there were gentry." Her husband's opinion obviously counted more, in Mrs. Callender's mind, than anything Rachel had to say about it. "He even saw Mr. Willing here, a rich man like him."

"You don't say?" Suddenly Rachel was paying extra close attention.

Mrs. Callender took another sip of her cider and seemed to be thinking back.

"Yes, it wasn't too long before Bridget died, actually. Mr. Callender said they were talking about Bridget. Can you believe it, they was talking about how she was pregnant. You could have knocked me over with a feather, you could. She never even told me, as close as we were."

"They? Who was Mr. Willing talking to?"

"Mr. LeClair, her father-in-law. He's one of our neighbors."

"What were they saying? Apart from her being pregnant, that is?"

"According to my husband, they were saying bad things about her. That she was a Jacobin whore and she'd pay for it someday. And look what happened."

Mrs. Callender started to cry, very silently.

"Poor, poor Bridget, she was like a child. There wasn't a lick of sense in her. Too sweet to live, she was. It wasn't her fault, not any of it."

"I'm sure it wasn't." The more Rachel heard about Bridget, the easier it was to believe it. "But think carefully, Mrs. Callender, it's important. Which one of them was it, who said she was a whore and she'd pay for it?"

Mrs. Callender thought carefully before she answered.

"Why, it was Mr. Willing, now that you ask me. Can you imagine? I know he's a moral, religious man, but why be so hard on a young servant-girl?"

"Are you sure?" To Rachel, this sounded practically like a confession. "Are you very sure?"

"That's what my husband told me."

Rachel leaned back in her chair, wondering what to say to Mrs. Powel. Should she even tell her? Mrs. Callender was only repeating what her husband thought he overheard, and it was months ago.

"Well, that's that." Martha came up to the table, interrupting Rachel's deliberations. "Now I'm done and I can join you. Would you like more cider?" She looked at them both in turn, first Rachel and then Mrs. Callender.

"Oh, no. I shouldn't be here at all." Mrs. Callender started as if awoken from a dream. "What if he did come home, Mr. Callender I mean, and was there waiting for his supper?" She hurriedly rose, threw on her cape, and made for the door. Just at the last moment, she turned back to them. "If you see him, please tell him to come home. And thank you."

"A good woman, that," Martha observed. "And with a husband like she has – he doesn't deserve her."

"Husbands!" Rachel said dismissively.

Martha smiled at her fondly.

"So how are you doing yourself? Tell me everything. Is Dobson still working you too hard? And is that doorkeeper still coming around, the one you were telling me about?"

Instead of answering, Rachel looked down and started absently toying with her glass of cider.

"Rachel, my dear, has something gone wrong?" Martha asked sympathetically. "I thought you rather liked him. And from what little I saw, he did seem quite fond of you. What happened? Was I mistaken?"

"Oh, men, you know. It's complicated."

"So tell me," Martha said encouragingly. "I've got time."

Rachel was just on the point of telling Martha everything when the door flung open and a man strode in. Martha recognized James Forten immediately. In his arms, he was carrying something – or was it someone? Certainly it was very awkward and heavy.

Martha looked at him closely and then shrieked.

"Jimmy! What's happened?"

"Where should I put him?" Forten's tone was calm but urgent. Jimmy was barely conscious and deathly pale. Blood was seeping out of the side of his chest through a hastily-manufactured linen bandage.

Without a word, Martha led him upstairs to her own bed. After a moment's hesitation Rachel followed them.

"What happened?" Martha asked once Jimmy was carefully tucked in and they were standing all together outside the room in the hallway.

"He was shot," Forten said grimly. "I don't think it hit anything vital or he'd be dead already, but there's been quite a lot of bleeding."

"Shouldn't I send for a doctor?" Martha hurriedly tried to think. Who could she call at this time of night to come down to a waterfront tavern?

"I think it will wait until the morning," Forten answered her. "One of the sailors I know took out the bullet and put a few stitches in him. He was a surgeon's assistant on a navy ship, once upon a time, and he knows about wounds from battles. The important thing for now is to make sure he doesn't bleed to death. The wound is staunched for now but it could start up again. Someone will have to keep watch over him."

Impelled by she knew not what, Rachel stepped forward.

"I will. I can watch over him."

Martha looked at her curiously.

"All right. I'll get you some extra candles and a chair and you can sit there by the fire. I'll come back when the tavern closes."

Once the customers were gone and things tidied up, Martha came upstairs.

"I haven't forgotten what you asked, about Mr. Willing," she said softly to Rachel. "We can stand just there in the hall and I'll tell you what I know. It isn't much, though."

"Thomas Willing did occasionally frequent the tavern," Martha continued, once they were in the hall. "It always seemed to be when he was meeting with someone 'a little bit on the shabby side.' Maybe he's thinking they'll do better with a drink, or maybe it's to make them more comfortable. He did meet here with Bridget LeClair once or twice, but I can't say as to how there was anything between them. They did sit close together, but there's other reasons for that. Like maybe he didn't want to be overheard, or maybe other patrons were talking too loudly. He'd meet here sometimes with her father-in-law too, so maybe it was something to do with his business."

Martha yawned sleepily. It had been a long day.

"I can ask around a bit if you want," she offered, "but for now that's all I can tell you. I'll be sleeping down the hall if you need me."

Rachel settled herself comfortably in the chair, preparing herself for a night of watching over Jimmy. As the hours went by, she found her vigil strangely peaceful. Now that the tavern had closed for the night, the building was still and empty. All she could hear was an occasional carriage horse clip-clopping down the street outside, the watchman crying the hours, and once or twice in the walls there seemed to be a scuffling, scurrying sound of some nocturnal creature. Jimmy lay as still as death, just barely breathing. From time to time she held her hand close to his face or over his heart to make sure he was still alive.

Sometime very early in the morning, well after closing but before the sun came up, Jimmy became suddenly restless, tossing from side to side and crying out softly. Suddenly alert, Rachel was terrified. What if he opened the wound and started to bleed again?

She tried to restrain him gently by holding down his shoulders, but that didn't work. It only made him struggle all the more. Desperate, she stroked his cheek and whispered softly in his ear.

"It's all right, Jimmy. I'm here. Don't worry. It's over."

He made a small mewing noise like a kitten and clutched her hand. It seemed to quiet him. He didn't want to let go, so Rachel moved her chair in as close as she could beside him. She sat there holding his hand until sometime after dawn when Martha entered. She had a tray with a plate of cold ham and bread and two steaming hot cups of tea, liberally laced with sugar.

"How are you doing? And how is he?"

"Well enough so far, I think. He's slept at least and he hasn't bled anymore."

Rachel carefully untangled her hand from Jimmy's and took a cup of tea. Martha drew up a chair and settled herself down beside her.

"Now tell me. What is this all about, with you and Mr. Mathers?"

Rachel slowly took a bite of the bread and a long sip of tea. Then she looked at Martha searchingly.

"Did you know that Jimmy was his son?"

"His son?"

"You didn't know? If I know about it, I thought everyone must know by now."

Martha shook her head.

"No, Jimmy never said a word." Then she grasped the fuller implications of the news. "So that's the problem between you and Mr. Mathers? Is that why you're not seeing him?"

"Well, part of it, anyway. What about his mother, where is she? Are they married?"

"Is that what you're worried about? My dear, you should have asked me. His mother is dead. She died some time ago. And before that, she was married to someone named Tucker. That's Jimmy's name, Jimmy Tucker."

Martha thought the news would set Rachel's worries to rest, but Rachel's expression made it clear that it hadn't.

"It scares you, does it? His having a son?" Martha guessed shrewdly.

"I like my life, just the way it is," Rachel said defensively. "I have my freedom, my independence."

"I understand," Martha said gently, and she was beginning to. "Is he asking you to give it up? Have you asked him?"

"He doesn't even know that I know about it. I haven't seen him since it all began. Not that I mind. In a way it makes things easier. Besides," Rachel added miserably, "he's not interested in my any more. He's taken up with some flighty housemaid, Miss Annie Dawson."

"Annie Dawson? Are you sure? I thought she was just someone he had to talk to as part of his investigation."

"I'm sure as sure. I've seen them together holding hands, about the time he stopped coming to see me. It wasn't just part of his investigating, believe me."

"We'll see about that," Martha thought to herself. She'd never met this Mr. Mathers but she'd see him very soon. Someone needed to go tell him what happened to Jimmy.

∽ 38 ∾

When Martha arrived at the Senate, Mathers was just inside, busily sweeping out the hall. The great front door was open. Having finally been paid for his services during the last extraordinary session several months before, he was humming to himself and feeling especially chipper.

"Good morning, Sir," Martha greeted him. "I'm looking for Mr. Mathers the Doorkeeper."

"Well, you've found him," he said cheerily. "Can I help you? You're here too early, if you want to watch the show. The Public Gallery isn't open yet. The Senate doesn't start till eleven."

"I'm not interested in watching the Senate." She came into the hall. "It's you I've come to see. My name is Mrs. Smallwood. I own the tavern called the Man Full of Troubles. Maybe Jimmy has mentioned me? It's Jimmy I've come to tell you about."

Seeing her worried look, Mathers felt a growing apprehension. He looked out the door and glanced up and down the street, to see if any Senators or Congressmen were coming. Seeing none, he closed the door and drew her further into the hallway.

"It's not good news, I'm afraid," Martha began abruptly. "But it looks like he'll be all right."

Mathers felt his heart lurch inside him.

"Is Jimmy hurt? What happened?"

"He's been shot. He was very lucky. It seems the bullet didn't hit anything too important. The bleeding has stopped and he should recover in time. He'll have to lie abed for a while, though."

Mathers looked at his watch. It was two hours before the Senate session started. This would be the time that he'd normally set things in order, tidy the Senate Chamber and set up the fires. Today, though, they'd just have to live with the room being messy and cold. He needed to go see Jimmy.

"I'll come with you now, if you'll take me. Just let me leave a note for Mr. Otis."

She waited as he lumbered up the stairs and down again and then they set off. Mathers walked so fast that, with his longer stride, she had to nearly run to keep up with him.

"Oh, by the way, Rachel was there all night," she told him as they neared the tavern. "Someone had to watch over him and she volunteered. She knows that Jimmy's your son. I don't think that Jimmy told her, but somebody did. You really ought to talk to her about it. And you'd better tell her about this housemaid, Annie Dawson."

Mathers felt as if she'd slapped him in the face, but he put it out of his mind until later. No time to think about it now. His concern for Jimmy took precedence. With Martha leading the way, they quickly crossed the tavern room and headed upstairs to the bedroom.

"Best be quiet," she cautioned him, "in case he's sleeping."

Mathers stood for a moment just outside the bedroom in the hall, gathering his courage to enter. Against the far wall was a four-poster bed with blue and white toile bed hangings, now drawn back and tied. In the middle of the bed, underneath a homespun coverlet, lay Jimmy, pale but peaceful. On his face was the hint of a smile. Mathers softly crossed the room to stand beside him.

He wanted sorely to stroke Jimmy's brow but he feared to wake him. After close inspection satisfied him that Jimmy was in no immediate danger, he walked softly back across the room. He joined Martha in the hall, where she was waiting for him.

"What happened?" he asked her quietly, once they made their way back downstairs.

"I can't tell you really. You'll have to ask Mr. Forten. He brought Jimmy here last night, barely conscious. We were so busy worrying about Jimmy that we didn't ask."

"Mr. Forten, you say?"

"Yes, he's a sail maker. He works just across from Willing's wharf, in a loft on the corner."

"What about a doctor?" Mathers said anxiously. "Has he seen a doctor?"

"A sailor took care of him last night. He was a surgeon's mate, Mr. Forten told me. Then Mr. Girard sent his own doctor over this morning. I don't know how he heard about it, but it's no great surprise. He seems to know everything that goes on around here. The doctor said that the boy should stay in bed a while, but with luck he would be fine in a week or so."

Martha glanced at the clock on her wall.

"The Senate starts at eleven, you say? Hadn't you best be going? Don't you have things to do there before they start? Jimmy's fine for now, and I'll let you know if anything changes."

Mathers suffered through the rest of the day in a state of restless impatience. In addition to worrying about Jimmy, he remembered Mrs. Smallwood's other news, that Rachel knew about Jimmy. And then too, there was Annie Dawson.

Even after the public had gone, he had to wait around. Senator Sedgwick, said Otis, needed him for some errand. Too nervous to sit, he waited in the hall, fidgeting and pacing.

Jacob, on the other hand, was feeling cheerful and relieved beyond measure. This morning, as he sipped his coffee in the City Tavern, he'd overheard something stupendous.

"You'd think that people could keep the ships straight, wouldn't you, with all that's at stake?" The speaker was behind Jacob, out of his line of sight, and the voice was unfamiliar.

"But here's a funny thing," the unseen speaker went on, "It seems there's been a big confusion when it comes to the Neptune."

Jacob's ears pricked up. The Neptune was the name of the ship his rice had been on. He glanced behind him to see who was speaking. It wasn't anyone he knew; not one of the regular crowd. The man was a ship's captain himself, from the look of him.

"Which Neptune?" asked the speaker's companion.

"Ah yes, that's the nub of it, isn't it," the first speaker responded sagely. "It seems that it's a pretty popular name. I guess people think it's lucky, to name a ship after the god of the ocean. There's the Neptune out of Philadelphia, and the one out of Charleston, and Lord knows how many others."

"And so?"

"So the one out of Charleston was taken by privateers, or so they said, but now it turns out it was the one out of Philadelphia. There's a story about it in the *Minerva*."

Jacob immediately went over to the newspaper rack, found the New York *Minerva,* and looked through it anxiously. Yes, there was the report, tucked away at the bottom of the second page. He'd have to confirm it of course, but it seemed that maybe after all he wasn't ruined.

The minute Jacob saw Mathers, however, he knew that something was dreadfully wrong. Jacob hurried over to Mathers's side, his own good fortune momentarily forgotten.

"What's the matter?" he asked anxiously.

"It's Jimmy," Mathers said miserably. "The fool boy's got himself shot. I saw him this morning. I want to go back to the Man Full of Troubles tavern and see how he's doing, but Senator Sedgwick wants me for some errand."

"We can leave right away," Jacob said firmly. "I'll take care of Senator Sedgwick."

He went back down the hall and found Sedgwick still in the Senate Chamber. He was sitting at his desk, leisurely sorting through his papers.

"I need Mr. Mathers to accompany me somewhere," Jacob told him curtly. "Whatever it is you wanted him to do, he can do it later."

"My dear Sir, –" Sedgwick began to protest, but Jacob cut him off.

"I'm afraid I must insist, Senator Sedgwick. My apologies," he added, not sounding the least apologetic.

He turned away and walked back down the hall, feeling better than he had in ages.

"Off to the Man Full of Troubles, then?" Jacob asked Mathers briskly.

"Whatever you say, Senator." Mathers gave him a weak sort of smile of gratitude.

Their stop at the tavern was brief, just long enough to see Jimmy (once again asleep) and to get a report of the day from Martha. She suggested they return about supper time, so they went off to see Mr. Forten.

The sail making loft was a vast, empty room with a smooth wooden floor, nearly covered with men on low benches, coils of heavy rope, and yards and yards of sail canvas. Some twenty men were sitting on the benches and sewing, their palms lined with leather. Some were white and others, like Forten himself, were free people of color.

When Jacob and Mathers entered, James Forten was in a far corner, talking with an old man who was bleached by years of sun and wind to a pale obscurity. They didn't recognize Forten, not knowing who he was, but the other man seemed clearly to be a former sailor.

Jacob and Mathers stood at the head of the stairs, watching the men at work and trying to decide which one was Forten. Forten, seeing them standing there, interrupted his conversation and called out to them.

"May I help you?"

Knowing that Mathers's emotions were still raw, Jacob took the lead in answering.

"I hope you may do so, Sir. I'm Senator Martin from South Carolina and this is Mr. Mathers, the Senate Doorkeeper. I hope that we are not unduly interrupting your labors. Mrs. Smallwood said that you were the one who found Jimmy last night. And saved his life, perhaps?" Jacob ventured.

"Yes, I suppose that's true." Forten seemed almost embarrassed to confess it.

Mathers stepped forward and made a low, formal bow.

"I thank you most profoundly, Mr. Forten," he said, his voice thick with emotion. "I don't suppose you know it, but Jimmy is my son. If there's anything I can ever do for you, just ask me."

"Well, I thank you," Forten answered, "but I only happened to be walking by. It's just lucky that I happened to be there."

"Don't you listen to him," called out one of the workers. He was sitting on a low bench, shoving a heavy rope through a hemmed channel on the edge of a giant sailcloth. "I saw what happened. He could have been shot himself. And it was the second time it happened."

"I told him to quit," Mathers said wretchedly. His own son, almost killed, and he blamed himself entirely.

"You shouldn't blame yourself," Forten said kindly. "I told him to stop as well. You know how these young fellows are, they don't listen to anyone. He was bound to find out who murdered Bridget."

"Bridget?" The old man in the back corner had been studying a tear in a sail, so motionless and intent on his task that he almost seemed to be in a trance. Now, suddenly energized, he shouted across the room. "You're talking about Bridget?"

"Bridget LeClair? Do you know her?" Jacob looked at him intently.

"She was a sweet girl," the man said softly. "She always had a kind word to say to me. No more meanness in her than would fill a thimble." He turned back to studying his sail, as if he'd forgotten their presence.

Mathers and Jacob exchanged looks. Was the man so old that he'd grown feeble-minded?

"But then she got sick with the fever," Mathers prompted him.

"Yes, so sad," the old man responded vaguely, and went silent.

Mathers shrugged. Perhaps it meant nothing. Then another, much younger man spoke up, hesitantly.

"I was there, at the hospital."

Instantly he drew the attention of everyone in the room. Feeling himself the object of all eyes, he sat up straighter and went on more confidently.

"Yes, I was working there at the hospital. You know how they say that we – that people of African descent – are immune? That's why so many of us were taking care of the sick and helping. Well, I worked there for a month, at the Wigwam, I never got sick at all, so maybe it's true. But then again, two of my cousins died, so maybe it isn't. Maybe it was my prayers, or maybe I was just lucky."

"Did you see anything that might be of interest?" Jacob asked. "In relation to her death, that is, her possible murder?"

Mathers held his breath, awaiting his answer. He'd talked to so many of the hospital staff and no one could tell him anything. After so many dead-ends, could he finally have found what he was looking for?

"Nothing bearing on her murder, I'm afraid. She didn't seem as sick as some of the others, so I didn't pay as much attention to her as to them."

"What about the last day, the day she died," Jacob pressed him. "Can you remember anything?"

"No, nothing important," the man said regretfully. Then, obviously trying to give them something, he went on. "She did have a visitor, though. Two visitors, actually. That was a rare thing. Most people were afraid to come. They were afraid of getting the fever themselves, I imagine."

"Ah," said Jacob very gently. "And who might the visitors have been?"

"One was an older woman. Pitifully thin she was, and so frail you'd think a strong wind could blow her over. The other was just another young chit," the man said dismissively, "like Bridget herself. Bridget seemed to know her pretty well, as she called out to her. Ann, she called her, or Anna, or maybe Annie."

"What did I tell you," Mathers muttered to Jacob, but Jacob merely gestured for him to be silent.

"Was there anything you can remember about the visit?" Jacob asked the man. "Anything at all? Did she give Bridget anything to eat or drink, for example?"

The sailor thought back, trying to recall.

"I remember she had on a black silk bonnet, tipped down low over her face. She had some rosemary with her and fanned it around a lot. Some people think it wards off the fever. I'm sorry, that's all I can say," he concluded apologetically.

No one else in the loft seemed to know anything else about Bridget, so Jacob and Mathers turned their attention back to James Forten. This time, Mathers took the lead, seeking all the details of Jimmy's two encounters with the ruffians. He questioned Forten relentlessly until Forten, worn out from all the questioning, called a halt. Then they left, with Mathers still thanking him over and over again and swearing his undying gratitude.

Afterwards, as Mathers and Jacob made their way back to the Senate, neither said a word. Each was lost in his separate thoughts, considering.

Finally, as they neared Congress Hall, Jacob broke the silence.

"Did Annie ever tell you that she visited Bridget at the hospital?"

Mathers replayed his conversations with Annie Dawson in his mind.

"That lying strumpet, she never did. I swear she murdered her."

∞ 39 ∞

There was a different air about Mathers today, when he entered the Old Stone House on Second Street. Derrick noticed at once and wondered at the reason. There was the usual awkward nervousness, of course – natural enough for a man come to court a would-be sweetheart. Today, however, there was something new in addition. Derrick saw it in how confidently Mathers opened the door, how broadly he was smiling, how he entered with almost a swagger.

"You're looking quite the fine gentleman today," Derrick greeted him. "Has some long-lost relative died and left you a fortune?"

Mathers's smile became even broader.

"Something like it," he responded proudly. "You're looking at the Senate's Sergeant at Arms. I've been promoted."

"Rachel," Derrick called out through the door to the back. "Come out and meet a customer who has some good news."

At the mention of Rachel, a wave of anxiety and resolution crossed Mathers's face. He'd promised Martha Smallwood that he'd talk to Rachel and explain things. It was the right thing to do, he knew, but actually doing it was a different story.

Rachel came out shortly, still wiping her hands on a dirty rag. Dobson had a pamphlet that needed to be printed right away to please a well-paying customer. So instead of tending the store today, she'd been setting type for it.

"Yes? What is it?"

When she saw who it was, she hesitated at the doorway, torn by conflicting emotions. She thought of the long months they'd been estranged, about what Martha had told her, and about the night she'd spent watching over Jimmy.

"Good day, Mrs. McAllister," he greeted her apprehensively, and then blurted out, "I have to say, I owe you so many things – my thanks, an apology, and an explanation."

She blushed deeply and was silent.

"Say, what's this?" Derrick interjected teasingly. "A lovers' tiff, is it? You'd better take yourselves out back to the alley, so you can kiss and make up."

So Mathers blushed as well, and then he and Rachel stood there, hardly daring to look at each other.

"Mr. Mathers has some news, my girl," Derrick went on. "Do you want to hear it?"

Rachel rallied and came shyly into the room.

"Yes, of course. What is it?"

"I've been promoted," Mathers told her proudly. "You're looking at the Senate's new Sergeant at Arms. Just what I've wanted, since the beginning. "

"That's wonderful." Rachel beamed at him. "But what does it mean? Won't you be the Doorman anymore? Will you still be coming around for supplies for the Senate?"

"I really don't know." It was, Mathers realized, a very good question. Was it time to give it up, now he had new responsibilities?

It was never really part of his job to begin with. Office supplies were part of the Senate Secretary's domain and Otis had fiercely resented his doing it. "But one way or another, I'll still be coming by. Provided, that is, that you want me to."

"So why have they promoted you now?" Derrick asked curiously before Rachel could reply. "Is it something to do with the impeachment?"

"That's it in a nutshell. I'm supposed to go off to Tennessee to arrest the fugitive Mr. Blount. I'm supposed to leave as soon as the session is over."

"You'll have some trouble arresting him, I should imagine," Derrick observed. "Down there in Tennessee, with all his friends around him and you there all by your lonesome. He's a pretty popular fellow there still, from what I hear. Maybe they don't want to see him arrested."

"So I'm thinking too, but I've got to try."

"But what about Bridget LeClair?" Rachel asked. "Have you found out who killed her like you promised?"

"Not yet," he admitted, "but from what I just learned, I'd wager you anything that Miss Annie Dawson is the murderer."

Derrick shook his head in disbelief.

"Annie Dawson? How can that be?" he protested. "Isn't she the one who started it all, with her 'suspicions'?"

"I think it was in case the poisoning was discovered, in order to turn the blame in another direction. It worked out that way, didn't it? She's a cunning, deceitful woman, to be sure. It's my lasting regret that I ever believed a word she told me." He looked at Rachel imploringly.

"That's as may be," Derrick said doubtfully, "but what about all the others? Before you go off convicting Miss Dawson, you'd better hear what Rachel's just learned from Mrs. Callender about Mr. Willing."

"Mr. Willing?" Mathers asked uneasily. Not more damning stories about Mrs. Powel's brother, he hoped. Not again. "She didn't say anything about him when I talked to her."

"Mrs. Callender came to the Man Full of Troubles tavern the other day," Rachel explained. "She was looking for her husband. I was visiting with Martha Smallwood and we got to talking, Mrs. Callender and I. She said her husband overheard Mr. Willing talking about Bridget to her father-in-law. He called her a 'Jacobin whore' and said 'she'd pay for it,' is what she told me."

Mathers felt a sinking feeling in the pit of his stomach.

"That doesn't sound so good, does it?" he said unhappily. "I guess I have to talk to him, Callender that is, but he keeps avoiding me. I guess I have to try again, to hear it directly."

He paused, trying to gather together his courage.

"Speaking of trying again, I said I owed you an apology and explanation, Mrs. McAllister." He looked up again, gazing at Rachel solemnly. "I'd like to talk to you before I take off for Tennessee. Would you be so kind as to let me take you to supper?"

Rachel hesitated, but Martha had made her promise to hear him out.

"I suppose so," she responded, surprised to realize that the prospect of seeing him again pleased her. "I should be free tomorrow night, if it suits you."

Fearing to tempt the fates, Mathers took her to the Calistoga Wagon instead of the Kouli Khan, and he ordered fried sausages and cabbage instead of pea soup and roast mutton. As they sat there nervously awaiting their food, they had a halting conversation about their work and the weather. Once the food arrived, Mathers ventured into deeper waters.

"As I said at the shop, I'm afraid I owe you an apology."

"It was rather hard," Rachel said honestly, "hearing about it, Jimmy's being your son and Catherine and all, for the first time from Lydia."

He hung his head, feeling sheepish and remorseful.

"The truth is, I didn't know how to tell you. And then you had your young man, and it seemed like it didn't matter."

"My young man? Whatever are you talking about?"

"The one you recommended for a job. I figured he must be some handsome young suitor. It's only because I thought you'd quit with me that I ever thought of seeing Annie Dawson. He never showed up, though, to apply for the job. Whatever happened to him?"

Suddenly Rachel understood what had happened.

"You dolt! The 'young man' I was telling you about, it was Jimmy."

"Jimmy?" Mathers echoed dumbly.

Rachel shook her head in wonderment.

"You mean, all that time, you thought I had some other lover?" Then she realized what she'd said.

"Other lover?" Mathers asked, suddenly beaming. "Other than me, you mean? Am I your lover?"

She blushed and looked away.

"Rachel, my dear Rachel." His voice was gruff and full of emotion. It was the first time he'd called her "Rachel" and not "Mrs. McAllister." "I'm so sorry."

She looked at him then and he held her gaze, until finally she looked away again.

"I accept your apology," she said softly, "but I still don't know how I feel about it all. Your having a son, I mean. And Catherine, and everything."

"It's all right, so long as I can see you from time to time," he said tenderly.

↫ 40 ↬

"**I** can't see Thomas Willing calling anyone a 'Jacobin whore,'" Jacob said flatly when Mathers reported Mrs. Callender's story, "except maybe some Republican Senator or Representative. We'd better talk to Mr. Callender ourselves. She must have gotten the story wrong."

Mathers had had a hard time before even tracking Callender down, much less getting the man to talk to him. Since Mathers needed to leave soon for Tennessee, however, they couldn't spend a lot of time trying to find him and get him to talk. They decided the chances of finding him at home were best if they stopped by late in the evening. They were prepared to roust the man out of his bed, if needs be.

So it was past ten o'clock when they knocked on Callender's door. As it happened, everyone was still awake. One of the children had the whooping cough and there'd been no rest for the entire household.

"What do you want?" James Callender opened the door a crack, clearly prepared to shut it again instantly.

"We need to talk to you, and this time we will." Mathers was prepared and he pushed the door firmly open.

Callender studied them for a moment and then stepped back from the door. Mathers's stance and his scowl made it clear that he had very little choice in the matter.

"Come in, then, if you must," he said resentfully. "But just in the hall. There's a sick child upstairs, so talk quietly. I can tell you though, you're wasting your time. I don't have anything to tell you."

"I think you do." Jacob's tone also brooked no argument. "According to your wife, you overheard Mr. Willing and Mr. LeClair talking about Bridget. That's what we're interested in."

"My wife?" James Callender turned and yelled up the stairs. "Mrs. Callender, come down here right away. I want to talk to you."

Jacob and Mathers exchanged a look. So much for the sick child, they were thinking.

Mrs. Callender came timidly down the stairs dressed only in her cap and threadbare shift, loosely covered by a much-worn bedgown. Her husband turned on her angrily.

"What did you tell these men? Didn't I tell you not to talk to anyone?"

"She didn't talk to us," Mathers said quickly, giving Mrs. Callender a look of apology. "It was only something she mentioned casually to Mrs. McAllister. And why should you mind, if it hurts Mr. Thomas Willing? Federalist that he is, surely you don't care about protecting him?"

"Thomas Willing's no friend of mine," Callender grudgingly agreed. "But you can't believe anything my wife says. I don't know what you're talking about."

"I'm sorry, I didn't mean to," Mrs. Callender whined piteously. "I didn't say anything I shouldn't. I only mentioned to her what you overheard, that time at the tavern when Mr. Willing and Mr. LeClair were talking. About Mr. Willing calling Bridget a whore and saying that she'd pay for it. I only thought –"

"You stupid woman," Callender interrupted her sharply. "Can't you remember anything right? You've got it all twisted. It wasn't Mr. Willing who said that, it was Bridget's father-in-law."

"Her father-in-law?" Mrs. Callender echoed in astonishment. "But why would he say such a thing? He cares about her. He's the one who suggested I give the candied oranges to her, when I found them by the door. He couldn't have been more concerned about her."

Her husband and Jacob spoke at once.

"Candied oranges? What candied oranges?"

"Mr. LeClair told you to give them to Bridget?"

Mrs. Callender paled, realizing what she'd let slip. Avoiding her husband's eyes, she turned and spoke instead to Jacob.

"I went out to the door and I found this little parcel, like I told Mr. Mathers here before. Then Mr. LeClair comes out, right afterwards. He sees me with this parcel and naturally he asks me about it."

"Naturally," Jacob said encouragingly, "and what exactly did he say? Can you remember it precisely?"

"He asks, 'What is that you have there?' and I says, 'I don't rightly know. I suppose as it's a gift for Mr. Callender.'" She looked at her husband pleadingly.

"But there wasn't any note," Jacob prompted.

"No, no note or anything, but they had to be for Mr. Callender. No one would give candied oranges to me." She said it simply, without self-pity or emotion. "And then Mr. LeClair comes over to see. 'Could it be sweetmeats?' says he. 'Candied oranges, perhaps?' So I look in the bag and sure enough, that's what it was."

By now, her husband was also listening closely.

"Then he looked so sad, he did." Mrs. Callender's eyes filled with tears as she recollected it. "I can't help but think of *ma pauvre* Bridgette,' he says. 'There she lies in the hospital, and she will soon be dying. They were her very favorite thing, the candied oranges, but alas I cannot afford them. She'll never taste a candied orange again.' He was so sad, he was near to crying. 'Well then,' says I, 'at least I can do that for her. I'll take them to her this very day.' 'Would you?' he says, all smiling. 'She would love that so very much. You are the very soul of kindness.' And so I went to the hospital and gave them to her."

Whatever else one might say about James Callender, there was no doubt of his intelligence. He looked at Jacob keenly, grasping the implications right away.

"The oranges were poisoned? Is that what this is all about?"

"Most likely so," Jacob answered him simply. "But were they for Bridget or for you, that's the question."

Callender turned to his wife.

"It's all right, my dear," he said, putting his arm around her thin shoulders with unexpected tenderness. "I know how you felt about Bridget and I forgive you. How did the parcel look? Was there anything at all, besides the paper and the oranges?"

She hung her head guiltily.

"It was tied with a silk ribbon," she confessed. "It was so pretty that I kept it."

"Could you get it now?" he asked her gently. She went back upstairs, came down again, and gave a length of ribbon to her husband. It was only a scrap of ribbon but obviously very fine. It was white, with a tiny fleur-de-lis motif woven down the center in pale blue, and thin gold edging and a deep blue stripe on either side.

"I know that ribbon," Mr. Callender remarked after studying it thoughtfully. "It's Mr. LeClair's. He'd had some to trim a waistcoat and it must have been left over. I remember because he showed off his waistcoat to everyone he met. He was quite insufferable, the way he went on about how the ribbon came from Marie Antoinette's own milliner. So, Gentlemen, I think that answers your question. Mr. LeClair has nothing against me that I know of, but he truly despised his daughter-in-law."

⦿ 41 ⦿

"So after all, it was Mr. LeClair," Martha Smallwood said wonderingly. "Who would have thought it?" She'd met the man once or twice and he seemed like such a gentleman. So old-fashioned, but surely harmless.

She was sitting with Jacob and Mathers at the Man Full of Troubles, waiting for the other guests she'd invited. She'd decided she would host a party to celebrate the end of the whole sordid affair, this very evening at her tavern.

"He'd been against the marriage from the beginning," Jacob explained. "He wasn't even sorry. When we confronted him, he explained all his reasons for killing her, as if we'd agree. She was English, a protestant, and weak-minded – the very opposite of everything he'd hoped for. If his son had lived, and if she'd had his child, in time it might have been smoothed over. As it was, though, his son died, she wouldn't come take care of him, and she had lovers. Worst of all, she got pregnant by another man."

Mathers drank deep of the punch, handed Jacob the bowl, and continued the story.

"He thought she'd trapped his son, you see, and he thought she'd killed him. Yes, killed him," he repeated, seeing Martha's look of surprise. "She was seeing other men, you see, even once she was married. She couldn't say no, and they took advantage. It's what killed his son, he said, her having affairs. Her being left a widow was God's punishment for her evil ways, but it didn't stop her. So he had to step in to do what God had left undone."

"He was the one set those ruffians on Jimmy? That courtly old man?" Martha still had trouble believing it.

"He said Jimmy deserved it." Mathers nearly choked with fury. "He said Jimmy was a troublemaker and ill-bred in the bargain. I would have throttled him then and there, if Senator Martin hadn't stopped me."

"He would have too," Jacob assured Martha solemnly and he looked at Mathers almost fondly. "In truth it was quite a scene. He had Mr. LeClair about the throat, or very nearly. If the constable and I hadn't stepped in, he'd have saved Pennsylvania the trouble of hanging him. Mr. LeClair said he was afraid that Jimmy might stumble onto something. He said he only meant to frighten the lad, but these fellows thought Jimmy needed a lesson, that he ought to be more scared of them."

"So who was the father of her child?" Martha was keen to learn all there was to know before the other guests arrived.

"We don't know who the father was." Jacob accepted this remaining mystery better than Mathers did. "It wasn't Mr. Willing, I'm sure, whatever he was up to. It wasn't just pity for her, though that was part of it. There was something between him and her husband, I think, some business matter, and as a result he felt he owed a debt to her. Whoever the father was, though, it doesn't really matter now. It had nothing to do with the murder. It's only that her being pregnant was too much for Mr. LeClair. That's when he decided to do away with her."

"So who stole the earrings?"

"That's another thing we don't know," Jacob began, but Mathers interrupted him.

"It must have been Annie, I'm sure of it. She stole the earrings and Mrs. Finch sold them for her. Then she was struck by guilt. That's why she visited Bridget in the hospital. Why else would she lie about it?"

"It's very possible," Jacob conceded, "but we really don't know." It wasn't the first time they'd had this discussion. "Maybe Bridget really did take them after all and she hid them where they'd never be found. She could have even given them to Annie."

It would be a miracle if the Walns ever saw the earrings again, but Mathers, Jacob knew, would never really stop looking for them.

Having satisfied her curiosity (as much as could be), Martha Smallwood somewhat regretfully resumed her role as hostess. She bustled about, setting out bowls of punch, platters of meats and cheese, and jugs of ale and cider.

By now the other guests were trickling in and, as they did, she hastened over to greet them. James Forten came with a few of the other sail makers, and Jimmy's dockside friends came too, Tim and Henry and the others. Mr. Callender came as well, having solemnly sworn that he'd write not a word about the guests or the party. Having inadvertently played a critical role, he was extremely curious to learn more. Primarily, however, he was drawn by the prospect of free rum and brandy.

Martha had also invited the neighborhood gentry, Mr. Willing and Mr. and Mrs. Waln (who didn't come, though they thanked her quite graciously for the invitation) and Mr. Girard (who did show up, along with his laundress mistress Polly).

Soon the party was well underway, with ample good-will, congratulations, and jollity. Mathers, however, didn't join in. He kept glancing at the doorway, trying to hide his look of disappointment.

"Don't look so downcast." Rightly guessing his thoughts, Martha patted his arm consolingly. "I'm sure she'll be here sooner or later. Derrick promised that, no matter what it took, he'd bring her with him."

Mathers was just about to despair nonetheless when Derrick burst in. He was followed, most reluctantly, by Rachel.

"Here we are," Derrick announced brightly to the assembled crowd. "I hope you've saved us something to drink. It's the devil of a time I've had getting away from Old Dobson to come here. He kept us late and wanted to keep us even later."

He strode cheerfully to the bar and poured himself a healthy glass of brandy.

Rachel stood there just inside the door, studiously looking anywhere but at Mathers. He just stood there quietly, look-ing at her.

I need time to think, she'd said finally that day at the Calistoga Wagon, and he hadn't pressed her.

Rachel took a step forward, then stopped, and then Martha called out to her. It was enough to break the spell. Mathers walked slowly over to her.

"Rachel, it's so good to see you," he greeted her softly. "Come, sit down by me and I'll get you something."

So many unspoken words lay between them, so many ques-tions, regrets, and hesitations. Now was not the time to pursue them, though. That would come later. He took her hand to lead her to a chair. She hesitated, and then accompanied him. Her mind was full of questions, but she was glad for the warmth of his hand holding hers. For the moment, she would enjoy their being together again.

∞ 42 ∞

J acob stood at the door of the President's house, wondering what awaited him inside. He'd known John Adams for many years, but he'd hardly seen him at all since he'd been elected President. Since then, most of their conversations had been unpleasant ones.

The footman let him in and led him upstairs to Adams's office. Adams was sitting at his desk, trying to look suitably Presidential. To Jacob's surprise, Senator Bingham was sitting there also.

"Senator Martin, at last," Adams greeted Jacob impatiently. "I see you've been off solving murders again."

"I can't seem to avoid it," Jacob answered warily.

"Never mind about that," Senator Bingham reassured him. "The President knows you're not working for the other side." He turned to Adams. "Don't you?"

"Harummph." Adams gave a grudging nod. "Anyway, that's behind us now. I'm more interested in what lies ahead of us. Senator Bingham's been telling me how things stand, about your motion."

"I beg your pardon?" Jacob looked from one to the other, mystified.

"Your motion," the President repeated irritably. "The motion that it's unconstitutional to impeach a Senator."

"Ah, yes?" Jacob braced himself for the inevitable torrent of abuse and criticism.

"I thought you were mad at first," Adams continued. "It seemed like another act of treachery. I thought – we all thought – that impeaching Blount would make the Republicans look bad. Now, however, things have changed. It's a different situation entirely."

"The House report has changed things," Bingham explained. "It's made it clear that there wasn't any French conspiracy. Not a word about the French being involved, just the British."

"It was always a crazy idea, to think the French had anything to do with it." Jacob couldn't help but feel a bit smug, recollecting the look on Senator Sedgwick's face when he'd waved the report at him. A childish moment of triumph, perhaps, but nonetheless very sweet.

"Well, maybe it wasn't or maybe it was." Adams waved his hand dismissively. "The point is, the impeachment proceeding was supposed to make the Republicans look bad, to tar them with the brush of treason. Only now, with the Report, it's the British who look bad and that makes the Federalists look bad. It looks like the Republicans are correct when they say our foreign policy is wrong-headed for being too friendly with the British instead of the French."

"And that's not the worst of it," Senator Bingham added. "It could get very ugly. Senator Tazewell's going to insist that Blount must have a jury trial for the impeachment."

"A jury trial?" Jacob immediately saw what a mess that could be. "It would be a circus. We'd lose control over the thing entirely."

"Exactly." Bingham nodded sagely. "Who knows what might happen? A jury might do any crazy thing – they might even say he isn't guilty. Tazewell will argue it's a matter of constitutional rights. It will look damn bad to argue against it."

"So you see," Adams concluded, "it's not working out the way it was supposed to work at all. Instead of making the Republicans look bad, it's looking bad for the Federalists. Deciding it's all unconstitutional might be just the thing to save us. And that isn't the only reason it's got to go. We've a foreign policy crisis on our hands, another one. Those bloody madmen in France have done it again."

"Marshall's dispatches from Paris have finally arrived," Bingham said grimly. "What he reports is catastrophic."

"Catastrophic?" Jacob looked at Adams questioningly.

"That damned scoundrel Talleyrand." Adams spat out the name disgustedly. "As you probably know, he's the new Foreign Minister. He asked for a bribe, that's the long and short of it. We need to give him $250,000, he says, and a ten million dollar loan to the French Government too, before they'll even talk to us. We need to soothe their injured pride, he says, and if we don't, they'll declare war on us."

Jacob was stunned.

"Surely we wouldn't pay?"

"Not as long as I'm President, by God!" Adams slammed his fist down on his desk. "If it's war, then it's war. First, though, I have to report this all to Congress. So you see why I want this impeachment business out of the way immediately, if not sooner."

"And that's where your motion comes in," Bingham smoothly turned the conversation back to the original subject. "It's a stroke of genius really. We can make the whole thing go away like it never happened."

Perversely, now that it seemed he'd won, Jacob felt like challenging them.

"I made my motion weeks ago and everyone ignored it. So now everyone thinks my legal analysis is right after all? Or is it only that it's useful to say so?"

"Does it matter why they agree, so long as they agree with you?" Adams looked at Jacob as if he were a simpleton. Adams hadn't gotten to be President by accident. When it came to politics, he was no fool.

"Don't look a gift horse in the mouth." Bingham clapped Jacob heartily on the back to encourage him. "You're the hero of the hour. Even Senator Sedgwick will have to admit you've saved us."

With that, Adams turned his attention to the papers piled on the desk. Clearly, in his opinion the meeting was over.

Bingham bowed to them both and hurried on his way. Jacob, still pondering the implications of Tallyrand's demands, lingered for a moment in the upper hallway. As he stood there, the door to the yellow drawing room opened and Elizabeth came out. She'd been having tea once again with Abigail.

"Good day Mrs. Powel," he greeted her politely but guardedly, remembering their last encounter at Dobson's bookstore. To his surprise, she smiled at him.

"What a strange coincidence it is," she said shyly, "that I should encounter you. I'm very sorry to say, it seems that I've been quite unfair to you."

Jacob just stood there, amazed. Twice in under an hour now, he'd been struck by unexpected good fortune.

"As I've just been explaining to Mrs. Adams," she went on bravely, "it seems that we were under a misimpression about the nature of your activities. It started with something my niece Mrs. Bingham said, or so I understood from Mrs. Adams. Well of course I would believe my niece," she continued on hurriedly, "only recently I happened to ask her about it."

She stopped to see how he was taking it all. Jacob, not sure where this all was going, merely nodded.

"Well, there it is," she said sadly. "It turns out my niece never said it. I began to see that the whole thing was a house of cards. I've done you a great injustice. I should have known better all along. I'm so very sorry." She looked at him pleadingly. "Could you bring yourself to accept my apology?"

For a long moment, Jacob was silent. Of all the things that he'd suffered through during the past few months, her lack of faith in him had hurt the most of anything. Then he looked in her eyes, and somehow it didn't matter so much anymore.

"Your apology is accepted," he said solemnly. "Let's consider it all behind us."

He followed her down the stairs and out the door to High Street, where he took her hand to help her into her waiting carriage. She left her hand in his a bit too long; her fingers trembled very slightly. With a burst of sudden resolve, he climbed in as well and, encouraged by the look that came unbidden to her eyes, he took his place on the seat beside her.

THE END

Author's Note and Acknowledgments

Secrets Worth Killing For is a work of fiction, but I have tried to make it as realistic as possible. The descriptions of late 18th century Philadelphia and the politics of the times are based on considerable research and most of the prominent characters – not only Adams and Jefferson but others such as Elizabeth Powel and James Mathers – were (with some literary liberties taken) real people. Jacob Martin is fictional but closely modeled after Jacob Read, the actual Senator from South Carolina. Rachel McAllister, Jimmy Mathers, and other fictional characters are modeled generally after the sort of people who might actually have lived in Philadelphia during this period.

Of the many people who have helped me with my writing in general and this book in particular, I'd like to give special thanks to the people who shared their historical knowledge of the period, including Karie Diethorne, Chief Curator of Independence National Park; Jack Gumbrecht, former Director of Research Services at the Historical Society of Philadelphia;

David Haugaard, current Director of Research Services at the Historical Society of Philadelphia; Catherine Kisluk, also with the National Park Service; David Maxey, author of *A Portrait of Elizabeth Willing Powel*; Alden O'Brien, Curator of Costume and Textiles at the DAR Museum; Deborah Peterson, expert on 18th century foodways; and Jack Wolcott, who must be the world's living expert on the Chestnut Street Theater.

I'm grateful also to "test readers" Sally Cummins and Julie Herr for their very useful suggestions, to Kimberly Walters and my other friends who have helped and advised me, and to Jason Orr of Jera Publishing, whose graphic design skills have greatly enhanced not only this book but also *Patriots & Poisons*. Last but far from least, thanks to my sister Lynn Selby for her continuing feedback, encouragement, and psychological insights, and to my husband Ted Borek for his loving patience and constant support.

You can read more about the historical background for this book and *Patriots & Poisons*, the first in the Founding Fathers mystery series, and also about me and my colonial girl children's books (similar to the American Girl™ Felicity series) at www.shrewsburypress.com. You can also find me on Facebook (https://www.facebook.com/JamisonBorek/) and on Goodreads (https://www.goodreads.com/author/show/7542530.Jami_Borek), and contact me via info@shrewsburypress.com. Your feedback (and reviews) are greatly appreciated.

Made in the USA
Middletown, DE
24 February 2023

25454706R00172